Shadowblood

A Novel of
Sherlock Holmes

Tracy Revels

Paperback ISBN 978-1-78092-047-4

ePub ISBN 978-1-78092-048-1

PDF ISBN 978-1-78092-049-8

Published in the UK by MX Publishing

335 Princess Park Manor, Royal Drive, London, N11 3GX

www.mxpublishing.co.uk

Cover artwork by www.staunch.com

For Colonel Openshaw

(Thanks for letting me kill you...)

This is a tale that can never be told.

This story must remain forever hidden, locked away in vaults far below the streets of London, in a library guarded by a figure as beautiful as she is immortal. This adventure cannot be added to those that have garnered my friend Sherlock Holmes his well-deserved fame. It is true that this case would reveal Holmes at the peak of his powers, and demonstrate his courage and resolve when faced with an opponent whose unnatural abilities were fuelled by demonic forces and drenched in human blood, but Holmes has forbidden me to ever publically chronicle these events. To share this story with the world would be to reveal a very different man, one whose knowledge and abilities extended beyond the mortal ken, into both brightest sunshine and darkest Shadows.

Still, I must write. It goes against my nature to leave the most exciting moments of our lives unrecorded. I must commit to paper our adventure, which took us from the pleasant countryside of England to the darkest corners of Paris and Prague, before leading us across the Atlantic to the steaming jungles of Florida. It was a quest that challenged my sanity and nearly claimed both our lives.

Perhaps, my Lady, you will be the only one who reads it and knows the truth. But if it meets your eyes alone, that is enough.

CHAPTER ONE

At first, there was only music.

I was suspended in a world of darkness. I reached out and touched nothing. There was no sense of ground beneath my feet, or of any structure surrounding me. I floated, lost in a vast, inky void, painfully aware of my helplessness, my inability to move, or fight, or even cry for assistance. I feared I was in hell.

But the music saved me. It came as a dark, sonorous tone, the rise and fall of a melody unlike anything I had ever heard. Played on a violin, bit-by-bit the notes began to connect, to come together as if they were taking physical form. I grasped at them and somehow, blindly, captured them. On that slender thread I was drawn from the darkness, reeled by delicate degrees toward a slowly emerging light.

I woke to the glow of a single candle and the smell of a sickroom. I could hear hushed voices, intense whispers, and the sound of long skirts brushing against the floor. A cough followed. There was the snick of a bag being closed, and a few moments later the creaking of a door. In sudden horror that I might once again be abandoned to the darkness, I struggled to turn my head. Blinking, I found only an indistinct form at a distance, a shadowy ghost at the very edge of my vision.

What had happened? Was I wounded, had I fallen in battle? Had I succumbed to some plague or been the victim of a horrific accident? My mind was filled with shadows. Instinctively, I called out to the only person I knew who could clear them.

"Holmes!"

My voice was nothing more than a belaboured, pitiful croak, and yet it brought a marvellous change. A figure emerged from the gloom, taking up the candle. In the sudden flare of illumination, I saw my friend's face.

"Watson. Thank God you are back."

**

The finest physicians of Harley Street were baffled by my case. It seemed that I had fallen into some form of catatonia or stupor, and for over a month I had lain in bed, often unconscious and always unspeaking, barely able to take the mildest forms of nourishment. Poor Mrs. Hudson was nearly hysterical with worry, and Holmes, I learned, had accepted no new cases or engaged in any consultations during my illness. Even Mycroft had come by to ponder my disability, while Gregson and Lestrade sent cards. I joked that I had never known I had so many friends in this world until I almost took leave of it.

It soon became clear that my convalescence would be an extended one. I had lost some twenty pounds and my muscles were stiff and nearly atrophied. As springtime gave way to summer, I could do little except eat delicate meals and wander aimlessly about our rooms. I insisted that Holmes return to work, as his temperament was not suited to nursing. It was enough that, out of respect to my lungs, he kindly abstained from filling our rooms with the vile smoke of his pipe or the retorts of any chemical experiments. I did not begrudge him the cases he accepted, all of which were, by his own admission, rather elementary.

But the hours I spent alone were not completely uneventful, and as I gained strength I struggled to recall exactly what I had been doing before my sudden lapse. I seemed to remember the vague outlines of a case in which I had served as Holmes's assistant. I could visualize a great yet crumbling manor, a row of opened tombs, and a dark-skinned woman crowned with a turban and clad in the clothing of another age. At times I glimpsed a golden bee and a long tunnel that I knew I dared not enter. Once, I woke from a nightmare in which the dead form of my old friend Stamford chased after me, his eyes unknowing and his limbs animated by some devilish evil that I could not define.

It would have been foolish to mention such waking visions and nocturnal fantasies to Holmes, for I knew from experience that he put no stock in dreams of any kind. I feared recounting these illusions would only strain his patience with me. But what had first been merely unusual recollections and ill-defined nightmares soon became vivid, almost constant hallucinations. I began to suspect that I might be sliding back into the mental quagmire from which I had just escaped and so, much to my embarrassment, I sought the council of a noted alienist. He could make nothing of my strange dreams or the fantastic scenarios that floated unbidden before my eyes. His only prescription was an extended period of rest, a long holiday taken far from the byways of London that seemed to generate these morbid fancies.

I returned to Baker Street rather discouraged, knowing that my meagre pension and the paltry royalties from my stories would be insufficient to finance the kind of escape my doctor had suggested. The best I could do would be a week's furlough in Brighton. The thought of sharing the seaside with flocks of horrid children and their pasty-faced nurses was equally as appalling as my nightmares.

"Watson, you have a guest!" Holmes announced. He had greeted me at the door, and personally relieved me of my hat and cane. I blinked and shook my head in confusion.

"I was not expecting anyone. Who is it?"

Holmes's eyes twinkled with mischief. "Come up and see."

I climbed the seventeen steps to our sitting room. Holmes threw open the door, gesturing to our fireplace, where a man of uncertain age stood. He was tall and slender, with buttery yellow hair and a trim moustache. He was dressed in almost foppish garb, but possessed the unmistakable erect carriage of a former military officer. Tossing a cigarette into the flames, he advanced with his hand extended.

"Doctor Watson! Surely you remember me!"

I did not. Nothing in his countenance brought back any memories. The man could have been a refugee from the street, a face drawn from a crowd. He strode across the rug and gripped my hand firmly.

I suddenly felt like a fool. Of course I remembered him! Thomas Darby had been a corporal in the Berkshires, and I had removed a bullet from his shoulder while under fire at the battle of Maiwand, just before receiving my own nearly fatal wound. I coughed and stammered over my embarrassment.

"Do forgive me, Darby, old chap. As Holmes has told you, I have been rather ill of late."

"You look a bit wane," he agreed. "I hope it was not that blasted enteric fever. I hear some fellows have relapses."

I waved away his concern. Holmes insisted on pouring drinks while encouraging us to reminiscence about our days as soldiers. But Darby was loath to dwell on the past and that terrible time in the colonies. Instead, he told me of his life since then, of how he had inherited Haven House, a manor on the western border of Surrey, and was spending his days renovating it and enjoying the duties and privileges of a country squire. He had wed, a declaration that surprised me as I recalled him as a staunchly-confirmed bachelor. To prove his truthfulness on the matter he produced a locket image of a lady of angelic beauty.

"You have done well for yourself, Darby."

"I'll admit I have enjoyed a bit of good fortune. But my life is rather tepid when compared to yours. What adventures you and Mr. Holmes share, chasing down thieves and murderers! I look forward to each new story, and I read them aloud to Isabella. I can only image how thrilling the exploits that you dare not record must be!"

"Perhaps Watson will recount those tales for you during his visit," Holmes said.

I looked up over my glass, taken aback by those words. "My visit?"

Darby grinned. "Ah, the cat is out of the bag now! I'll be straight with you, Watson. Your friend Mr. Holmes wrote to me and told me of your illness. It gave me quite a fright to think of you succumbing to something as simple as a fever when you should be saved for some villain's snare, eh? And so naturally I said, 'Let me come to London and fetch Watson away, keep him in the country for the summer to get his bearings back.' You will say yes, I trust? You must say yes, Watson, or Isabella will not let me return to Haven House! She insisted before I left, 'Come with Watson in your carriage or do not come at all.' Quite the Spartan matron, my missus!"

I was astonished by this offer. I glanced at Holmes, knowing that he was its author. Even though I had not shared my dreams and

9

hallucinations with him, he had somehow deduced my afflictions and anticipated the diagnosis.

"You should go with Darby," Holmes said. "I will be engaged in number of investigations throughout the summer, but they are all petty and criminally unimaginative. There is no reason for you to have to suffer the dreadful city heat in these stuffy rooms when you could take advantage of the fresh air and wholesome exercise of the countryside."

"Do come with me," Darby insisted. "We will have a grand time."

It seemed like manna from heaven. I gave my consent, and arrangements were made for us to leave on the following morning. Darby departed to finish his business in the city. Over dinner that evening I finally found the words to thank Holmes for engineering my rescue.

"Think nothing of it, Watson. It would be obvious, even to the dullest mind, that you need rest and recreation. I shall expect you back in September a changed man, as fit as if you had sipped from the Fountain of Youth."

I shook my head. "But how on earth did you track down Thomas Darby? I have never, to my recollection, mentioned him. I haven't even thought about him in years."

Holmes favoured me with his most mysterious smile. "A magician gets no credit if he gives away his secrets!" He pushed an extra slice of cake in my direction. "I trust your holiday will be pleasant and uneventful."

That wish was not to be. As I packed my bags and anticipated long, lazy days, even my tortured imagination could not have conjured the strange twists and turns the journey would bring, or the truth that would once again be revealed in spectacular and hideous fashion.

CHAPTER TWO

Darby arrived early the next morning. A short journey from Waterloo station took us to the town of Leatherhead, where we had our luncheon in a small restaurant near the station. I recalled an earlier journey through that place, one that Darby urged me to recount, but I was unable to finish my tale because throughout our meal both gentlemen and labourers stopped at our table, warmly hailing my companion. It was clear to me that my former patient was a popular and respected member of his community, which gave me even more reason to expect a long and pleasurable summer.

We were collected by one of Darby's men driving an elegant brougham. As we took a leisurely drive to Haven House, Darby pointed out the unique features of his neighbourhood. The landscape was doted with both quaint cottages and stately manors, many of them dating back to the Tudor period and others a product of the Restoration. Darby regaled me with stories of the families who inhabited these edifices, of loyal cavaliers and stern-faced Puritans alike, and how the region had been the scene of many battles during the war between king and parliament. He spoke of ghostly troopers who marched across the fields without leaving footprints in the soil, and of bright, flickering fairy lights, which the superstitious locals claimed were lanterns carried by the wee folk on their midnight rambles. Despite my dark dreams, I found these tales fanciful and amusing, a pleasant way to pass the long drive. At last we turned a corner and started down a path lined with the most magnificent beeches I had even seen. The mighty trees seemed to twinkle and sparkle in the sunlight, welcoming us properly.

Haven House was a queer yet pleasing dwelling, a strange amalgamation of Norman and Gothic styles with long, narrow windows and sturdy grey towers. Despite its outer appearance of great age, Darby assured me that inside his 'castle' was every modern comfort. Mrs. Darby waited for us at the doorway, and I immediately saw that the photograph within the locket had done poor justice to her ethereal beauty. Her flawless skin glowed from within and her golden blonde hair formed an enchanting nimbus around her head. She greeted me warmly, proclaiming that she was my greatest admirer. I found myself as bashful as a schoolboy in the glow of her praise. My embarrassment served as a vast font of amusement for my friend.

The weeks that followed passed in an unexceptional manner. We engaged in such pursuits as country gentleman traditionally enjoy, including hunting and fishing and sleeping late whenever we chose. Darby took me on long walks through the dales and his lady often joined us on picnics. The Darbys were social creatures, hosting many dinners and card parties, so that I soon became acquainted with the best people of the region. A fellow from the local newspaper requested an interview, and after his article appeared in print, Darby's guests often called upon me to narrate one of my adventures with Holmes. I became so in demand as a dinner guest that Darby playfully threatened to bill himself as my agent and begin collecting fees.

I could not have asked for better company, or a more restful season, but I soon found that I missed Holmes. Even his eccentricities left voids, so that from time to time I wished to hear the screeching of his violin or smell the toxic fog that was inevitably the product of a three pipe problem. I composed rather lengthy letters, filled with word pictures of my surrounding, but found I could never mail them. Holmes was not an admirer of my attempts at 'poetry,' and so I limited myself to brief messages assuring him of my comfort and continued recuperation. I received short telegrams of reply, and some indication that he was kept busy with a sudden flood of cases that were as profitable as they were easy to solve.

One Friday afternoon, as August gave way to September, Darby suggested that we take an invigorating gallop. It had been long years since I was last mounted, and I convinced him that a canter would be the extent of my equestrian daring. He accepted in good humour, and we spent the better part of the morning exploring the fields and lanes. We rode some two miles to the east, coming over the crest of an untilled hill. Darby reined in his horse and pointed into the small valley before us.

"There's something odd, Watson. Do you see that copse of ancient oaks? It looks as if the sun refuses to shine there, does it not?"

Just as he said, the area surrounding a dark and rather ramshackle house did seem gloomier than its surroundings. I glanced to the heavens, expecting to see some heavy clouds overhead, but the sky was clear and blue.

"What a strange effect."

Darby leaned forward, patting his mount's neck. "And a man who is just as strange lives there."

I encouraged him to share his local gossip.

Darby laughed heartily. "I doubt this fellow could compare to some of the characters that you and Holmes have encountered, but he is weird enough for at least a sketch in your memoirs. His name is Telfair, and he is an American millionaire. He purchased that crumbling old pile a year or so ago, I don't remember the exact date. He lives there with his daughter, but with no servants and no wife that we've seen. They keep to themselves."

"Always?" I asked, wondering how anyone could abide being isolated in such a dreary spot.

Darby nodded. "There's no church or clubs for them, and the hand of friendship which I tried to extend, as their closest neighbour, was firmly slapped away."

"Perhaps he wishes to live like a medieval hermit."

"Well, he hardly looks the part," Darby chuckled. "He is short and tremendously stout. It's simply vulgar, the way Americans put on weight to go with their prosperity, don't you think? He also has a thick head of black hair that looks rather like a dirty mop atop his skull, if you ask me. Stranger still, he appears to be barely thirty, only a decade older than his daughter."

"So you have seen the girl?"

"She was pointed out to me in the station just after they arrived. Naturally I was curious to learn more about my neighbours. A few months ago I gained access to Telfair's house when I called upon him to ask him to serve as a witness in a local squabble over grazing rights. He received me in his study, but only long enough to tell me he had no intention of appearing in court." Darby waved his hand in bravado. "But while I was in his lair I pretended I was Sherlock Holmes. I made detailed observations and sniffed out every clue."

With this announcement Darby twisted his face, making an expression that perfectly mirrored Holmes in his foulest temper. I laughed so heartily I startled my horse.

"And what did you learn?" I asked.

"Only that Telfair is a collector of strange objects. I saw weird things from around the globe. I recall mummy cases and African fetishes, along with big brass boxes and great piles of scrolls and old books. A thief would fare well, if he could separate the valuables from the debris in that room. I tried to ask Telfair about his intriguing inventory, but he shoved me out of the door before I could even phrase the question."

"Well, if my time with Holmes has taught me anything, it is that reality is far more improbable than anything fiction can create," I said.

"And Telfair is an example," Darby agreed. "But enough of wasting time speculating about our local crank. I'll wager a guinea you can't jump that stream! Tally-ho!"

An hour later we were in the stables, turning our poor lathered horses over to the lad who cared for them, when Crenshaw, Darby's ancient, stiff-backed butler, appeared in the doorway, alerting us to his presence with a discreet cough. The expression on the old servant's face made it clear that he found this announcement distasteful.

"There is a Mr. Telfair to see you, sir."

Darby nearly dropped his riding crop on his foot. "Are you certain, Crenshaw? It is really Telfair?"

The retainer nodded. "Indeed, sir. I did not recognize him, nor did he offer a card, but his accent is pronounced." Crenshaw flicked cool eyes at me. "There are no other Americans in the neighbourhood."

He spoke the nationality with the same disgust that one might use when noting the presence of rats. Darby chuckled.

"Well, this is rather unexpected, but at least now you'll have a chance to meet the odd duck. Come, Watson, let's not keep him waiting."

Without changing our attire, we followed Crenshaw to the parlour. The man pacing inside was short and big-boned, flabby at first appearance, but when he turned to face us I could see that his girth had once been ponderous. Now his flesh sagged around his face and folded into greasy, dun-coloured layers around his neck. Its looseness was evident beneath his ill-cut suit and even his wrists, where they protruded from a dank, stained shirt, seemed draped in excess skin. Small, piggish eyes peered out from bloodshot sockets, and despite some distance I could smell the fetidness of his breath. I was relieved to see that Mrs. Darby had not returned from her afternoon shopping expedition and so was not forced to receive a man of such low quality and foul habits.

I glanced to my friend. He looked baffled, his brows drawn together. He gave a quick shake of his head, as if trying to drive away an unpleasant thought. I could tell that it required some courage on his part to even speak to the strange man who now was glaring at me and making harsh, snorting noises.

"You are Watson?" the man demanded, overriding Darby's attempt at pleasantries. I found myself bristling, easing a half step backward even as he lunged forward.

"Yes, I am Doctor Watson," I corrected, uneasily offering my hand. "And you are...Mr. Telfair?"

He ignored me, his fingers clenching into tight fists. From the corner of my eye, I caught Darby's continued expression of astonishment. "Where is Sherlock Holmes?" Telfair demanded. "I must speak with him immediately."

"I am afraid my friend did not accompany me on this journey," I answered, striving to remain polite. There was something about this loathsome man that made me itch to seize the fireplace poker and apply it to his nearly hairless skull. The reaction took me aback even as I spoke to him. I had met many strange and grotesque characters in my adventures with Holmes, yet there was something so utterly repugnant about this man that I wanted to remove him from existence.

"Then you must summon him!" Telfair shouted, waving one hand as if prepared to strike me with it. "You must get him to come, immediately."

Darby could take no more and stepped between us. "See here, Telfair, Sherlock Holmes is a busy man. I'm sure he does not have time for an idle holiday in the country."

"This is no holiday," Telfair snapped, his blackened stubs of teeth clacking together. "This is life and death and more!"

Darby laughed. "There is nothing more than life and death, old fellow."

Telfair's eyes narrowed. His voice emerged in a hiss. "What an idiot you are!"

"If this involves a case, I could send a letter to Holmes," I offered, fearful that a brawl was about to commence. "But I must warn you that my friend has been very busy and may not be able to spare the time for your concern."

Telfair rounded on me. "You will send a telegram, immediately! And he will come. He must come, in the morning. I will expect him before noon."

"But if Holmes---"

"Before noon!" Telfair shrieked. He turned and stomped from the room, slamming the door loudly as he exited.

Darby gave a low whistle. "'Pon my word, Watson, I knew he was an eccentric, but I had no idea Telfair was a monster. And what in blazes has happened to him? I barely recognized the man. He's changed so hideously in such a short time. He must have contracted an especially vicious disease." Darby shuddered and seized a decanter, pouring us both a drink. "You certainly should ignore his request. Or, should I say, his order!"

I heard the words emerge from my lips before I had any real thought of speaking them. "I will send the telegram, immediately." I shrugged at Darby's look of astonishment. "Sherlock Holmes enjoys cases that present some element of the bizarre," I explained. "He no doubt would have deduced a dozen things about Telfair while you and I were merely dumbfounded by his rudeness."

Darby waved a hand in front of his nose. "Well, I deduce the fellow needs a bath! Unless your exertions are at fault for generating such a stench."

I was tempted to make a boxer's jab at Darby, and he danced back as if reading my mind. I settled for passing him my emptied glass. "If I reek so badly, perhaps I had better ride into town and send the telegram before your missus returns, so I will have ample time to bathe before dinner. I would not wish to offend my hostess."

And so, an hour later, I entered Leatherhead and dispatched a message to Holmes. I kept the lines terse, as I knew he preferred them, saying only that a grotesque character named Telfair was requesting his services for a matter beyond life and death. The young lady in the telegraph office was a local beauty, and I indulged

19

myself in a bit of innocent flirtation with her, losing track of time in the process. When I swung back into the saddle it was almost sundown. The sky was a strange tint of scarlet and purple, the darkness descending rapidly. I eased the horse into a sharp canter, hoping I had not tarried long enough to delay my host's dinner.

As I approached the final quarter mile to Haven House, I noted a figure on the side of the narrow road. The descending night seemed to be swallowing him, making him more indistinct as I approached. The man was small and bowed down by the weight of a great box on his back. I thought perhaps he was a peddler with a cumbersome crate of wares. Maybe his wagon was stuck and he was loath to leave his valuables behind. I was pondering how I might assist him while I closed the last of the distance between us. At just ten yards away, I realized that it was not a container of old clothes or a steamer trunk that he carried on his back.

It was a coffin.

My horse was suddenly skittish. I drew alongside the fellow, and in a quick glance saw that he was dressed in the strangest of clothing, with a cowl over his head, a crude tunic on his body, and moth-eaten hose on his legs. His feet were wrapped in bands of cloth tied with leather strings. He was the very picture of every medieval peasant I had ever encountered in a Sir Walter Scott romance.

I spoke a greeting, and he lifted his face to me.

Even now, so far removed from that encounter, I can feel the chill that raced to every limb and the cold hand that seemed to close around my heart. The countenance he presented was pale and splotched, with hair-filled warts on his chin and right cheek. His half-open, gray-lipped mouth revealed broken teeth and a mutilated tongue. But it was his eyes, one green and one yellow, that seemed to freeze my very soul.

His hideous maw drew into a smile. At that instant, some part of the spell snapped. I spurred the mare mercilessly and she broke like a champion of the Wessex Cup, speeding to the crest of the hill. I pulled hard on the reins and my horse reared, hooves pawing at the moon. I hated to abuse such a fine animal, but something told me to turn back, to take a final look at the vile, coffin-bearing man in the dust.

He was no longer there. I scanned around, but the land on either side was bare and offered no convenient hiding place. The darkness was growing thicker, but I was certain I could see him had he still existed.

A sudden nausea swam over me. I could smell the sickroom odours again and a sweet oblivion beckoned. I shook it off, wary of falling from the horse and lying in the path for hours. I resolved to say nothing of the strange encounter. I had no desire to frighten my hosts for either my sanity or my health. Summoning calmness, I returned to Haven House and hurriedly bathed and dressed for dinner. The evening passed in a convivial, uneventful way. We concluded it with a game of cards in the parlour, where the cloying fragrance of lemon suggested that Darby had summoned his housemaid to scrub the room free of Telfair's evil essence. I retired that evening still somewhat perturbed by my strange vision, but also convinced that I must forget it, lest I leave myself open to whatever bizarre ailment had plagued my mind in London.

I hoped to dream of my long-lost darling Mary, and if she would not return to me, then to dream of the winsome telegraph girl. Instead, I wandered long, endless lanes, chasing hideous men made of shadows.

CHAPTER THREE

The next morning, I had just descended to breakfast and was chatting with my host when the door flew open and, to my great astonishment, Sherlock Holmes crossed the threshold. Clad in his great cape and soft cloth hat, he was a welcome, if shocking, sight. Darby laughed heartily as Holmes filled the empty chair between us and began vigorously applying marmalade to toast.

"I take it Watson's summons has brought you down?" Darby asked. "Or rather, I should say, Mr. Telfair's orders are being obeyed?"

"I have heard certain rumours about Mr. Telfair," Holmes said, "which make me rather eager to meet him. This seems an excellent opportunity to satisfy my curiosity."

"Oh?" Darby countered, one eyebrow lifting. I guessed that he was surprised to hear the local eccentric's fame had spread as far as the metropolis. "And what have you heard?"

I could tell, from the carefully-schooled neutrality of my friend's face, that he was not prepared to tell Darby everything. I had known Holmes long enough to be aware when some bits of data were being carefully guarded. "Only that Telfair is a collector of antiquities of the most arcane and eclectic nature," Holmes said. "Perhaps he will grant me a tour of his collection as payment for resolving whatever conundrum he presents."

"He's certainly an odd bird," Darby said. "And if you persuade him to discuss his baubles, you will have bested me. I barely had time to glance at them."

Holmes shifted the conversation smoothly to other subjects. An hour later, Darby rose and announced that he had business in the city, but that his boy would have the dogcart readied for us. Crenshaw had already taken Holmes's meagre bag to a guest room, and we wasted no time in setting out for Telfair's manor, which Darby informed us bore the rather unimaginative name of Oakhurst.

In strange contrast to the bright, clear morning, the moment we entered the copse of trees that surrounded the estate a dark, dank miasma enveloped us. A putrid smell rose from the ground, trapped by the heavy canopy of aged, lichen-covered trees. I felt my spirits sink, but Holmes gave no impression of being affected by the sudden gloom or the stagnant air. A slight tightening of his jaw and a firmer snap to the reins was the only indication that he found our new environment disturbing.

There was no sign of life as we approached, despite the fact that Holmes had sent Telfair a note earlier that morning, telling him when to expect us. Holmes tied the horse to a rusted hitch, pausing for a moment to slide a soothing hand down the mare's forelock. I was about to inquire whether Telfair had been sincere in his desire to consult with Holmes when the heavy door creaked open and the master of the house peered through the gap.

"Are you Holmes?" he barked. His manners had obviously not improved in the past twenty-four hours.

"I am. And do I have the honour of addressing Mr. Edgar Telfair, owner of the Arkham Manufacturing Company?"

The man staggered backward, as if Holmes's pleasant greeting had been a physical blow. He jabbered his words. "I...I have...it is true...worked for that company many years ago---"

Holmes had walked halfway up the short flight of steps, but now he halted abruptly and raised a hand in signal for me to do likewise. "Mr. Telfair, let us be clear from the start. If you wish to engage my services, it is essential that you be honest with me. I do not waste my time with dissemblers."

I fully expected the man to explode with rage, as he had the previous afternoon. Instead, Holmes' commanding presence cowed him, and he hung his head like a whipped child. Moving awkwardly, he pushed the door further open and silently invited us inside.

I was immediately struck by the pervasive gloom of the place. No lamps were lit and all the curtains were drawn. Illumination was provided only by a few flickering candles in odd niches and corners. I could barely make out the lines of the walls and contours of chairs and benches. We followed Telfair's slumped shoulders as he led us toward the rear of the vast and silent building. As we passed other open doorways, I had fleeting glimpses of rooms decorated in the style of a century before, with crossed swords above the mantels and oppressive landscape paintings on the walls. Dust and mould assailed my nostrils, making it obvious that a woman's touch was lacking. Recklessly, I put that thought into words.

"You are a bachelor, Mr. Telfair?"

His reply was grunted and vicious. "A widower, if it's any of your business, which it is not. This way."

He opened a door and led us into the only room in the home that was adequately illuminated. It was a library, its walls lined with bookcases, cabinets, and glass-covered boxes holding strange objects and artefacts. What had once been an elegant study now resembled a cluttered attic. Boxes and trunks were strewn on the floor while manuscripts and folios were thrown around carelessly, their papers fanned and torn. Telfair moved behind a desk that was laden with carvings, totems, and what appeared to be a book so long and wide that it would require two readers to turn a page. Belatedly, our host realized there was nowhere for us to sit, and hurried to clear away debris from a pair of straight-backed chairs. As he worked, I marvelled at other bits of décor, including a suit of samurai armour, an Egyptian mummy case, and a box worked in purest ivory and gold, a reliquary that might have once graced a Catholic cathedral.

"Now, Mr. Telfair," Holmes said, settling down. "I am told that you would like to engage my services. Please tell me why."

"It is my daughter," the man said, dropping back behind his desk. "She has been stolen from me. Kidnapped!"

As he spoke, he drew a small photograph from a drawer and passed it to Holmes. My friend's gaze flicked over it so quickly that I wondered how it was possible for him to draw any conclusions from such a cursory glance. He handed the picture to me, and I was immediately impressed by its subject. Miss Telfair was a very beautiful young woman, with a gentle expression and doe-like eyes. Her lustrous hair was worn loose, and to my surprise she modelled a dress in a style that had been fashionable at mid-century, one with vast round skirts and a low, lace-framed bodice.

"Her name is Alice," Telfair said. "She is all that I have. Mr. Holmes, you must find her. Waste no time and spare no expense. I am a rich man, I can reward you."

"Tell me the circumstances of her disappearance," Holmes answered, with a curtness that surprised me. As repulsive as Telfair was, no one could deny his distress and concern for his child. Telfair pulled a soiled handkerchief from his sleeve and dragged it across his brow.

"When my wife Edwina died, her loss was a great blow to my girl, for she was very devoted to her mother. We led a retired life here, and I was concerned that Alice would fall into a deep melancholy without some distraction. She wished to go to Paris, to see an exhibition, and so I permitted her to travel. I hired a lady chaperone to accompany her, but, on the first day of their travel, my spirited girl eluded her and completed the journey alone. Alice returned to me five days ago, and while I was stern with her about her lack of regard for her reputation, I was grateful to have her home. But only three days later, I came back from a business meeting in London and found her missing."

"Why do you assume she has been taken, Mr. Telfair?" Holmes asked. "She is of age to marry, and many otherwise respectable young ladies have been known to abandon stern fathers in lonely manors for handsome lovers in exciting cities. Was there any sign of struggle in her rooms, or elsewhere in the house?"

Telfair's sallow cheeks took on twin spots of colour. "No. None."

"And her clothes?"

"I do not understand."

"Was her clothing missing?"

Reluctantly, Telfair nodded. "Two travelling trunks were gone, as were a number of her books. But her jewels were left behind."

"A most obliging criminal, to allow your daughter to gather her attire and her library, but to leave precious stones untouched."

"I... yes...I suppose it seems...rather extraordinary."

Holmes leaned forward and slapped a palm to the desk. Telfair jumped in reaction, one hand lifting to his jaw. My friend's eyes blazed, but his voice was icy.

"I will give you one last opportunity to tell me the truth, Mr. Telfair. But if you attempt to spin another of these ridiculous fables I will wash my hands of you." Holmes glowered at the man, who seemed to curl down into himself, crumpling like a slowly-deflating balloon. "Your daughter has left you; that in itself is unexceptional. Perhaps she has even eloped. But why is it so essential to find her and bring her back that you would cover a perfectly natural event with such a clumsy lie?"

Telfair took several wavering breaths before speaking. "I could tell you the truth, but you would not believe me. It is too fantastical."

Holmes's lips twitched. "You would be astonished by the stories I have been told. Your tale cannot be any stranger."

The wrinkled man shuddered. "It will be. Oh yes, it definitely will be stranger than any you have ever heard." He slumped in his chair, taking a few moments to gather his breath. "To begin," he whispered, "how old would you say my daughter is?"

He pointed to the photograph that I was still holding and, from time to time, secretly admiring. She was truly a striking girl. Holmes looked to me, one raised eyebrow indicating that it was my expertise on the fair sex that should be consulted. I coughed and stammered out a reply.

"No more than a day over twenty, I should think."

Telfair smirked, but there was an odd and sudden sadness in his eyes. "Alice is almost a century in age. Her lost mother reached the age of a hundred and fifty years, and I was born in the year of our Lord sixteen ninety-five."

Holmes's expression was one of cool and calm acceptance. He leaned back in his chair, as relaxed as he was when seated in our rooms at Baker Street.

"Intriguing," Holmes said. He placed his fingers together in a steeple. "Mr. Telfair, do continue."

CHAPTER FOUR

Telfair rose and plucked an ancient, leather-bound journal from the shelf behind him. He placed it on the desk and turned it so that we could see pages covered in antique script, with dates in the eighteenth century clearly marked.

"I was born in Boston, to Puritan parents of modest means. I was a very smart lad, a boy of much scholarly promise, and my father worked hard to save enough money to send me to Harvard College. He wanted me to become a minister of our faith, but I was not made for such a life. I grew into a wild young buck, fonder of drinking and carousing than conjugating Latin verbs or memorizing the scriptures. At last the inevitable happened: there was a girl and a scandal. She was the daughter of my theology professor, and I fled the colony rather than live up to my responsibilities. I never saw my heartbroken parents again."

He looked to us, clearly expecting mockery or more anger. As for myself, I was too astonished to attempt speech. Holmes merely nodded for him to resume his story.

"My wanderings took me from the safety of the English settlements to the far reaches of the Spanish holdings in the west. I was gifted with languages and acquired a fair understanding not only of Spanish but also of many native dialects and pagan tongues. I became an itinerant merchant, a trader along the lonely trails. Something of the scholar remained in me, however, and drew me to the settlement of Santa Fe. I had always been absorbed by antiquities, and in this crude settlement I found much that revived my boyhood passion for the past. I conceived the idea that I would write a treatise upon the history of the little town and my adventures among the savages. This, I hoped, would win the fame my churlish behaviour had robbed me of in Boston.

"It was in Santa Fe that I met Father Olivarez. He was a strange character, a tall and extraordinarily lean man who wore the ragged robes of a Franciscan friar. A great brass cross circled his neck, but he allowed his hair and beard to grow to such lengths that he could braid them both into long plaits which dangled off his scalp and jaw. From the local gossips I quickly learned that some indiscretion had removed Olivarez from the Church, and that he had no official sanction to perform the sacraments. Yet he was often called to the bedside of dying outlaws and harlots, where he ministered to them more gently than any respectable man of the cloth would have done. He was somewhat solitary, but I made his acquaintance one day while studying the records of a local mission and, as we were both outcasts in that strange land, we fell into a kind of fellowship.

"Father Olivarez shared my love of history and arcane topics. Many a night I sat in his adobe hut and discussed long dead kings and wizards. His tales were so vivid I once asked if he had been in the marvellous courts he described. A shadow passed over his face as I said this to him. Something in my innocent remark made him uncomfortable, so much that he drew the evening to an abrupt end. But a few days later he hailed me in the graveyard, where I was scribbling tombstone inscriptions into my notebook. With a few kindly words, we were good fellows again.

"Early one summer morning, I felt something slither across my chest, rousing me from a deep sleep. Instinctively I struck at it, and the fiendish black scorpion that had crawled into my bed stung me with all of its venomous fury. My screams brought the doctor, who told me there was nothing he could do to save me. I had been fatally poisoned. I could feel my body swelling, the fever clouding my mind. I shrieked when I saw Olivarez approach my bed, no doubt to administer his unorthodox last rites.

"Instead, he pulled a dark bottle from a canvas bag, forcing it to my lips and urging me to drink. Water gushed into my mouth and the next instant I felt an odd tingling followed by a rush of blessed coolness, as if my body had been submerged in the deepest stream. I slipped out of consciousness and when I awakened a day later, I found myself in perfect health. The ugly wound of the scorpion's sting had vanished. I felt no nausea or lingering weakness. Even more startling, when I walked to my basin and washed my face, lifting my countenance to the mirror, I saw that my hair--which had thinned so much that I might have been mistaken for a monk--was now thick and lustrous, as black as it had been in my childhood.

"I dressed and hurried to Olivarez's house, filled with gratitude and curiosity. How and why had he hidden his talents as a healer? Surely a man who could concoct a potion that was both an antidote to poison and a stimulant to bodily repair should share his wondrous medication with the world. I babbled all this to him, but he only shook his head. It was not his secret to share, he averred, as it was something he had stolen.

"All that day, he spoke in vague terms of a magical Fountain in the Spanish colony of Florida where mysterious, life-granting waters flowed, and of a map he had acquired, the only one in existence that would reveal the location of this marvellous place. It was a map that no man could copy. He had tried, he said, to draw it on paper, but it had a way of suddenly dancing about, the lines and symbols on it changing whenever he made the effort of replication. I asked him to show me this map, but he would not. He claimed that ever since he snatched it away from its rightful owner, a dark shadow had followed him. This unseen thing gave him a sense of foreboding and caused him such misery he could never reside long in one place.

"I begged him that if he would not share the map with me, would he at least take me to the spring. I offered him what little wealth I had acquired, with the promise of more to come, but again he refused. This spring was a curse on the world, he warned, a terrible and unnatural thing. And more than the map was required to find it, for a dreadful mist, which only a wizard of exceptional power could lift, surrounded the Fountain. Olivarez claimed that no mortal was meant to know of this place, or drink its water for, while the water healed the flesh, it also brought on a subtle corruption of the soul. He had only given me a draught out of pity to save my life because of our friendship. He ordered me now to return to the English colonies and forget I had ever known him.

"Such a thing was impossible. For days I brooded over his words. Perhaps he was mad and his story was merely the working of a crazed mind. Or maybe he was mocking my credulity with a dark fairy tale. Yet when I looked at my hair, or felt the renewed vigour in my limbs, I could not discount the wonder that only a few swallows of the water had worked.

"And so I decided that I must have the map. I purchased several bottles of strong liquor and went to Olivarez's house at night. I told him I was leaving Santa Fe in the morning, and that I did not want us to part as anything less than true friends. I knew he had a weakness for drink, and by candlelight I coaxed him to consume more than was prudent, so that just after midnight the defrocked priest collapsed on the dirt floor, snoring loudly. I searched his small dwelling, and to my great surprise found a metal ring set into the floor beneath a shrine to the Virgin. This I pulled on, opening a door and descending into a vast cellar. There I found nearly a hundred bottles, all carefully sealed with wax. I also found a locked wooden chest. With an axe I smashed the lock, then pushed back the lid. Inside the chest was a brittle parchment covered in marvellous designs. I took the paper and as many bottles of water as I could stuff into a sack before making my way from Olivarez's dwelling.

"I had all intentions of gathering my things and fleeing, but my conscience stopped me. I began to regret my treatment of Olivarez. I had betrayed a friendship and robbed the man who saved my life. Guilt wrapped around me, and I moved as if weighed down by chains. By the time I finished strapping my meagre possessions to my horse, I knew I could not commit the crime I intended. Filled with shame, I rode back to the padre's house, wondering if I could somehow return the map before he roused and slink away into the night without him ever knowing of my perfidy.

"A single lantern still burned within; I could see its glow through the open window. As I tied my horse to the rough-hewn post, I noticed that Olivarez's flea-bitten cur was crouched at the corner of the dwelling, wide-eyed and trembling in terror. This should have been a sign, but at the time I was too tangled in my own mortification to notice. The door was ajar---another warning I failed to heed. Instead I entered, prepared to confess everything.

"Two paces within, I saw Olivarez on the floor. Or, rather, I saw the thing that had once been Olivarez. He was mutilated, so horribly torn asunder that his body had only the general shape of a man. Bones and vital organs were visible, and blood was everywhere, the metallic odour of it so strong it nearly overwhelmed me. The old man's garments had been stripped from him, and lay in tatters across the floor. His few possessions were likewise destroyed with exceptional violence. I should have run away immediately, but some perverse, terrible curiosity drew me to the open door in the floorboards. I took two steps down the ladder, far enough to see that the remainder of Olivarez's precious bottles had been shattered and his trunk broken to bits amid the glass.

"It was then I realized my folly. I had trod in Olivarez's blood, left the marks of my boots around his corpse. The residents of Santa Fe all knew me and knew of my peculiar friendship with the man. This deed could not be concealed, and I would surely be blamed for it. The defrocked priest had admirers among the fiercest men in the territory. Even if the officers of the law released me, the bandits and cutthroats would track me down and avenge their friend. I had to flee their wrath. I mounted my horse and galloped away into the night.

"I made my way cautiously across the wilderness, going to great extremes to protect the dozen bottles so carefully wrapped in my pack. At last I settled in the city of Providence, where I went into business as a clerk in a merchant company. I prospered, I wed, and a son, Alexander, was born to us. But despite my happiness, I could not forget the map, which I kept locked away in the most respected bank in the city."

"And how did you use the water?" Holmes asked.

Telfair sighed, drawing one crooked finger along the top of his journal's open page, as if working an invisible equation. "The water I carefully rationed; never more than a swallow was needed to affect the most superb rejuvenation from any illness or accident. We withheld the water from our son until he was twenty, for even before he was born we had noted another consequence of the water's frequent consumption. By taking regular draughts we ceased to age, remaining physically as sound as two people in their third decade of life. Only when Alexander reached the full bloom of young manhood did we share our elixir, rejoicing in our belief that we would live forever as a family. Of course, this unnatural state necessitated many moves, for people would start to notice our lack of aging and whisper about us, and the thing we feared most was our secret being discovered. We vowed never to share our precious tonic with the world." His face suddenly clouded. His bottom lip quivered as he forced out another sentence. "But then we learned the truth, that we were not immortal after all."

"How did you discover this?" Holmes inquired with a professorial air, showing no sympathy for Telfair's distress.

"In the most painful way imaginable. In the year of the Peace of Paris, Alexander was thrown from his horse in the street outside our home. He was killed instantly, his neck snapped. I poured an entire bottle of the water over him, but he did not revive. With his passing I understood the bargain we had made: my family could not escape death if it came in a violent or unnatural fashion. We could only seek to avoid it by evading any form of illness and maintaining our supernatural state of youthfulness."

Holmes considered. "Even with the most meagre consumption, your supply must have dwindled."

"It did," Telfair agreed. "And after Alice was born, I knew that I must find the Fountain."

He opened a drawer and laid a yellowed book upon the table. I turned it so that I could read its title: *The Territory of Florida*.

"I left my family behind, for Florida, which was only recently made a state, was a wild and lawless place. I took up residence in the tiny town of St. Augustine, the nearest settlement to the location of the Fountain. For weeks I wandered through the swamps and hammocks, certain that I had found my goal. But whenever I came close, a kind of green fog descended, veiling the spot where the map indicated the Fountain should be. Once, I foolishly wandered into that deep, putrid mist. I was instantly disoriented, unable to see, or hear, or even feel the ground beneath my feet. It drove me nearly to madness, those hours that I struggled to make some progress in that dank void. At last, the fog itself seemed to gather me up and hurl me from its depths, vomiting me onto a dirt trail. I travelled back to town, only to find the city much changed, filled with visitors who wore clothing of an unfamiliar style. The streets were wider, the homes finer. I staggered into a tavern, seizing a newspaper someone had discarded on a table. I read the date with horror. More than ten years had passed!

"I at last heeded Father Olivarez's warning: the Fountain of Youth could be discovered only with the map and with magic. I would need to find a conjurer, one who understood the strange rites necessary to part the fog and give access to the spring. But where could such a man be found? I pondered whether I should go to Europe to seek out mages in the shadowy lanes of crumbling castles, or to the Orient, where Chinese wizards were said to dwell atop cloud-covered mountains. But then I recalled stories I had heard of Negro slaves who knew hoodoo and other forms of dark work. I made discreet inquires, and in another year I learned of Old Gator, a bondsman who was said to have exceptional powers. By good fortune the slave's master was heavily in debt and eager for ready cash. It was not a happy trade, for in buying Old Gator and taking him to St. Augustine, I removed him from his wife and many children. But I promised him freedom if he would help me find the Fountain, and he agreed, though with great reluctance. He warned me that the spring I sought was cursed, but I was in no mood for his ignorant superstition. All that mattered was his ability to work the spell, lift the fog and find the water.

"I hired a small craft to take us up the San Sebastian River. We went as far as Devil's Creek, where we disembarked with a horse and wagon while the boat tied up to await our return. We pushed along the narrow, winding banks of the stream, which led to a point where we could go no further, for just beyond, creeping through the trees and vines, was the strange, green-hued mist. It hung heavy and thick, as well defined as some vast velvet curtain.

"Old Gator bent down and gathered a handful of mud. He mixed it in his palm with leaves and twigs, grinding the mass together until blood trickled from between his fingers. He flung his concoction forward, into that heavy fog. The mist rippled and quivered, reacting to the assault as if it were a living thing. It parted, rising to form an unnatural archway. Old Gator led me through it, down a tunnel of impenetrable darkness. Abruptly, just as I was certain the spell had failed and I was once again lost, we emerged into open ground and bright sunlight. I marvelled at the change, which my slave explained was a working of the Fountain's magic.

"I had never seen a more beautiful vision. Majestic palms swayed above a small, perfectly oval pool. The water twinkled beneath the outcropping of a moss-covered cliff. Peering over the edge, it seemed that I could see downward for miles. In the spring's depths I beheld marvellous things: bejewelled palaces, ivory-paved roads, great tabernacles to ancient, mystic gods. I would have fallen from the precipice, tumbling headfirst into the water, had not Old Gator seized my jacket and pulled me back. He warned me that these visions were mere illusions. If I could see the pool for what it really was, he warned, I would go mad.

"I had room in my cart for well over a hundred bottles, each of them carefully wrapped in soft woollen cloth and padded by cotton bolls. For long hours we worked, side by side, the daylight never fading in that magical place. When the task was near completion, I slipped a revolver from my pack and hid it in my pocket. I ordered Old Gator to fill one last bottle and, as he knelt at the water's edge, I stepped behind him, aimed my gun, and put a bullet in his brain."

CHAPTER FIVE

I had sat in astounded silence throughout his tale, but this admission drew an exclamation of horror and disgust from my lips. Telfair blinked, as if emerging from a trance. He considered me with jaundiced eyes.

"What else could I have done? Old Gator could not be permitted to talk and give away my secret, or lead others to the site. I could not afford the luxury of his survival." Telfair shook his head. "He was only a slave."

Holmes was considering Telfair with the same disdain one would adopt when viewing a loathsome insect. I shuddered as I imagined Old Gator's body sinking into the depths of the spring, his blood spreading out like the slow opening of a scarlet flower. "There were no questions asked when you returned alone to the boat?" Holmes said.

"None. I told the captain the slave had taken fright and run away into the woods." Telfair shuddered at his memories. "But I had nearly paid the price for my treachery. The tunnel began to close on me as I travelled back through it. I could feel the clamminess even before the mist came down, as the very darkness of the tunnel seemed to condense, becoming smaller and smaller. But I whipped the nag unmercifully and emerged at a point only a short distance from my transportation."

Holmes nodded. "Your researches must have taxed your wealth by this time."

Telfair coughed harshly. "My accounts were almost completely exhausted. But I had gained knowledge during my travels. I understood that the states of the South were very different to those of the North, and would one day be sincere in their determination to be free of the Union, something that many northern businessmen were unwilling to believe. With the last of my funds, I founded the Arkham Manufacturing Company and began producing rifles in great numbers. When the Confederate rebellion broke out, I was excellently placed to take advantage of the many government contracts that came my way. I expanded my business, and soon offered the government not only arms, but uniforms, shoes, and medical equipment. I acquired a new fortune, one vaster than any I could have dreamed."

"Why did you leave America?" I asked, wishing such a repulsive man had stayed on the other side of the ocean.

Telfair's hands began to twitch. "Because my money was also ill-made, Doctor. My goods were what we Americans call 'shoddy.' My rifles were prone to jamming, and the uniforms I provided were often threadbare in a matter of weeks. No one could march more than a mile in my boots, and the foodstuffs we sent to the army were filled with maggots and weevils. Such practices lined my pockets and those of my partners, but eventually drew the ire of powerful men in Congress. Investigations were called for, with the threat of prosecution. I decided that it was time to move on, and so with my family, my fortune, and my precious cargo of water from the Fountain of Youth, I travelled to Europe.

"We lived the life of wealthy vagabonds, residing for periods in the great cities of the continent. My money gave me the leisure to once again pursue my beloved studies of antiquity. The collection you see around you has been built over the last forty years. Nothing was beyond my grasp. See here, see what I found!" A new kind of animation, driven by avarice and hideous to behold, washed over Telfair's face. He leapt up, pulling more books from his shelves and

40

toppling boxes filled with strange objects. "The *Book of the Dead*, the breastplate of Constantine, the bones of St. Jerome---all are mine, and will be, for as long as...as..."

He dropped back into his chair, gasping like a fish hurled on a riverbank. His skin had turned an ugly shade of greenish grey and was emitting a soured, sickly odour. His chest heaved. Grotesquely, he began to weep. Holmes picked up one of the scattered artefacts from the desk, a knucklebone set with diamonds, examining it closely as he spoke in a scholarly tone.

"So tell me, Mr. Telfair, why did your daughter steal your map?"

"But...I have not said..."

"I grow weary of this tale, and of you," Holmes interrupted, with sudden bite. "Only the theft of your precious map, the one thing that guarantees you an unnaturally-long existence, could affect you in such a way."

Telfair clumsily wiped his face with the back of his hand. "Two years ago, we were living in Paris. Alice had inherited my love of scholarship, and nothing pleased me more than to indulge her wish to spend hours in the great library of the Sorbonne. Edwina was, by comparison, a dull woman who cared only for her clothing and jewels. I confess that I ignored my wife in favour of my daughter, but when my wife rebuked me for my neglect and bragged that she had taken a lover, her betrayal enraged me. There was a dreadful quarrel, and I shoved Edwina down the great staircase of our mansion. When I reached her, I saw that she was desperately wounded, but not expired. I could have saved her life, I could have given her the water, but despite my daughter's screams and pleading, I refused. Before our eyes my wife withered, the evidence of the great age she had attained racing back upon her as her life flittered away. When she died, only minutes later, she was as withered as a mummy, and at Alice's touch she crumbled into dust.

"I suppose it is my fault, what happened next. Alice could never forgive me for her mother's death. Her manner to me was cold and, though she stayed with me, I could see in her eyes that a fierce hatred of me now burned beneath her icy civility. She devoted herself even more intensely to her books and soon surpassed me as a scholar, especially of occult topics. In fact, though it grieves me to confess it, I came to fear her. Had she lived in another age she would have been burnt as a witch for the experiments she made, the dark forces she toyed with as carelessly as another woman might don a bonnet. I tried to confine her here, deep in the countryside, where her research into black magic could be conducted in private, but she insisted on travelling and acquiring more books and relics. She was in America for a time, and I know nothing of her activities there except she wrote to me that in Boston she had found a companion who would grant her any favour. She returned home alone, and I thought all was well between us, that perhaps she had abandoned her obsession with black magic and granted me absolution for my sin. But two nights ago, she must have placed some type of spell on me or slipped a drug into my wine. I awoke late the following day, still slumped in my chair. She was missing, some twenty bottles of water had been taken, and the map was gone from my safe. It was then that I recalled reading of your visit in the local paper, Doctor Watson, and knew that if anyone could help me, it was Sherlock Holmes."

Holmes sighed. I could tell that Telfair's story, as fantastical as it had been, had wearied him. His tone indicated that his patience had been pushed to the breaking point.

"It is only natural, sir, that a spirited young woman should not wish to be confined with her elderly father in a dreary house. I would counsel patience, Mr. Telfair. You may find yourself deprived of your prized possession and, I fear, saddled with a son-in-law not to your liking. But many men have experienced worse, and from your own admissions your daughter is in no immediate peril." Holmes rose. "For the entertainment your narrative has provided, I will forgo my usual consulting fee."

Telfair leapt to his feet. "You do not believe me!"

"I did not say as much. I do, however, assert that your daughter is in no danger, and if you are half the wretch you have confessed yourself to be, you are receiving no more than your due in misery."

Telfair gasped. "But you must find her. You must! Not only has she taken the map, she has broken all the remaining bottles!"

I had likewise risen to depart, but Telfair's words, screamed at Holmes's back, rooted me to the spot. The pathetic man whirled on me, holding out his hands in supplication.

"You see it, Doctor? I have imbibed for too long, I am dependent upon the water now. In only two days I have begun to wither, to shrivel and decay from within! I must have the water, I must consume it regularly in order to maintain my life, to keep all the years at bay!"

Holmes said nothing. I shook my head. Telfair gave another hideous screech and dashed around his desk. Panting like a dog, he grasped my friend by the lapels.

"Wait---you cannot leave---there is more I must tell you. The shadow, the dark, unseen and unknown thing that Olivarez feared---

43

I have felt it, too. Yesterday, for the first time, I sensed it just behind me, watching me, biding its time. I could not tell you what it is, or describe it, I only knew it was <u>there</u>, so close! Mr. Holmes, whatever this undefined, unnameable thing may be, I am certain that it wants my life. It is going to kill me!"

I looked to my friend. His face was like a stone.

"You are more than overdue for death, Mr. Telfair," Holmes said, firmly detaching the man's hands from his jacket. "I bid you good day."

CHAPTER SIX

Holmes was silent on the ride back to Darby's estate. The expression on his countenance bore such gravitas that I was afraid to question him, and so held my peace on our journey. I was amazed to find that we had been at Oakhurst for most of the day, and that a soft twilight was beginning its summer descent, bathing the landscape in ethereal colours.

Holmes stated his intent to return to the city, but I pleaded with him to spend the night at Haven House. Darby and his wife were delighted to have him as a guest, insisting that their cook prepare a French feast in honour of Holmes' most recent triumph in service of that republic. As we dressed for dinner, I finally summoned the courage to ask the question that was foremost in my mind.

"Holmes, the tale we were told...could it have been real?"

In truth, I expected to be mocked or even insulted for my credulity. Instead, Holmes turned slowly from the mirror, stilled in the act of straightening his tie.

"What do you think, Watson?"

I was shocked to be asked to give an opinion. I decided to be logical; or rather, to try and rationalize what I had heard.

"Springs of water have long been credited with miraculous properties. I spent a week in Baden-Baden once, and would have sworn that I felt revived by half a decade, at the least. Is it not possible, then, that some fountain, whose healing properties have not yet been examined by science, could exist? And that Telfair is telling the truth?"

"I had not expected you to be such a fervent supporter of hydrotherapy, Watson!" Holmes said, in a manner that bordered on patronizing. "How then would you explain the map?"

"That is easily dismissed as fiction. Any map can be copied. Telfair was foolish to never attempt it."

Holmes nodded agreement. "Let us assume that such a miraculous spring does exist, one capable of producing youth and unnaturally long life. Let us also agree that everything happened as Telfair said, and that the young woman, wishing vengeance on her father for the wilful murder of her mother, did steal the map and destroy his supply of the life-giving liquid. Should my advice to him change in the least? Is there anything I could do, at this point, to save such a creature?"

"No, I suppose not. But what about his insistence that he is being followed, his overwhelming dread?"

"Again, presuming that this remarkable tale is somehow true, it stands to reason that a man who has committed theft and cold-blooded murder, and is responsible for the sufferings of untold numbers of American soldiers, should feel guilt to the point of paranoia. I find nothing especially remarkable in that." Holmes secured a cuff link and scowled at me. "Watson, again I offer you a hypothetical. What if everything Telfair said is true, but there is no natural explanation for the Fountain's properties? What if magic exists in this world, magic beyond any scientific explanation? What would you make of it then?"

I found myself forced to chuckle at my own folly. "If so, then I would pray that my dreams were true and that you are the wizard my mind has so often conjured you up to be!"

Holmes rolled his eyes. I realized, abruptly, that I had punned on the word. I was ready to apologize when Crenshaw appeared, summoning us to dinner.

As always, it was a treat to be the guests of the Darbys. The meal was exquisite, and Mrs. Darby, lush in a rose-colored gown that flattered her perfect porcelain skin, was a delight for the eyes of even the world's most confirmed bachelor. At Holmes's insistence, we did not discuss Telfair, despite Darby's obvious curiosity about his eccentric neighbour. The evening might have ended in a game of cards or with a serenade from the musical couple, but the sudden appearance of a man in a long coat, his hat pulled low, intruded on our pleasantries just as Crenshaw was bringing in dessert.

"Inspector Larson," Darby said, "what on earth are you doing here?"

The man was grim-faced. "I am sorry to have to intrude on your party, but there has been a rather ghastly occurrence at Oakhurst. I had heard in the village that the famous Mr. Holmes was visiting and…" As he drew his hat off, we could tell that he was shaken. His skin was gray, his lips bitten bloody. "Do give me a brandy, Darby, that's a good fellow."

He dropped into a chair as we hurried to offer him a strengthening draught. He downed half of it in one swallow. With a tremble in his voice he begged Mrs. Darby to depart, as what he had to tell us was not proper for a lady's delicate sensibilities.

"It's a bad business. In all my years, I've never seen such a thing," he muttered once my friend's wife had reluctantly left the room. "Not even in the colonies, among savages, have I laid eyes on anything so hideous. He's dead, sirs. Mr. Telfair has been brutally murdered. At least…I presume that thing in the study is his corpse."

His strange words ignited immediate action. Darby remained behind, unwilling to leave his wife in the care of just the servants, should some madman be on the prowl. Holmes and I rode with Inspector Larson and a constable to the American's manor. If the place had seemed gloomy and despondent in the daytime, by night it was more spectral, as dark and rank as a tomb. I could barely breathe by the time we reached the door, where two more policemen were stationed. By the glow of their lanterns, I could see that both men were in a great state of agitation, their eyes wide and their features drawn into grimaces.

"Have you been back inside?" the Inspector demanded. The men shook their heads.

"No sir, not on my life!" the younger of the pair answered.

"It's not worth even my pension!" the other exploded. "We must have a cannibal loose in our midst."

The inspector seized a lantern and signalled for us to enter. The house was still lit only by candles, which glowed like solitary ghosts in the empty rooms. We retraced our path to Telfair's study. Several lamps had been lit, but the effect was not comforting. Their yellow light fell on the most gruesome thing I had ever seen.

It was a human body without its skin. Clothing, ripped into bloody tatters, was cast aside. The corpse's limbs were flung wide, its mouth opened in a final scream. Horrid eyes stared lidless at the ceiling. Blood had soaked the carpet and the floor beneath the body. I could trace the lines of muscles; indeed, the remains before me resembled the illustrations of anatomical specimens in medical textbooks.

Except that even as we watched, the figure that had once been Telfair appeared to be dissolving, melting with a hiss and a bubble of blood. His tissue was dissipating, as if being slowly cooked by an unseen force.

"God in heaven," Inspector Larson muttered, turning and bolting from the room. I could hear his retching sounds in the hallway.

"He has been flayed," Holmes said dispassionately, kneeling beside the body. A stench was rising from it, but Holmes continued his close inspection undisturbed by the vile aroma. His calmness in the presence of such an atrocity was both astonishing and alarming. He leaned back, brows drawn together. "One wonders, where is the rest of him?"

"What?"

"His skin, Doctor. Where did it go?"

For a moment, the room wavered and I feared I would embarrass myself by being as sick as the inspector. Holmes climbed to his feet and turned me away from the hideous object on the floor.

"Go and see who found the body. Talk to that witness if he is still here."

I nodded, grateful to have a way to be helpful without being forced to remain in the room with the loathsome evidence. Larson directed me to the kitchen in the very rear of the house. A man sat there, unattended by any of the official force. From a distance of several feet, the odours emitting from him told me he was a drunkard, just as his filthy attire and wooden right leg marked him as a mendicant. He shivered when I approached him, but I assured him I was a friend.

"Cor, you don't think they'll pin this on me, do you?" he demanded. However intoxicated he had been hours before, the sight in the study had sobered him.

"Tell me what happened," I said. "I am certain Sherlock Holmes can convince them of your innocence," I added, though such advocacy would hardly be necessary. He was a small man, and besides the loss of a leg, his hands shook convulsively. Even if, despite his handicaps, he could have overpowered and killed Telfair, it would have been impossible for him to dispose of the remains in such a gruesome manner.

"I came by hopin' for a place to stay...been travellin' around, you see." The beggar motioned to a crude pack on the floor. "Thought maybe there would be a barn, or a shed I could sleep in. Came to knock like a proper fellow should, but the back door was ajar. More than that, it was open, swingin' back and forth. Thought I'd had the good luck to find a place that was empty, where I could live like a king for a night of two. Then I walked in and found him! God! Oh, God!"

The man began to sob, rocking back and forth in his chair. It took some time for me to coax the rest of the tale from him, of how he had gone screaming into the night, hobbling away in a panic and not stopping until he reached the village. Inspector Larson had been slow to believe his story and insisted on dragging him back to the house, despite his entreaties to take sanctuary in a church. He begged to be allowed to pray for what he was certain was his now-imperilled soul.

"There's evil here! More than just that thing in the study," the poor man babbled, tearing at his hair. "I feel it! Feel it in my bones!"

I tried to be reassuring, but failed. The man continued to shudder and sob; he had worked himself into such a state I doubted his heart would stand the strain much longer. I called the inspector in and, upon my advice, he sent the witness away to the hospital in the care of one of his officers.

"You'll swear he has no part in this?" Inspector Larson asked.

"He's a beggar and a drunkard. He has neither a reason nor the ability to kill a man in such a manner."

The inspector nodded. He seemed relieved that someone else had concurred with his thoughts. "I barely knew Mr. Telfair," he said. "Quite the hermit he was. But I can't imagine why anyone would murder him and take nothing." He stroked his trim beard, his face set in a mask of confusion. "There was gold in his desk, and plenty of valuable curiosities and baubles scattered all about, yet nothing else was disturbed, as best we can tell. If you don't mind getting Mr. Holmes's opinion on the matter, I would be most appreciative."

I understood immediately: he did not want to go back into the study. I steeled myself to enter where even hardened policemen feared to tread. The door was still open, and I could hear whispered conversation. I stepped inside without preamble, thinking to find Holmes talking with the boldest of the officials.

Instead, I found my friend conversing with a human head resting inside an ivory and gold box.

CHAPTER SEVEN

I must have made a sound, perhaps a gasp or small cry. Holmes looked to me and lifted the box he held, so that I might have a better view of it.

"Watson, I charge you to recall your words of just two hours ago," he said, "and to remember everything."

It is difficult to describe what happened next. It felt like I was standing beneath a great waterfall, but instead of a cold, thunderous spray of water, what I was being showered with were memories. Fractured scenes, snippets of recollections of faces, voices, and actions pounded down upon me. A great roaring enveloped my hearing. My knees wobbled, I staggered forward and grasped a chair for support.

I suddenly saw them all: the Lady Hypatia, Marie Laveau, Spring Heeled Jack and Baron Samedi, the glittering monstrance that held the heart of Saint George, the London Stone, the ravens in their cage. Titania's crown glittered and my soul swirled like smoke in a jar. I was walking through the lost Library of the Arcane and bowing to my Queen in her chapel as her ghostly servant glowered in disapproval. I was fighting for my life; I was saving my friend from certain damnation. And then, as everything snapped back into place and the grand puzzle in my brain was completed, I saw Sherlock Holmes standing beside me, keeping a firm grip upon my shoulder.

I knew both who and what he was.

"Once more unto the breach, dear friends," Holmes stated. "You are an exceptional man, Watson, with a mind powerful enough to rally against one of the most powerful enchantments ever devised. Your soul returned easily, but your memories had to fight a bit harder. Welcome back."

Dumbly, I nodded. I looked to the box, which my friend had tucked under his right arm like a rugby ball. Its front side was open, revealing a wizened human head. The head was mummified, its eyes shut, but reddish hairs were still visible on its scalp and chin, as was a prominent mole and a scar on one cheek. Bizarrely, the visage seemed familiar to me, as if I had seen it somewhere before. But surely it was a long dead thing, the remains of some person who had been deceased for centuries. Perhaps I had imagined that it was somehow animate.

Its eyes opened. Bright blue orbs stared at me as the thing in the box spoke.

"*Bonsoir, Monsieur le Docteur.*"

I was so taken aback I blurted out the painfully obvious. "It's French."

Holmes regarded me with wry amusement. "A brilliant deduction, Watson. May I present His Royal Highness, King Henri IV of France. Perhaps you remember him from your school days? He brought the evils of the French Wars of Religion to a close and was the author of the Edict of Nantes, which provided a modicum of toleration for the Huguenots. He is most famously known for saying, upon his conversion to Catholicism, that 'Paris is well worth a mass.'"

I stared at the thing inside the box. "How is this possible?"

Holmes continued as if giving a lecture to a museum's guest. I would be prepared to swear that the decapitated head was smirking at me, its dry lips twitching at their corners.

"In 1793, revolutionaries desecrated the vaults of the Basilica of St. Denis, that great royal necropolis where Henri and his ancestors were entombed. His head was removed and used as a football before being rescued by a citizen who was appalled by such profane behaviour. Later, the king's head was sold, and somehow our late associate Mr. Telfair acquired it."

"But how can it talk?" I demanded, backing away when Holmes once again lifted the box, considering its contents. I was reminded of Hamlet with Yorrick's skull.

"Through an animation spell," Holmes answered. "One of unfortunately limited duration. Forgive me while I complete this interview."

As I watched, Holmes continued to speak to the strange being in the box, asking what it had witnessed. The head replied softly, retaining a strange dignity in the perfectly accented words.

"*Je n'ai rien vu. J'ai entendu quelques paroles.*"

"What did you hear?"

"*Il parlait espagnol. Il demandait la carte.*"

Holmes nodded. "And then?"

"*Il n'y avait que des cris terribles.*"

"Yes," Holmes replied. "I imagine that the scream was horrible to hear." He put one hand to the dropped side of the container. "Thank you, Your Majesty."

The head closed its eyes. I perceived a bizarre weariness in the desiccated features. "*Veuillez me laisser dormir,*" it finished and, with another soft thanks, Holmes closed the box and placed it back on the nearest shelf.

"Good God," I whispered.

Holmes turned and brushed off his hands. "I am sorry to have startled you, Watson, but his was the only possible testimony to what occurred in this room. Our villain was careful to leave no traces, and soon even the body will be gone."

He gestured to the form on the floor. It had crumbled in my absence. At this rate of deterioration in moments it would be only an unsightly stain. I closed my eyes and took several deep breaths. I sensed Holmes slowly approaching me.

"Are you well?" he asked, in an uncharacteristically gentle tone. "Can you bear this?"

I somehow managed to answer in the affirmative. I felt again that I was coming up to take air, surfacing from a deep pool of fantastical experiences. "How could I have lost such vivid memories?" I said. "How could I have not known that you are a wizard?"

Holmes addressed my confusion with his usual brisk efficiency. "When you took back your soul, months ago, your mind refused to accept the cleansing enchantment that normally follows such an action. I had warned you that it was unlikely you would recall anything, but you seemed determined to retain your memories. I was not prepared for your mind to fight so hard, to actually go to war with your body in order to retain those recollections of your journey into the world of the Shadows. That struggle nearly killed you."

"My long illness was caused by this conflict?" I said, wrestling with strange new thoughts.

"Yes. You gave us all quite a turn, Doctor. And when you awoke, it became clear to me that you would eventually regain those memories. I suspected that if you stayed in London, they would return too fast, before you were physically able to endure them. Thus I sent you off to the country." He glanced back at the morbid thing near our feet. "But now the past has caught up with us, and I will need your help."

"But how can I aid you in this?" I murmured. The weight of my resumed knowledge pressed against me, like a great cloak that I was being forced to don. "I am no magician."

"Whether my investigations are in Sun or Shadows, I want you by my side," Holmes insisted. His sardonic humour returned, along with a twitch in his cheek. "I would be lost without my Boswell."

"You know it is my greatest honour to assist you," I murmured, disturbed as the last of the gory remains of Mr. Edgar Telfair disappeared into the ether, leaving only a rank odour behind. "What did you learn from the king?" I asked, sending myself a mental order to charge forward, rather than retreat.

"Your French is not adequate?" Holmes asked.

"In a restaurant, yes. From the mouth of a long dead and decapitated monarch, no!" I replied, with some heat. Holmes held up a conciliatory hand.

"He said that he saw nothing and heard only a few words. The intruder spoke Spanish, demanding the return of a map. One can easily reconstruct the rest. When Telfair did not have the map--

and there could be only one map that his visitor wanted--his inopportune guest assaulted and killed him. One might even say he took his pound of Telfair's flesh."

"But who was this murderer?"

"I do not know. I know only that he spoke Spanish." Holmes nudged his shoe against a bloodstain. "It seems rather out of the Black Legend, does it not? Something from a torturer's dungeon."

I shook my head. "Holmes, how will this help the police?"

"I fear it will not. I can hardly make the authorities aware of my unique informant. I can only tell them that Mr. Telfair was murdered by a person or persons unknown."

A ghastly idea occurred to me. I did not wish to speak it, but I felt it necessary, even as my revulsion with the thought caused me to stumble over my words. "Could it have been his daughter?"

Holmes stroked a finger against his lips. "It is possible but not probable. She had already taken revenge on her father for her mother's death in a way that would lead to a grisly demise. Why return and inflict a different, if even more hideous, form of execution? And there is the question of the Spanish that the king heard a male voice speak."

"Telfair said his daughter mentioned a companion."

"An excellent counterpoint, Watson. But is that individual male or female? Telfair never clarified the gender." Holmes moved to the door. I skirted the circle of blood, following him. "We must leave the local authorities to their own devices. My suspicion, however, is that this case will soon pass into local folklore, and Oakhurst will become a haunted house."

"Alice Telfair must be notified."

"If she can be found," Holmes countered.

We took our leave of the authorities. I noticed that Holmes never informed them of our earlier interview with Telfair; perhaps he feared we would be considered suspects in the man's murder! Inspector Larson was kind enough to return us to Haven House, where we found both Darby and his lady still awake, eager to hear the news. Holmes provided a somewhat edited version of the events, telling them of the gruesome mutilations, but omitting the works of sorcery.

"How horrible!" Mrs. Darby exclaimed. "Do you think there is any danger to the neighbourhood?"

"No, I am certain that this was an act of private vengeance," Holmes said. "Telfair was the target, and he had a premonition that he was being stalked."

"Still, I'll keep my gun at my side, at least for the next month or so," Darby proclaimed. "Will you stay to investigate further?"

Holmes demurred. "I must return to London in the morning. And I fear I am about to rob you of your guest. I need Watson's help as I pursue this matter further."

The Darbys strenuously protested the loss, but at last Crenshaw was summoned to help me pack. I got little rest that night, for my dreams returned with such vividness that it seemed I was once more fighting the evil witch-queen Marie Laveau and waging war against zombie minions.

Holmes woke me before dawn. My gracious hosts were already dressed, ready to bid us farewell as we loaded into a dogcart, bound for the station. But as we rattled away, a suspicion that had been growing since my memories were unlocked began to nag at me.

"Holmes," I said, "was Darby really my friend? Or yours?"

"Watson, you are truly back in fine form," Holmes chuckled. "What gave them away?"

"For one thing, it was odd for an old army companion of mine to appear so conveniently out of the blue. And I did not even recall anything about him until he shook my hand."

"For good reason," Holmes said. "You had never met him, Watson. He was not even a military man!"

"How did you manage such a deception?"

Holmes looked unbearably pleased with himself. "It was not my magic at work, but his. Thomas Darby possesses the ability to plant suggestions in the mortal mind; in fact, all of his kind do. It is how they have managed to move so easily from the world of Shadows. I offered the hint that he was a former companion, and when his hand met yours that brief contact gave him access to your consciousness, allowing him to place perfectly harmless, though completely false, impressions in your brain."

Some part of me felt I should be offended by this manipulation, even for the kindest of reasons. I worked to place an appropriate amount of annoyance in my voice. "There was always something about them that seemed a bit unworldly. I never could place my finger on it, however."

Holmes reached into the pocket of his cape and pulled out a small set of field glasses. "I owe you a thousand apologies, and I confess my meddling, but it was essential for you to get some rest. I also wished you to be guarded by one of my allies, in case those true memories returned all at once. Look through these," he commanded, handing me the glasses. "They will allow you to penetrate the mental fog that Darby created. Gaze back and tell me what you see."

I was certain it was too dark to pick out anything, especially now that we were just beyond their drive, but I obeyed and put the device to my eyes. To my astonishment, through those lens the scene was as bright as day! I could see Haven House and its occupants standing in the yard.

All were transformed. The house itself was now a true castle, with great swirling spires and majestic towers. Silken banners waved in a breeze, one that we did not feel. At the gate, Darby was no longer a gentleman in jodhpurs and jacket, but a slender elf, with long golden braids hanging behind pointed ears. His spouse was of similar form, and dressed in a gown of glistening fabric so fine it seemed spun of cobwebs. Both husband and wife were ethereally beautiful.

Holmes plucked the glasses away from me. "Careful, Watson. No mortal was meant to gaze on elves in their natural bodies. They have a way of unsettling mortal senses."

"They are...friends of yours?"

"Relations, on my mother's side."

"Good heavens," I whispered. Holmes snapped the reins, encouraging our horse into a canter.

"I could have sent you to my kinsmen in Yorkshire," Holmes said with a smile, "but I suspected elfin company would be much more congenial."

CHAPTER EIGHT

There was a small pyramid of letters and telegrams waiting for Holmes on our Baker Street breakfast table. With a groan, he sank into the correspondence while I busied myself with restoring my wardrobe to its proper place. By noon Holmes was gone, citing the need to deal with investigations he had abandoned when he received Telfair's summons. I had the distinct impression that, despite the grotesque nature of the murder, Holmes now attached relatively little importance to the case. He said only that Miss Telfair should take care, for perhaps she had inherited the curse that seemed to follow the map.

"Should we not attempt to warn her?" I asked, as Holmes was putting on his hat. He waved his cane in the air.

"I doubt that she would listen," he replied, exiting our rooms with a jaunty salute.

Weeks passed, during which Holmes attended to his affairs and I did little except take aimless walks while I worked to set my mental house in order. I once again reconciled Holmes the mortal detective with Holmes the Halfling wizard, a man born in the Shadows. The more I considered the thing, the more I felt assured that London had never been so well protected. With all the dark and horrible creatures that had escaped the Shadows to become the beasts and terrors of legend, mankind was fortunate to have such a gifted defender as Sherlock Holmes.

But as summer gave way to fall, and fall to a miserably early winter, I was surprised to see no signs that Holmes might renew his interest in the case of Alice Telfair and the map to the Fountain of Youth. Instead, he delved deeply into more mundane matters, and that season was one of his most productive. A dozen cases or more were laid at his doorstep and cleared in a fit of energy that was almost frightening to behold. My recovery now complete, I was once again invited along on investigations, and my notes for that period grew so copious that I was forced to purchase addition cabinets for my files. Holmes seemed unusually happy, eager in his work and, as always, blatantly unconcerned with any rewards beyond the pleasure of completing a puzzle and seeing justice was done. I have no doubt that had he charged more regularly for his services, or accepted all of the many tokens of appreciation that were offered, he could have retired a rich man by the arrival of the holidays.

None of his cases, however, touched on magic or dipped into the Shadows. My few attempts to probe deeper into his hidden nature or to ask questions about that dark mirror of our sunlit world were met with stony silence and the occasional raised eyebrow. I soon understood; Holmes had no urge to recall or discuss the powers that he had inherited. He wanted to be mortal, to live within his mind rather than his preternatural abilities. As much as my curiosity tugged at me, I resolved to respect his wishes and not raise the subject further.

There was, however, one person whom I could not so easily dismiss from my thoughts, and that was the Lady Hypatia. Her beauty, intelligence, and courage were an inspiration to me. I wished to speak with her again, but I knew I would never find the entrance to the Library of the Arcane on my own. I would need to enlist Holmes as a kind of chaperone and, knowing his dislike for any interaction involving the softer passions, this would be a difficult thing to request of him, especially in consideration of his determination not to return to the dark path of his Shadowborn inheritance.

A week before Christmas, I had dreamed of the Lady Hypatia and was considering how I might ask Holmes to grant me the favour I most desired. I was seated at our breakfast table, pondering whether I could phrase the request the way a child might hint at a much longed-for Christmas gift, when Holmes thrust the morning newspaper at me. He jabbed a long finger at a small article buried in the back pages.

"See what has become of your case, Watson!"

"My case?"

Holmes tapped more urgently on the paper. I looked down and read the following:

Lunatic Claims Devil Amuck In Surrey

Yesterday, a Mr. Leonard Fishwick, well known as a mendicant in the neighbourhood of Leatherhead, was committed for life to the Cane Hill Lunatic Asylum. The court proceedings were interrupted in a most unpleasant manner when Mr. Fishwick began to scream and struggle, claiming that the devil was loose in the community and had killed a local citizen, Mr. Edgar Telfair, in a shocking manner. Indeed, before he could be restrained, Mr. Fishwick described mutilations so foul that several female spectators in the courtroom fainted. He also accused the local police of having refused to investigate the matter properly. This reporter spoke with Inspector Jared Larson, who assures our readers that while it is true Mr. Telfair's absence from the community has not been satisfactory explained, no demonic suspects are being sought for questioning.

The newest resident of the Cane Hill Lunatic Asylum is, of course, entitled to his opinions, but this reporter holds that the only thing Satanic in Surrey is the prices charged by the local hotels.

I looked to Holmes. "Does he think this is funny?"

Holmes lit a cigarette. "Of course. The anonymous reporter, forced to do nothing more interesting than chronicle the minutia of a commitment hearing, was grateful for anything to liven up his paragraph." Holmes blew smoke skyward. "And I see that Inspector Larson has managed to cover up this outrage rather effectively."

I folded the paper. "Do you consider the matter closed?"

Holmes's eyes narrowed. I sensed an internal debate, one he finally resolved by snubbing out the half-smoked cigarette and asking me to join him on an impromptu trip to Paris.

"Paris!" I exclaimed.

Holmes rose and pulled the jack-knife from the mantel, freeing a message that had been affixed by its blade. "Brother Mycroft seeks a favour. I am inclined to grant it."

And so we were once again travellers. It had been many years since I had toured the City of Lights and, as the nature of Mycroft's favour was diplomatic and therefore secretive to a degree, I spent most of my time in sightseeing. Bundled in my heaviest coat, I climbed the Eiffel Tower, strolled along the Champs-Elysees, and basked in the smile of the Mona Lisa in the Louvre. I paid an admission to go into the vaults of St. Denis, where the remains of King Henri IV had once resided, wondering as I did if he missed his former resting place.

Holmes, it appeared, had no real concern for the fate of Miss Alice Telfair, but now that he had dubbed the matter my case, I found I could not so easily banish the young woman from my thoughts. As I rambled through the great city, her sweet, innocent face drifted before my eyes. Holmes had frequently warned me that

I should never judge an individual solely by appearance, but the more I considered the case, the more certain I became that a woman of such youth and naiveté could not be culpable of occultism, thievery, and what was, in essence, a slow form of murder. Her father was already unhinged by his exposure to the magical water; perhaps this explained his babbling words against her. Olivarez had warned him that consuming the water would work a corruption in his soul. If this were true, then Mr. Telfair had been lost to us for some time. As his daughter, Alice was younger and healthier, and would have required less of the water to maintain her appearance. Surely her personality was not already altered or stained. If Holmes would just apply himself to this investigation, and locate the young woman, I was confident he could persuade her to give him the map and renounce her unholy researches.

I halted in my tracks. Holmes had decided this case was without merit, but I would not simply fold my hands. The life of a beautiful girl was in the balance. It hardly mattered that, according to her father's statement, she had been born when my parents were young. To my mind, she was only a child and thus worthy of rescue. With boldness fuelled by chivalric impulses, I set a new course, determined to launch my own investigation.

I entered the great library of the Sorbonne and after some negotiation (which taxed both my grasp of the language and my patience with imperious French academics), I was ushered into an office where a librarian of great age and exaggerated dignity sat. I presented my card to him, informing him that I was an agent of Sherlock Holmes. I was pleased to see my friend's name had the desired effect. The librarian puffed up a bit and inquired how he might assist an associate of the "great detective."

I told him we were seeking a young and beautiful lady who had availed herself to researches in the Sorbonne. I hinted that an inheritance was at stake and that we sought the lady to help her claim her rightful due. But much to my surprise, at my mention of Alice Telfair's name the official's face turned purple with rage. What followed was a flurry of French denunciations. He spoke so rapidly and with such palpable fury I feared he would suffer an apoplectic seizure. At last I was able to calm him, and as he mopped his brow he told me, in clearer terms, that he suspected Alice Telfair of thievery. She had gained access to the oldest and most unusual books in his collection, a privilege not normally given to non-students. Her father's wealth had garnered special treatment for the young woman, including the right to consult texts that the librarian deemed most improper for a lady.

When I asked what these texts included, the librarian spewed an entire bibliography of unfamiliar volumes. Seeing my confusion, he scribbled a list and thrust the paper at me. These, he claimed, had been found missing after her departure. Other books had been left in their place, books with nearly identical covers, so that the theft was not discovered until some months later.

"It is not their cost," he shouted---or so I translated---"but their danger. These tomes should not be in the world."

I did not prolong the uncomfortable interview. That evening, Holmes announced his business successfully concluded and a great danger to the British Empire averted. As we sat in a sidewalk cafe along a grand boulevard, we drank celebratory champagne and discussed spending Christmas on the continent. With some embarrassment, I confessed my boldness in attempting to investigate the Telfair matter on my own. Holmes arched an eyebrow, but made no comment until I unfolded the paper with its inventory of stolen books.

The change in his expression was remarkable. The lightness and pride vanished, to be replaced with a stern meeting of the lips. He scowled as he read.

"This is very bad, Watson."

"But what does it mean?"

"That Alice Telfair is far more dangerous than I imagined her to be. As a mortal, with no touch of the Shadows about her except the consumption of the Fountain's waters, she has no access to the Library of the Arcane. But, in her determination to learn dark magic, she has made the most of the occult information available to humanity. Some of these works might be viewed merely as salacious biographies of famous magicians. But others...for a woman determined to become a witch, they are recipe books for the most hideous black magic spells."

"You should not have dismissed her father's concerns so blithely," I said, my remark earning a rather unfriendly look from Holmes.

"I fear that may be my weakness," he admitted, when I refused to retract my statement. "I have a bad habit of underestimating women."

At that moment there was a shout and flurry of disturbance in the crowd. I recalled the recent activity of anarchists and feared we were about to fall victims to terrorism. Women screamed, men shouted. Waiters stumbled, tossing plates and glassware into the air.

I pushed my chair back as something large and grey descended upon our table in a blur of dark wings. To my astonishment, the form proved to be a magnificent falcon with a golden badge around its throat. Holmes smiled and put a hand to the bird. It gentled at his touch.

"Well, now," Holmes said, looking more bemused than startled. "This is certainly a surprise."

"My word, Holmes. Is this one of your familiars?" I asked, *sotto voce*. I could not imagine any other reason for a trained bird of prey to suddenly swoop onto our table.

Holmes shook his head. "Not mine, but another's." He indicated the glittering medallion on the falcon's breast. "She belongs to a fellow sorcerer. But this is hardly a place to receive and decode a message from a mage of such illustrious reputation. Let us retire to our rooms."

He coaxed the bird to his wrist. I was stuck with the task of settling our bill and enduring the angry glares of fellow patrons and staff as we made a rather hasty departure from the restaurant.

CHAPTER NINE

I closed the curtains and locked the door of our hotel room. Holmes sat in a chair, clucking merrily to the falcon. Our feathered companion had caused much amusement in the lobby below. The desk clerk and the porters were probably discussing the odd English addiction to sport and hunting even as we rode up in the elevator.

"To whom does she belong?" I asked, studying the bird. The elegant female was the most beautiful specimen of her species I had ever seen, with feathers that glistened like dark, polished marble. Her talons were, on close inspection, gilded with silver, and so sharp that I feared for Holmes's safety as the bird flexed her feet against his sleeve. Her alertness was intense; her head jerked from side to side, seeking prey in the dark corners of the suite.

"She is the familiar of Doctor John Dee. Have you heard of him?" Holmes asked.

"I have not. Does he have a medical specialty?"

Holmes chuckled softly. "No, he is a Renaissance man in the truest sense of the word. A mathematician, prophet, alchemist, and astronomer, he was also the closest, if the most secret, advisor to the Virgin Queen. It was Doctor Dee who cast the horoscope that determined the day of her coronation." Holmes motioned for me to settle in the chair at the room's desk. "I trust you recall the Spanish Armada?"

"Not personally," I answered, matching his humour. "But, of course, I read of it in my school days. It was the greatest invasion fleet ever assembled when it sailed in 1588. Had it been successful, England would have fallen to Spain."

"Imagine the consequences of such an event," Holmes mused. "The execution of our beloved sovereign for heresy, the dismantling of Parliament, and the installation of all the horrors of the Inquisition! Had the Armada been successful, our fair isle would have been devastated."

"We were fortunate in having such able soldiers and sailors to defend us," I agreed.

Holmes smirked at me. "No offense is intended to the sea dogges like Hawkins and Drake, but the greatest thanks should be offered for the timely storm which battered the clumsy Spanish vessels and sent most of them to the bottom of the sea. Perhaps you recall the line 'Jehovah blew with His winds, and they were scattered'?" Holmes touched the medallion that graced the falcon's breast, drawing my attention to the Greek letter delta engraved on the badge. "And we must also recall that meteorological elements may be manipulated by those with unique talents."

"Are you implying the Almighty had some assistance?" I asked.

"It is a matter of historical record that Doctor Dee remained in his tower all that day, alone with his books and sensitive instruments. When the gale was done, his servants testified that their master was exhausted. I leave it to you to draw the logical conclusion," Holmes said coyly.

"You speak as if you know the man."

"Because I do," Holmes replied. "He was one of my tutors, in my youth."

I suddenly caught on to the joke. "Holmes, are you having fun at my expense? Doctor Dee has surely been dead for over two centuries!"

"One of the advantages of being a Halfling wizard is that death is an uncertain suitor. Doctor Dee is a product of a human and immortal union. His mother was a lady in the court of King Henry VIII and his father a satyr. When age and exhaustion threatens his mortality, Doctor Dee slips back into the Shadows, where no one dies."

I looked to the bird. "So he sends you his familiar from the netherworld?"

"Perhaps. Or it may be that the good Doctor is back in residence in one of his favourite haunts. Over the centuries he has acquired homes in a number of cities. Let us find out what he wants of me."

I fully expected the bird to begin to speak, as it seemed to have the intelligence and bearing of a human of noble blood. But to my surprise, and with the bird's squawking protest, Holmes plucked a feather from its tail. He passed the glittering item to me. Before I could question, he slid an inkwell and tablet of stationary closer.

"Write," he commanded.

I was about to ask what it was he expected me to pen, when the quill itself took control of my hand. It forced its tip into the inkwell. I watched in wonder as the feather began to scratch feverishly across the paper. I had heard of the automatic writing practiced by spiritualist mediums, but I had never imagined myself as a participant in such a fantastic process.

Words took shape on the page, my hand creating them without my consent. The quill seemed possessed, charged with a kind of intelligence. I tried to read what was being scrawled, but the motion was too fast. At last the feverish pace stilled and my fingers dropped the instrument. Each digit cramped from the feverish action, requiring me to massage my hand. Meanwhile, the quill trembled against the page. Abruptly, the feather rolled itself into a ball, flew up into the air, and vanished with a loud pop. No stage conjurer could have performed a more breathtaking illusion.

I was still staring at the space where the quill had disappeared, but Holmes was already removing the paper and reading from it. I was grateful that he could translate, as the fractured swirls and curlicues the enchanted pen had produced were as mysterious to me as the hieroglyphics of ancient Egypt.

"The message is simple, Watson. Doctor Dee requests my presence to consult over a most distressing matter. He is maddeningly vague as to the details, however, but he hints that blood magic has been worked."

I asked him to elaborate. Holmes rose and moved across the room to open the curtains.

"Blood magic is the foulest form of enchantments a human witch or wizard can call forth. It occurs when sacrificial murder is used as a source of fuel; thus the practice's rather unwholesome name." After a moment of studying the sky, Holmes raised the window and returned to the falcon, which had fluttered onto the back of his chair. "But I suspect there is more," Holmes continued. His face had taken on a grim and thoughtful cast. "Doctor Dee, despite his great age, is perfectly capable of dealing with a meddling mortal. He would scarcely tolerate such repulsive practices as blood magic in his own fiefdom for long. How like him, however, to not tell

73

me what else is truly amiss, to make the matter so mysterious he knows I cannot resist heeding his call. He is well aware that I have retired from the Shadows, but he also knows that a good puzzle has the potential to draw me back to my unnatural home."

"You will go to him?"

"We will go, Watson, unless of course, you have another pressing engagement."

I thought of the Lady Hypatia and how I wished to see her again. I thought also of Alice Telfair, whose strange thefts had so disturbed both the Sorbonne librarian and Holmes. This matter of Doctor Dee's, whatever it was, could hardly be connected to the matters that intrigued me most. But habit, and long years of association, made me agree readily to Holmes's plan.

"Of course I will go with you."

He smiled as he coaxed the falcon back onto his wrist. "I thought I knew my Watson. Now be a good chap and fetch my cigarette case."

I retrieved the article from my friend's travelling cloak. At his further request, I opened it. As before, a great golden light appeared, so bright and intense that I was forced to look away. A bee flew out, leaving a glittering trail in his wake as he circled the room.

This was Holmes' familiar, the tiny creature best able to do his magical bidding. Holmes held out his palm and the bee landed within, waiting obediently as Holmes whispered to it in a strange language. He next placed the bee on the bird's back, tucking it into the soft feathers between the strong shoulders. Holmes returned to the window, releasing the falcon into the air. I rushed forward, watching as the noble creature soared across the cityscape of Paris, growing more and more indistinct as it flew to the east.

"The bee will deliver my message," Holmes said, as plainly as if announcing the dispatch of a telegram. "Doctor Dee will know we are coming."

"But why did you put the bee on the bird?" I asked. "Did it not know the way to Doctor Dee's residence?"

Holmes feigned offense. "Watson, how dare you cast aspersions on my familiar! Of course it knew the way. But Prague is a substantial distance for even a magical bee to fly."

"Prague!" I exclaimed. "So Doctor Dee is not in London."

"No, and I fear it may be some weeks before we see that picturesque pile on Baker Street again," Holmes said. "Would you be good enough to go down and make arrangements, let the clerk know that we will be vacating this fine establishment for the morning train?"

I nodded my assent and left the room. It was the hour for the hotel's most fashionable guests to seek out the cabarets of Paris. A gaudy crowd awaited the lift, and I took my place at the back of the line, behind women in scandalously low-cut dresses and men with glossy silk hats. At last the cage of the elevator arrived, and its door was drawn back with a loud rattle. Men and women filed inside. I hoped to take the last available spot.

The operator, a small man clad in the bright blue and gold livery of the hotel, lifted his face and looked at me.

It was the man from my nightmare, the same hideous being I had seen on the country road, carrying a coffin on his back. He stood upon a box, needing the height gained to work the lift's controls. His repulsive mouth drew into an evil grin and the dangling hairs in his warts twitched like insect antennae. He beckoned to me, but I retreated.

"Well, come along," a burly gentleman in the front of the throng ordered. He was clearly annoyed with me for delaying his party's departure. I shook my head and begged their pardon, fleeing as rapidly as I could down the hall. I had just reached our door and was pounding upon it when I heard the most hideous sound imaginable.

It was a metal screeching, followed by a scream raised from a half dozen throats, followed by what could only be the resounding crash of the elevator.

CHAPTER TEN

Our departure for Prague was delayed for two days. The horrible accident in the hotel, which claimed the lives of six people, was thoroughly investigated by the Parisian authorities. Holmes assisted the *gendarmes*, joining the inspectors who carefully removed all the mechanisms of the fatal device. The twisted metal and frayed cables were laid in a ballroom, where engineers of all stripes inspected them. Holmes aided their efforts as I watched from a corner. I had no doubt that, as he studied each damaged piece of metal through his lens, he was seeing more than others could envision and conducting tests that no elevator expert, however well trained, could replicate. But it was all for naught, as neither the representatives of the lift company, the hotel managers, nor the police could find a cause for the tragedy.

"So it was magic," I said to Holmes, as we finally took our leave of the city. "And I did not imagine that hideous man. He was there, wearing the uniform of a lift attendant."

Holmes settled into the compartment, spreading a collection of European newspapers across the seat. He shook his head. "There was no trace of magic."

"You do not believe me," I said, saddened that not even my closest friend accepted the veracity of my tale.

Holmes blinked, then leaned over and patted my knee. "On the contrary, Watson, I not only believe your observation is accurate, I am grateful that you made it. Had you boarded the lift heedlessly, you would have paid with your life."

It was the very thought that had plagued me for days. I wondered if the ghoulish figure had been responsible for the disaster or if, in some wicked way, he had been the agent of my salvation.

His remains had not been found among the bodies of the victims. No one had seen such a bizarre character in the hotel, and the real lift operator, a lad of fifteen, had snuck away from his post to smoke a cigarette when the accident took place. I was the only person who could testify to the presence of the strange fellow. The Paris police had dutifully taken my statement, but I had later heard them murmur things about '*l'idiot*,' which I assumed applied to me.

"Let us put it from our minds for now," Holmes suggested. "It does the brain no good to churn without proper data. The lack of traceable magic does not necessarily imply that magic was not used. There are several forms of enchantment so ancient and subtle even I could not detect them."

That statement did not give me confidence. I turned to the window and tried to divert myself with the changing scenery of the French countryside. Holmes passed an hour in digesting the newspapers he had collected. He gave a soft exclamation while reading one from Berlin.

"I wonder if this incident may explain our summons."

"You will have to translate," I demurred, when he offered the newspaper to me. "My German is not so serviceable."

"Then allow me to simply summarize the facts," Holmes said, glancing again at the text of the report. "The terrible event occurred in a suburb of Prague. It seems that a Mr. Gelder and his wife, an aged couple living in quiet retirement, were butchered in their home. Their maid discovered their bodies. Someone using a sharp implement, a small axe or hatchet being the most likely weapon, had assaulted the pair. They were attacked as they slept, and there is the strong probability that the lady awoke and attempted to defend her husband, as there were wounds to her arms and chest. However, her struggles were in vain."

"Killed in their own bed!" I exclaimed. "By whom?"

Holmes rolled a hand to indicate the bafflement of the police. "The authorities have no suspects. The only servant, the housemaid who found them, lived away from the home and her husband and daughter swore to her innocence, that she was with them at the time of the murders. Nor did she have any motive for the ghastly deed, as she testified that the Gelders were an exceeding generous couple. She had been happily in their service for over a decade. The Gelders had one son, a mining engineer who lives in Berlin, and who was likewise accounted for at the time of the crime. A poll of the neighbourhood indicated the couple was well-esteemed, a quiet pair with no known enemies."

"It must have been a robbery."

Holmes shook his head. "The Gelders had only modest wealth, but the detectives on the case have gone to some pains to indicate that nothing was taken. A jewellery box in plain sight of the bed was unopened, and a sizeable pile of gold coins was free in a drawer. Herr Gelder's silver watch and stickpin were likewise left upon the nightstand."

"Then why were they killed?"

Holmes folded the paper. "I do not know. It could be the source of the blood magic that Doctor Dee cited." My friend's eyes became hazy, losing their sharpness, as if he were looking through time rather than across distance. "For blood magic to be effective, it must follow a pattern. The sacrifices must always be the same. In ancient days, it was easier to acquire infants, slaves and female virgins. In this modern age, as more and more elderly are abandoned by unfeeling offspring, perhaps our fiend has found a new and ideal flock to be harvested."

I begged Holmes to speak of other things, and we passed the rest of the day's journey in a rambling conversation on golf clubs, the aesthete movement, and the possibility of socialist revolutions in Russia. Unfortunate delays, including an avalanche that had to be cleared along the tracks, slowed our progress. We arrived in Prague almost a week after we had been summoned. I asked Holmes why we had not simply journeyed through the Shadows, as we had done once before, but he avoided answering my question.

Walking past Prague's ancient astrological clock, whose carved apostles kept time and brooded over the snow-draped city, I was reminded of the King of Bohemia, one of Holmes's most notorious clients. I playfully suggested that we pay a social call on His Majesty who we had learned was in residence in the castle awaiting the birth of yet another heir. Holmes demurred, sarcastically stating that we were no longer on the king's level.

"We will, however, come within the shadow of His Majesty's domicile," Holmes said. "Doctor Dee has once again taken up residence in the Golden Lane."

"When did he live here previously?" I asked, as we made our way through the Old Town quarter, along the narrow, winding streets toward the Charles Bridge.

"During the reign of the great Holy Roman Emperor Rudolph II," Holmes replied. "Perhaps you have not heard of him? He was on the throne from 1576 to 1612, and during that time he had little concern for the religious conflicts that were brewing all about him. His interests ran to the arcane and the occult. He collected magi from across Europe, rewarding those who could hold his attention and help him elude his most persistent melancholy. He studied the Kabala and the works of Arab prophets, and tinkered with a variety of mechanical devices. His devotion to alchemy was such that he created vast laboratories in his palace, devoting long hours to his search for the fabled Philosopher's Stone. His cabinet of curiosities was unrivalled among royal collections, said to contain a unicorn's horn and a fairy's wings."

"Did it?" I inquired as we crossed onto the Charles Bridge. This great stone edifice, graced with a number of statues of sad-faced saints, had witnessed many triumphant processions during the centuries it had spanned the Vltava River. I felt as if the unseeing eyes of the sculpted martyrs were monitoring my progress as we strolled past the entertainers who made the bridge their stage. "The cabinet of curiosities, I mean. Did it actually contain those items?"

My friend seemed to give my question ponderous consideration. "Many collectors in that time displayed a unicorn's horn, but this marvellous artefact was always the horn of a narwhale, a creature then unknown to science. As for the fairy's wings," at this he gave a wink, "I know of no flightless relatives."

We continued our climb up the narrow lanes, passing magnificent churches and prosperous homes. The smell of baking bread and the chatter of merchants as they swept their doorsteps made the journey seem more like a pleasant tour than a secretive mission. The great St. Vitus Cathedral suddenly loomed over us, dark and stark. Consulting his watch, Holmes decided we had an extra hour before our interview, and so we wandered through the magnificent structure, admiring its fusion of Gothic and Baroque art. Remarkably, the cathedral was still under construction, but we avoided workmen and scaffolds in favour of antique chapels and chancels. I gawked before the solid silver tomb of St. John Nepomuk, a figure of unique devotion whose monument was a wondrous example of Counter-Reformation excess.

"Below us, in the vaults, are the remains of some of the most powerful rulers who ever lived," Holmes said, "as well as a number of intriguing warriors and martyrs. The Bohemians have quite a taste for the bizarre. Ludmila, one of their favourite saintly protectors, was murdered by her own daughter-in-law."

I had already suppressed a shudder at some of the more vivid crucifixes. Holmes now showed me a statue of a woman in court garb. She was slumped forward with a garrotte around her neck.

"Perhaps they could have used your services several centuries ago." A wild though came to me, riding on the tail of that flippant comment. "Holmes...exactly how old are you?"

His only answer was an enigmatic smirk. "I think it is time for our appointment. This way."

I should have known better than to expect clarity. I followed Holmes to a small street behind the great palace, where the houses were ancient and narrow, painted in shades of amber and yellow. I observed a few shingles that advertised the shops of goldsmiths and jewellers, but for the most part the neighbourhood had the appearance of a place where a traveller should carefully guard his wallet. One house, so small and modest it seemed to disappear, crouching shyly between its neighbours, was our destination. Holmes approached the door and knocked sharply.

The door flew open and a gun with a long, wicked barrel was thrust under Holmes's chin.

CHAPTER ELEVEN

"Gotz!" Holmes said warmly. "How good to see that you are still in service."

I had swallowed my instinctive cry, but my cane was still raised in a futile effort at defence. Holmes waved for me to lower it as the owner of the gun stepped into the light. He was a bull of a man, with broad shoulders and a massive head. His black beard thrust forward, and cold, steel-gray eyes considered us with fierce calculation. More astonishment filled me as I saw that the firearm he wielded was not carried in his hand. Instead, it was his hand, extending as a metallic continuation of his arm.

"This is not a proper way to greet the good Doctor's guests, however," Holmes chided, in the same spirit that one would scold a puppy for jumping onto one's trousers in exuberant welcome. "And I despair for any poor peddlers or tradesmen coming to collect their bills."

The man muttered something in guttural German. Holmes frowned.

"That bad, is it? I find it difficult to imagine anything that could make Doctor Dee wary."

"Who is he?" I asked, as the fearsome giant turned, leading us into the little house. The man moved rapidly, and I gained only the briefest impression of a perfectly ordinary, cheaply furnished dwelling, before we began climbing a narrow set of stairs.

"Our guide is none other than Gottfried von Berlichingen, knight of the Holy Roman Empire. He is more simply and famously known as Gotz or Gotz of the Iron Hand. Have you noticed his unusual prosthetic?"

"I could hardly fail to see such a monstrosity," I hissed. "How did he acquire it?"

"Gotz lost his right arm to a cannonball during the siege of Landshut in 1504. Surviving such an event was miraculous, but rather than accept his new status as an invalid, Gotz had a blacksmith construct an iron hand, complete with articulated fingers. The device was so clever that Gotz could write with a quill pen, stroke a lover's hair, and continue to whack at his enemies with a sword."

The man halted at the top of the stairs. A large iron appendage was laid upon a table, and as I watched, Gotz removed the gun from his sleeve and strapped on the metal arm as a replacement. Holmes continued to talk as if Gotz could not hear him.

"My mentor has, as you see, made some improvements to give Gotz variety and make him more useful. I suspect that any metallic, steam-driven device can now be snapped into place on Gotz's stump. Tell me, Gotz, has the Doctor gotten around to taking my suggestion and constructing a dough kneader for you?"

The stalwart servant's answer was a mere grunt. I shook my head.

"Holmes, if he fought in the sixteenth century..."

"He should have been dead for some time. Indeed, that would be the natural order of things. But allow me to finish my story. Gotz turned to banditry and mercenary endeavours, and for another forty years he was the terror of the continent, raping, pillaging, and murdering as he pleased, shouting his battle cry of *'Leck mich im Arsch!'*"

At Holmes's use of the profane statement, Gotz turned. Something like a smile crossed his bloodless lips. It was enough to freeze my soul.

"But he erred when he tried to make Doctor Dee stand and deliver," Holmes continued, wagging a finger at the knight. "Annoyed by his effrontery, my mentor spellbound him, and turned him into a ghoul."

"A ghoul?" I asked.

"A wizard's base servant, a creature that maintains a semi-immortal existence on uncooked flesh. As long as the knight consumes the raw carcasses of fowl and swine, which have been further enchanted by his employer, he will continue to dwell upon this earth. But he can only be assured of this existence by remaining in the service of Doctor Dee. Should he attempt to escape or otherwise displease his master, he would soon find himself with a new overlord, in the depths of Hell."

Gotz snorted and opened a door at the end of a narrow hallway. Holmes passed through, and with some trepidation, I followed.

"Holmes! Confound you, you are late!"

A small, elderly man rose from behind a desk. His back was stooped, and his gray beard, knotted and unkempt, hung to his waist. In many ways he was the very picture of a magician from a children's book, dressed in deep purple robes with a long, pointed cap upon his head. Zodiac signs were embroidered in the rich fabric of his gown, and he grasped a knotted staff as he rose to move around the desk. He walked with a strange, lurching gait, his upper body preceding his legs. To my surprise he threw open his arms and embraced Holmes, even as he continued to berate him for his tardiness.

In that motion, his gown swirled, and I deduced the reason for his peculiar stride. Instead of human legs, his lower limbs were the hindquarters of a stag, with cloven hooves. I recalled Holmes's words, that Doctor Dee was the offspring of a human woman and a satyr. Once again, the marvellous world that I had unwittingly entered seemed to swirl around my vision and I had to take a deep breath and remind myself that I was a British soldier and therefore not prone to fits of vapours. Doctor Dee turned from Holmes, considering me with eyes that twinkled with youthful mischief. The bright blue orbs seemed bizarrely out of place in his wrinkled, age-stained face.

"A fellow practitioner. Welcome, Doctor Watson. I trust your travels were comfortable?"

I felt something implied behind the words, but I merely acquiesced that our journey had been a pleasant one. Doctor Dee lurched toward a bookcase, removing several volumes.

"I am grateful that you were able to view more of the lovely hills and vales of Bohemia during the holiday season. But at what cost did such leisurely travel come?" He spun around and slammed the books to his desk. Anger replaced the bonhomie of moments before. "Holmes, the bird has flown! I lay this at your doorstep."

Holmes ignored the taunt, signalling for me to take a seat. I was reminded of our interview with Telfair. Indeed, the queer oval chamber we found ourselves in was reminiscent of Telfair's study, its walls lined with old books and many strange artefacts on display.

But this room bore an air of comfort and pleasantry that the millionaire's home had lacked. Doctor Dee's study was brightly lit, though no source of illumination, such as candles or lamps, were visible. The chairs were overstuffed, and gilded on the arms and legs. My only complaint was the slight musty odour, the smell of age and antiquities.

"You were perhaps too canny in your summons," Holmes replied. "Tell me all that has happened."

Doctor Dee shook a gnarled finger at my friend. "There has been a summoning. Some fool worked the Circle of Faust!"

Holmes lifted both eyebrows. "Indeed? And you have not noticed another wizard, of either the human or Shadowborn variety, in the neighbourhood?"

"Would I have summoned you if I had?" Doctor Dee snorted.

"I see. This explains the blood magic." Holmes looked to me. "Calling up a demon is an act that normally requires great skill acquired through decades of conjuring. Doctor Dee would have sensed another wizard of equal power, had one been in residence in Prague. This nefarious deed has been performed by a novice, who used blood magic to rush the process."

Doctor Dee scowled and took my friend to task for his calm expression. "You do not seem to recognize the seriousness of this! The Faust Circle has not been worked for over a century. Who knows what mischief has been done? A wizard willing to do blood magic is a dangerous rogue, and must be dealt with!" As he spoke, with increasing passion, small bursts of coloured light, like miniature fireworks, popped around the room. "We must learn who he is and destroy him."

"There is a very simple way to discover his identity," Holmes said, removing his cigarette case from his pocket. He snapped it open, and in response a golden light rose from the pages of the book that had been tossed to the desk. The magic bee, Holmes's tiny familiar, returned to its home with a buzzing that somehow projected happiness. "I am only surprised that you have not already attempted it."

Doctor Dee bristled. "You do not imply that I should also summon Mephistopheles?"

"I do," Holmes countered. "He is certainly the best witness to this crime, and you are powerful enough to bind him to do your bidding. Only you, Doctor Dee, can make a devil tell the truth."

I could see a war of emotions on the elder's face. Clearly he was flattered by the compliments Holmes had offered, but he was also loath to accept my friend's suggestions. His gnarled hands twitched nervously, stroking the tangles in his beard.

"This is no game, Holmes. Men have lost their souls for less."

"But we are not ordinary men, Doctor."

The ancient wizard leaned back in his chair. For long minutes he was silent, pondering my friend's words. A quick glance at Holmes confirmed that he was confident in the ultimate decision. He had the proud look of a schoolboy who had stumped his tutor.

At last, Doctor Dee snorted and pushed himself up from his chair. "Mephistopheles is no minor minion to be trifled with. He is a prince of Hades, a lieutenant to Satan himself. We must not call up what we can not put down."

"I have no doubts as to your ability," Holmes replied.

The ancient conjurer's eyes narrowed. "You are toying with me, Holmes. Do you really wish to get to the truth, or are you merely eager to satisfy your curiosity? I know you have never called forth a demon."

"I promise, I am not in this for sport. If you raise this devil, I will subject him to an appropriately harsh inquisition and get to the bottom of this mystery."

Doctor Dee finally nodded and signalled to Gotz. "Go to the Faust house and make sure that its residents are...elsewhere."

I shuddered at what such an order might imply. As the ghoul stomped out, Doctor Dee uncorked a bottle of wine and poured three glasses. "I am too old to be raising demons," he muttered. "And I much prefer the company of angels."

Holmes gestured lazily. "Perhaps you have read the great classic that recounts Doctor Dee's work with the heavenly messengers—*A True and Faithful Relation of What Passed for Many Years Between Dr. John Dee and Some Spirits*? No? Watson, your education was sadly neglected."

I did no more than touch the wine to my lips. If we were truly about to speak with denizens of the lower regions, I wanted all my wits about me.

"Why would a novice wizard call up a demon?" I asked. Doctor Dee gave me a look indicating he considered me little better than the village idiot.

"There is only one reason," he stated. "He wished to sell his soul for youth and lust!"

"I beg to disagree," Holmes said, pushing his own barely tasted wine aside. "It is more likely that such an impatient character seeks wisdom, more knowledge of the dark arts. Carnal pleasures always follow power." Holmes tapped long fingers together. "Or, another hypothesis: our foe is dying, and has no time to acquire the proper skills. He wants to extend his life, to enjoy the fruits of his magical labours for more years than the Fates have dealt him."

"A human practitioner can not lengthen his own life by magic?" I asked.

"Only the Shadowborn have that privilege," Doctor Dee muttered. "It is impossible for a human to cast such a powerful spell upon himself, for that would negate his power to break it."

Holmes nodded. "Watson, you once saw me take the shape of a bird, if you recall. A human wizard who tried such a trick would find himself eating worms for the rest of his existence."

Doctor Dee harrumphed into his wine. "I never thought we would face such a problem again. In truth, I thought the world had finally turned, and that mankind was at last slipping free of his fascination with the Shadows, that human witches and wizards would become extinct. What need is there for magic-workers in the age of steam and electricity?" He seemed in a mood to reminiscence, like an old soldier holding court in a pub and spinning tales for new recruits. "When I was young, mathematics was considered a dark art, dangerous to study. Now the engineers rule empires, buildings challenge God in His Heaven and ships dive to the bottom of the ocean. What use does man, with his metal servants and mastery of natural philosophy, have for magic?"

Holmes concurred gently. "Our kind will soon be nothing but a legend. A day is coming when even childish curiosity about the

Shadows will be extinguished." He traced a finger around the rim of his chalice. "But when that occurs, mankind will lose something priceless. It will be a sad day indeed when imagination dies."

"We are not there yet!" I exclaimed, concerned that their conversation would soon be too philosophical for me to follow. "This person, whoever he is, still believes in magic enough to kill innocent people in order to work it!"

"Watson will keep us on task," Holmes said, saluting me with his cup. "Tell me, Doctor Dee, have you gathered any information on this individual?"

"I am a wizard, not a detective!" the aged mage snorted. "I felt the blood magic when it was worked, and the next day I also sensed the flaring of the Circle. Before I could drag my weary bones to the house to investigate, the business was done and the malefactor vanished."

"What of the residents of the home?" my friend asked.

"They were drugged, all of them. There was enough opium in their food to leave them in a stupor for more than a day."

Holmes became suddenly alert, like a hound that hears the hunter's horn. "You are certain? They were sedated rather than enchanted?" His eyes glittered at Doctor Dee's affirmative. "That is even more suggestive of our foe's lack of talent. He could not afford to waste the energy of the blood magic on subduing the people who stood between him and the Circle. But he also did not use physical force, did not strike them or bind them or..."

My friend lapsed into silence, yet his face shown with natural intelligence, the rapid working of the ideas in his brain reflected in a sudden, dangerous smile.

"I know who this practitioner is!" he said.

Doctor Dee and I exchanged a glance. "Well then, name the man!" the ancient wizard ordered.

"I cannot," Holmes replied. "But I will allow Mephistopheles to confirm my deduction. Surely Gotz has cleared the path for us by now. I seem to recall him as a most efficient servant. Into your coats, Doctors, and let us interview Hell's most loquacious agent."

CHAPTER TWELVE

We made our way down from the Golden Lane, flanking the elderly man who leaned heavily upon his cane. Despite the icy conditions of the streets, Doctor Dee dismissed my friend's offer to call a cab, saying that he preferred to walk. I wondered what the other pedestrians made of his hobbled gait and elaborate robes. Perhaps they considered him merely a local eccentric, as not one resident of Prague turned or gave him a puzzled glance.

At Doctor Dee's direction, we made our way back to the Charles Bridge, passing spectacular gardens and fountains turned into twinkling wonderlands by the snow. Crossing over, our guide took us into the section of the city known as Nove Mesto, or 'New Town,' despite the fact that it had been founded, Doctor Dee informed us, by Charles IV in 1348. I saw signs of modern, insipid architectural renovation, but many of the old mansions and fine churches were mercifully untouched. Just at the corner of Charles Square, near a refreshing little park where, Holmes informed me, in springtime students from the nearby university often took picnic lunches on the grass, was a striking Baroque dwelling. Gotz stood at its door, looking grim and surly.

"They are gone, Master," he spoke, after Doctor Dee commanded him to use English for our benefit. "To the theatre," he added, perhaps at my expression of concern.

"It is a bit early for a matinee," Holmes noted.

"But not for a puppet show," Doctor Dee said. "They are the bane of this place! Everywhere, the marionettes! Bah!"

Gotz opened the door for us. The house was clearly home to a family of wealth and taste, judging by the exquisite furnishings and antiques. There were signs that it had been abandoned only minutes before: a half-filled teacup rested on a table, a child's wooden blocks were scatted in the parlour, and a broken pink satin ribbon, perhaps from a too-hastily-tied bonnet, sagged helplessly across a threshold. We once again climbed a flight of stairs and entered a small upper chamber.

This was clearly being used as a nursery. A crib and a rocking chair were the main items of furnishing. A number of toys were scattered around, and the room's walls were painted with bright scenes from fairy tales. I stood to one side, enchanted by a clever rendering of Jack and the Beanstalk, as Holmes and Doctor Dee pushed the crib and the chair to a corner and pulled back a woven rug from the centre of the floor.

"Ah, still here," Doctor Dee muttered, as Holmes closed the curtains. I turned up the gas and stared at the floorboards. I could see nothing more than warped, age-stained wood.

"I doubt it will ever go away," Holmes agreed. "Faust did a fine job of making sure his hubris would grow into a legend."

"I do not understand. Where is the Circle?" I asked, knowing that their vision saw layers no human eyes could penetrate. Holmes waved a hand and whispered a word.

The Circle erupted on the floor. Some six feet in diameter, it was a ring with an outer rim of strange symbols engraved around it. These tokens, like the edge of the Circle itself, glowed with an eerie blue luminescence. I felt something quiver in the air, an unnatural vibration that raised the hairs on my arm in alarm. Holmes began to step forward, but Doctor Dee seized his arm and held him back.

"I will handle the summoning!"

Holmes almost smiled. "Of course. You were interviewing demons long before I was born. I yield to your vast experience."

He joined me as Doctor Dee began to pace around the Circle. "What is he doing?" I asked, as the wizard drew vials from deep pockets within his robes. I watched as he poured small libations and scattered debris around the ring.

"He is sealing the Circle. The ring itself acts as both a corridor from Hades and as a prison. The demon cannot violate a Circle closed with holy water and salt, held fast by charms and relics."

I felt an odd sensation, a kind of trembling. Before, I had raced into Holmes's world blindly. Now, I realized, I had a choice. I could stay and stand witness, or I could excuse myself and go downstairs. Nothing was forcing me to remain and watch as unhallowed things were conjured from the depths of the inferno.

Yet despite the suddenly unsettled state of my stomach, I did not wish to leave. I found myself as fascinated by these acts of wizardry as I was by Holmes's feats of deduction. And, I reminded myself sternly, our ultimate goal was not a mere flirtation with evil, or to satisfy idle curiosity, but to learn what villain was committing such horrendous acts of blood magic. We were on a quest as real as any investigation from the past. Holmes's methods were perhaps unorthodox, but the purpose was noble. He wanted to catch a murderer and save lives. If he had to call up the Devil to do it, he would. Nothing could stop Sherlock Holmes once he was on the scent of a wrongdoer.

"Watson, if his makes you uncomfortable, you may certainly exit," Holmes offered. My mind already settled in the matter, I offered a loud snort.

"I have no fear of hooves and horns," I said, a bit more theatrically than I had intended. There was no doubt, from his expression, that Holmes saw through me. But he merely folded his hands over the head of his cane and looked at much at ease as if we were about to view a horse race or a military parade.

"Very well. Doctor Dee, are you ready?"

The old magician nodded and laid aside his cane. He removed a long wand of twisted oak from his sleeve. Raising his arms, he began to chant, murmuring words in a strange mix of languages. I caught a smattering of Latin, and a phrase of Hebrew, stirred liberally with Greek and Arabic. The room grew dim. The gaslight went out completely, leaving only the blue phosphorescence of the Circle. The glowing ring became more brilliant, flaring up into a solid wall of vivid blue light. Its intensity was such that I was forced to throw up my hands and close my eyes, but even with those shields I felt a burning, searing pain that was almost too much to bear. Doctor Dee's chants rose in equal intensity, concluding with a shrieked crescendo.

I blinked and slowly turned my head. The glow had faded, but the Circle was now rimmed with aqua-tinted flames. Within the flames stood the demon.

I had expected the creature carved on a thousand church walls and immortalized in hundreds of medieval manuscripts, a red-bodied thing with a long tail and a pitchfork, bearing horns upon his head and exhaling brimstone and smoke. Instead, the figure who stood confined within the wall of purified light was a slender man, well-dressed in the German style. He wore a fitted frock coat, with a glistening diamond pin in his tie and a high silk hat upon his head. Rather than hooves and talons, there were patent leather boots on his feet and soft, mauve gloves on his hands. His skin was fair, his hair blond. A neat goatee gave his chin an arrogant point. He opened eyes of the purest blue and smiled with perfect white teeth. Indeed, his whole aspect was so pleasant and charming, so washed in masculine beauty that he drew me in. I wished to offer him my hand, beg to make his acquaintance.

Holmes's arm barred my way. I came back to myself in a rush of shock.

The demon---who wore the shape of a handsome man with elegant ease---winked at me as he spoke.

"Who dares to summon Mephistopheles, Satan's right hand?"

Doctor Dee waved his wand. The imp's head swung to the side, as if the magician's action had activated an invisible lasso. Mephistopheles's lip curled. He sneered in contempt at the one who had bound him.

"Ah, my old friend Doctor Dee. Why do you meddle?"

"You will answer Sherlock Holmes's questions," Doctor Dee commanded. "Speak no more, except in answer."

Mephistopheles's eyes narrowed, drawing focus on my companion. "The great Sherlock Holmes, is it? I am pleased to meet you. We know your name rather well in the nether regions."

Doctor Dee twitched the wand again and the demon winced. Holmes lifted his hand.

97

"I am gratified to know my fame carries so far below. But let us keep this interview brief. I wish to know who called you forth, just over a week ago."

The demon smiled. "Why should I tell you? Like any good businessman, I prefer to keep my dealings private, lest some competition hone in on my clients."

Holmes nodded to Doctor Dee. At a word, the Circle light flared again. The demon abruptly howled in pain. He dropped the cane he had held, sinking to his knees.

"No! Stop it! Please!" Mephistopheles shrieked.

The action horrified me, and I bit back an instinctive, sympathetic cry. I could not imagine a torture so vicious it would make a devil beg for relief. Doctor Dee dropped the wand, reducing the light. Inside the ring, the demon removed his hat and wiped a sweat-drenched brow. He ground his teeth together as he spoke.

"My master will pay you back for that, wizard!"

"Answer my questions and you may return to Satan's presence," Holmes snapped. "Who gained possession of this house and summoned you?"

"Alice Telfair," Mephistopheles snapped, slowly climbing to his feet. "The American witch."

My chest tightened. I could not believe he was telling us the truth. Alice Telfair was not an ugly hag who would offer her body and soul to a devil in a dark Sabbat ritual! In my mind I still saw the beautiful face of the sweet, innocent girl. I could not imagine her so debased, so unnatural.

"What did she want?" Holmes asked, giving no indication that he found this information startling. I recalled what he had said---he could not name the <u>man</u> who had worked the Circle. For once, I did not appreciate his sense of humour.

"What do they all want?" the imp sneered, placing the hat back on his head. "More power, complete knowledge of all magic. She understands that she can never master the intricate, arcane rites of the Shadows, because she is a mere mortal."

"And she must have the key to these rituals, especially if she wishes to lift the guardian mist that surrounds the Fountain of Youth," Holmes said, with the air of a man thinking aloud. The demon's face drew into a hideous mask. I could see bizarre ridges of misshapen bones as his skin pulled tight.

"If you knew this, why summon me?! I have better things to do than converse with Halflings!"

He spat the word out as a curse. Holmes ignored his temper. "She spoke to you of the Fountain."

It was not properly a question, but Mephistopheles answered it, perhaps because Doctor Dee was sighting down his wand like a hunter with his gun. "She declared her intention to go to the Fountain, immediately. She showed me the map, so I suppose she knows the way."

"Thus you accepted her payment of her soul and gave her what she desired," Holmes said.

The demon cackled. His merriment shook the walls of our chamber, knocking pictures to the floor. "You fool. Do you think we are in the business of purchasing shoddy goods?"

That word, <u>shoddy</u>; Alice Telfair's father had used it. Holmes scowled at his prisoner.

"You would not make a deal with her?"

"Pathetic Halfling. Do you think we are so desperate for souls in Hell that we would negotiate such poor bargains? There was no need to bicker for the pale shade of Alice Telfair---she is already committed to the path of evil, and is so spotted and blotched that there is no reason to corrupt her further." The demon turned his eyes to me. "Let me make it plain, sir, for I perceive you are confused. We only give a supplicant power because we see his potential for evil. The deals are for corruption, to drag a naïve, deluded person further into the abyss. No one can truly sell his soul---he can only give us permission to turn it so black, so soiled that he will reject every hope of salvation! Alice Telfair needs no persuasion in that regard."

"So she is already damned," I heard myself whisper.

Mephistopheles winked. "Perhaps. Perhaps not. I leave it to you to decide." He turned back to Doctor Dee. "I have satisfied your curiosity, magician. Now let me go."

Holmes held out his hand. "One more question. Did you give Miss Telfair a gift?"

There was a silent moment. Bit by bit, the demon's sensuous lips drew back. "Clever Mr. Holmes," he drawled. "You understand how it works. A bargain is not necessary, but a little gift will bind her to evil forever."

"What did you give her?" Holmes demanded, unimpressed by the devil's gloating.

The demon laughed. "Just a tiny bit of magic, something she could not quite master, a silly little trick she can amuse herself with, provided she fuels it with more blood. I will tell you no more."

"Dismiss him," Holmes said to Doctor Dee, who seemed poised to once again strike Mephistopheles with his wand. "He is of no further use to us."

The imp smirked. "Good luck on your quest, Mr. Holmes. Send Alice Telfair to us soon; she is a pretty wench and will brighten our brimstone ballrooms."

With that, Doctor Dee cast another spell and the Circle flared like an exploding star. The force rocked me backward on my feet as my hands once again flew up to protect my eyes.

When my vision cleared the room was empty and the floorboards were nondescript. Doctor Dee busied himself with retrieving the small charms and relics that he had scattered around. Holmes was lost in thought, one finger pressed tightly to his lips.

"Why did you ask about a gift?" I whispered.

"Because the more gifted one is, the more likely he will fall. It is an encouragement to hubris, the feeling that one is too powerful to be brought down by the Divine. Such 'free' gifts are, as Mephistopheles said, generally more effective than contracts."

"You know this woman, this Alice Telfair?" my friend's mentor asked.

Holmes did not immediately answer. He seemed to have slipped away, to another place, where he was unaware of his two companions. I noted how Doctor Dee rolled his eyes. Perhaps this was a reaction he was familiar with, from centuries before. At last, Holmes thumped his cane on the floor and turned to face us.

"Doctor Dee, I thank you," he said. "And I assure you that Prague is in no more danger from this witch."

The ancient wizard frowned. "How can you be certain?"

"Because she has exhausted her resources in Europe. She must now travel to America, to seek the Fountain of Youth and, since Mephistopheles would not give her ultimate magical power in exchange for her soul, she must also find a wizard capable of lifting the fog which surrounds it."

"And you will follow her," Doctor Dee said.

"No," Holmes said, "I will not."

CHAPTER THIRTEEN

We took our leave quietly. Holmes offered no explanation for his startling decision. Doctor Dee was clearly astonished, but Holmes merely bade him farewell and, with a playful admonishment to Gotz to be a good servant, strolled from the house. I followed mutely. For a street or more I walked behind him, uncertain of his intentions. At last he stopped, waiting for me to move to his side.

"When last I was here, there was a hovel near the Storch house in the Old Town Square that served exceptional dumplings and goulash. Let us take our luncheon there before returning to the hotel."

I nodded dumbly. For three hours we sat in the café, talking only of things that lacked significance. Our conversation wandered over dozens of banal topics. When we were done, Holmes consulted a timetable and announced that we could catch an early evening train. We had a short time to pack our bags and settle the bill but, by good fortune, the train was delayed and we found ourselves cooling our heels inside the station. There, at last, I worked up the courage to question my friend's judgment.

"Holmes, surely you are not planning to dismiss this case?"

Those steely gray eyes, so capable of levelling a gaze that could make even a hardened murderer confess his deeds, now considered me. "Watson, there is no case."

"How can you say that?! Miss Telfair---"

"Is no concern of mine. You heard Mephistopheles say that her soul was rotten to the core. But nowhere is such spiritual immorality also illegal, and I could hardly prosecute her for witchcraft without opening myself to charges of wizardry."

"But what of the murders?"

"They were committed by ordinary means, through the judicious application of a hatchet, if the newspaper's report is correct." Holmes lit his pipe, shaking out the match. "I am not here to make up for the inadequacy of the local police, and I cannot be expected to investigate every murder that occurs in our major metropolises. It is true the deaths were used as a kind of harvesting, to build up Alice Telfair's limited mortal powers, so that she could summon the demon prince, but that also could not be proven in a court of law."

"Since when do you care about courts and the law?" I demanded. "This is a matter of justice."

My friend favoured me with a scowl of annoyance. "Watson, I must make something clear to you. Until that day when Titania entered our rooms and demanded I search for her crown, I had renounced the world of the Shadows. I was happy to have abandoned my strange heritage, and glad that I no longer worked the magic in my blood. I would have ignored her summons completely, but she was clever and vicious enough to put your soul in peril."

"And had you still ignored it, Marie Laveau and her ilk would have ripped down the veil between the worlds," I reminded him. "We would even now be dead!"

Holmes lifted an eyebrow. I saw the error in my assumption. "I would be dead, with most of the mortal world," I amended. "You, and the other residents of the Shadows, would be the overlords of a forever-darkened earth."

Holmes did not reply. For a long time we simply sat in mutual silence. Finally, the whistle sounded and I saw a puff of smoke ascending over a low row of houses.

"If you see no merit in this case, I do," I said. "Because, unlike you, I believe that even a single life, and one lowly soul, is worth saving. If you would only apply your talents to find Miss Telfair, then you could rescue her."

"Why would she require a rescue?"

"Because you did not truly listen to Mephistopheles's words," I snapped. "Her soul is not yet damned. It may be blackened, but she still has time to repent. You could show her the error of her ways, coax her off the path of dark magic and help her to once again walk in the light."

"I am no priest, to be proselytizing!"

"But you are part human!" I argued. "And therefore you also have a soul! You should care. You should not wish to see another human's soul irrevocably lost."

Holmes considered me through a cloud of smoke. "Your chivalry does you credit, Watson. But I am also no knight upon a white horse, ready to ride to the rescue of an enchanted maiden."

I summoned my wits, attempting to marshal another argument. The station conductor strutted by us, a figure of pride in his brass buttons, with a gleaming silver whistle around his neck. His very presence gave me an idea. If I could not reach Holmes through his humanity, perhaps an appeal to his curiosity and his vanity would work.

"There is a central question you have not answered, and that will remain unanswered unless you pursue it. What does Miss Telfair want so badly that she would risk her soul to attain it? She already possesses an assured form of near-immortality, she is eternally beautiful, and now, with her father dead, she is even wealthier than before. What more does she desire?"

Holmes looked bored. "Knowledge. The devil said as much."

"But knowledge of what? Of mere magic? As long as she consumed the water her father had stored, she had centuries to acquire that knowledge. She did not need to be so hasty. So why did she take such a horrific risk in summoning a demon to bargain for further powers, in order to penetrate the mysteries of the Fountain? She must want something more."

I felt I was making progress. My friend's expression changed. I could see him beginning to give my inquiry more dutiful consideration.

"She had the water," Holmes mused, "before she broke her father's hoard she gathered up a personal supply. This is about the Fountain of Youth itself, something she seeks to find at the source."

I knew I should encourage him, be his transmitter of the light of ideas. Striving to stitch words together, I turned from him and looked to where the crowd was assembling on the platform, awaiting the arrival of the train.

In their midst, I saw the fiend.

It was the little man, the hideous dwarf I had spotted near Haven House and in Paris. He was now clad in the uniform of a station porter. He stood atop a travelling trunk covered with stickers from many destinations. I gave a startled shout, pointing to him. Not waiting for Holmes to question my reaction, I leapt from my chair and ran toward the figure.

"Stop! You there, halt!"

I was too late. The man spotted me, grinned at me, and hopped from his perch. A woman with a perambulator sailed between us, and I nearly went flying over the infant's carriage. My clumsiness through the crowd produced a barrage of oaths in Czech and German, along with a few salty words in French. Still, I elbowed my way closer, until at last I reached the place where the man had stood.

There was nothing in that spot but a collection of hatboxes being guarded by a prune-faced matron. The man and his strange container had vanished.

"Good heavens, Watson, what possessed you?" Holmes asked, arriving just as I was catching my breath. "You nearly caused an international incident. Do you wish to plunge our country into war?"

"Holmes, the dwarf. That evil face! He was here!"

All amusement fled my friend's countenance. He turned, scanning the crowd. The train whistle blew again, as the huge locomotive rolled into the station.

And then another, shriller sound split the air. The station conductor, who had been so resplendent in his scarlet and gold uniform, was somehow airborne, flying above the track. He could not have jumped so high, nor been pushed with such a force. He seemed to hover in midair, as if suspended on invisible wires. The incident took only a moment, yet time seemed to stall and stretch, as everyone in the station watched, alerted by the horrific intensity of his scream.

We all saw him collide with the train. Falling, the poor man was ground to a bloody pulp beneath the locomotive's wheels.

CHAPTER FOURTEEN

We made our way back to London with all possible speed. Holmes said little during the journey, but spent long hours smoking his pipe and staring out the window. I could tell some form of mental battle was being waged, that he was torn between his vow to stay free of the Shadows and both his curiosity and his sense of justice. People were dying; a witch was killing them. Did it matter if this murderer was using magic or more prosaic means of dispatching her victims? Did he not owe it to the world to bring such a villain to heel?

And perhaps more importantly, he had to know the answer to the question I had posed. He had to learn why it was so important to Alice Telfair to seek the Fountain of Youth when she already had access to its waters.

It was not until we were at the door of 221 B Baker Street that Holmes announced his intentions.

"Watson, I will take this case."

I confess that after many hours of trains, cabs, and boats, and very bad food consumed hastily at stations, I was so tired I almost failed to comprehend his words. "You will investigate?"

"I will find the witch Alice Telfair, hopefully before she reaches the Fountain of Youth. I will learn her purposes and I will stop her nasty little habit of murdering people to fuel her magic. If possible, I will show her the error of her ways and save her soul. Is there more that you require?"

I shook my head. "Can you start in the morning?" I asked.

Holmes chuckled. "Good old Watson! Take yourself to bed. I will sort through the correspondence and over breakfast we can draw up a plan of action." Our bags made a resounding thump on the floorboards, and with a yawn I puttered off to my room, too tired to even shed my jacket or undo my collar. Removing my boots was the extent of my disrobing. It seemed I had only closed my eyes when Holmes entered the room and slapped my shoulder.

"Watson, I was a fool! Why did I not foresee this?"

I shook cobwebs from my brain. Holmes rattled a sheet of stationary before my face.

"This arrived two days ago, from Inspector Larson. Alice Telfair returned to her home, long enough to be interviewed by the police, who have rather stupidly declared her above suspicion. Of course she went home, she expected her father to have crumbled to dust by now and she had an inheritance to claim. Up, man, you are the one who wants to chase this game to ground!"

Bleary-eyed, I rose and, feeling akin to those zombies we had once vanquished, travelled with Holmes to the station, where we boarded the earliest train. Holmes conducted his interview with the inspector over breakfast at the same small establishment where Darby and I had dined, under much more pleasant circumstances. The good officer seemed puzzled to find himself abruptly summoned to a conference with the London detective.

"Yes, she was here. Just a week ago it was. One of the messenger boys saw her arrive and diverted her to us. Poor thing, she was quite hysterical when we told her about her father."

"Feminine hysterics have a way of clouding rational male minds," Holmes countered sourly. "Where did she claim to have been?"

"Travelling on the continent, she said, and she had ticket stubs to prove it," Larson answered. I could see he did not appreciate my friend's tone. "Not proper for such a young lady, I thought, but I suppose she is an orphan now and has no choice but to make her journeys alone."

"So there was no companion?" Holmes asked.

"She did not mention one, and no one came with her." Inspector Larson shrugged. "It was not something I saw reason to inquire about."

Holmes scowled. His questions had all the charm of a cross-examination conducted in a cold prison cell. "Did you tell her what actually happened to her father?"

"That's hardly fitting details for a woman," the inspector huffed. "I merely told her that he was killed and his body had suffered mutilations. She swooned at the first mention of blood."

Holmes rolled his eyes. "Of course she did. And did she ask about your investigation?"

The inspector nodded. "I told her we were rather confounded by a lack of evidence. She suggested someone from America might have murdered her father, in revenge for his shoddy dealings during the late war. It seems rather a stretch to me, but we are making inquiries."

Holmes sighed. "It will be a waste of your time to chase phantom Yankees, Inspector. How long did she stay in residence?"

"Only long enough to reclaim some of her personal items from the home. Her father's accounts had been frozen at the bank, and she urged us to keep them sealed, saying that the murderer

111

might return and claim to be a relative. I thought that very clever, Holmes, for her to allow us to bait the trap that way."

"She took none of his money for herself?"

"Not a shilling. She said she had her own accounts, in London." Inspector Larson daubed his napkin to his lips. "She did ask for some of her jewellery back, and I saw no harm in letting her collect her own possessions. I rode with her to Oakhurst, where she showed me the necklace and earrings she was placing in her bag. My father was a goldsmith, so I know the value of a lady's baubles! These were Tudor pieces, set with emeralds and rubies, worth a king's ransom. For the life of me, I still can't understand why her father's assassin didn't make off with such loot, especially when it was lying about in plain sight on a dresser."

Holmes pushed aside his untouched plate. "Did she mention her future plans?"

"Only that she would resume her travels, as she had nothing left to hold her in the country, and would return when we had finished our investigation." The inspector sipped the last of his coffee. "We'll give it a bit longer; I still believe I can catch this devil! But if I haven't found him by the springtime, I'll notify Miss Telfair via her bank and leave her to her fortune."

Holmes made no comment. He rose and silently offered his hand. Inspector Larson studied him with an air of confusion.

"I don't know what more you could expect of me, sir. The girl was clearly on the continent when it happened, and she had no reason to kill her own father. If it was money she was after, she seemed in no hurry for it!"

"There are many motivations that we find difficult to understand," Holmes said. "I am in no way critical of your work, Inspector. No one could have been more diligent."

"Well, I hope you will remember that, should she come to you."

Holmes went rigid. "You told her of my involvement?"

"Of course I did! I wanted her to know I brought in the very best man and did everything I could to find her father's killer." He looked even more confused than he had that night in Oakhurst, with a flayed body upon the floor. "Quite frankly, sir, I assumed that was why you wished to speak with me. I thought she had come to consult you!"

It was uncharacteristic of Holmes to swear, but on the ride back to London he muttered a string of oaths that would have made a sailor proud, punctuating them by beating his fist against the seat.

"She must have been surprised to learn that someone hastened the process of her father's death for her," Holmes snarled. "But Larson was an idiot to tell her of our presence in that house. We have lost the advantage of surprise, Watson. Now the lady will be wary. Before, she had no reason to hide, to pretend to be anyone other than who she was. It stands to reason that she will take a disguise." Holmes massaged his brow with his lean fingers. "I suppose I must be grateful that she can only avail herself to costumes and paint, rather than taking on a glamour."

The word confused me. "What do you mean?"

"A glamour is an act of conjuring which changes one's appearance and persona completely, even to the minutest details of speech and mannerisms. The act itself is untraceable, but requires tremendous energy to produce and is draining to sustain." Holmes hissed in air through his teeth. His headache must have been excruciating. "It is akin to the effect the elves attained, if you will recall. Only a Shadowborn wizard or witch can produce it."

"Then her disguise will be something prosaic. You will be able to see through it easily," I said, attempting to be encouraging. "Most likely she will dress as an old woman or as a young man." Holmes ignored my enthusiasm and my predictions of how easily he would detect our prey. After a moment's consideration, I rubbed my face and spoke more solemnly. "I am grateful I am not trying to elude you, Holmes. I would make a rather ugly female with this moustache."

My friend lifted his fingers away, scowling and no doubt pondering just how stupid I had become. Then he laughed, catching on that I was having a bit of fun at my own expense in the effort to change his sour mood.

"Watson, our good Queen should strike a medal for you," Holmes said, "to honour your service to the empire in tolerating my ill humours. It is just that I fear Alice Telfair will take special care now that she knows I have shown an interest in her father's murder. She would be wary enough of me as mortal agent, and if she has somehow learned that I am also a Shadowborn Halfling, with a wizard's power, she will seek ways to completely shield herself from me. Her efforts will require greater power, and that will require further sacrifices."

I nodded my understanding. "More people will die in the service of her blood magic."

Holmes remained lost in thought until we reached our destination. Upon disembarking, he went promptly to the telegraph office, where he dispatched so many messages that it required the funds in both our pockets. As I watched my last shilling disappear, I asked what he was doing.

"Alerting my network. It stands to reason that Alice Telfair has returned to London to gather funds and prepare for her journey. I want to know what ship she is taking, and, if possible, the nature of her thus-far-invisible companion. That individual interests me as much as Miss Telfair does."

"And why is that?" I inquired.

"Because for blood magic to work, the magician must not sully his hands. Like some pagan priest, he works the magic over the collected blood and gore, but an assistant must perform the sacrifice." Holmes scribbled out a final note and passed it through the brass bars to the attendant. "I want to know who is wielding the axe."

CHAPTER FIFTEEN

Holmes's labours quickly bore fruit. As always, the many strands of his web astonished me. In a matter of hours he could gather information by both legal and somewhat questionable means. He soon learned that there was no account in any London bank for a woman named Alice Telfair. He summoned the Irregulars and gave them a good look at Alice Telfair's picture (which, in my clumsiness, I had slipped into my pocket during our interview at Oakhurst), ordering the boys to loiter around the better hotels with the hope of spotting her in residence, on the slender chance that she was not already attempting any form of disguise.

"That's quite a twist!" one of the boys declared, earning a cuff on the head from Wiggins, who was ever the disciplinarian of his troops.

"I must agree with your assessment, as does Doctor Watson," Holmes said, with a playful wink to me. "She is a rather lovely girl. And we believe that she is travelling with a companion, most likely a strong man."

"And a swell one, I'd wager," another of the lads offered. He ducked Wiggins's attempted swat. "Why would she step out with an ugly bloke, eh?"

Holmes gave the urchin an extra sixpence for his smart thinking before sending them on their way. "The child makes an excellent point, Watson. Alice Telfair is beautiful enough to attract handsome men. Even if she lacked magical enchantments, which we know she does not, her natural beauty would be enough to bind a man to her. And while a gentleman of rather less pleasing appearance might work even harder for her favours, her feminine pride would suffer to be seen with a feeble specimen."

Later that same day, a note arrived from one of Holmes's informers in Whitechapel. He beamed as he deciphered the code the man used.

"Watson, you have often wondered why I allow certain elements of the criminal class to go free. Here is your answer! What good would it do to send a fellow to prison for stealing a cheap watch when, on the street, he can finger much greater offenders, the worst of the cutthroats and thieves?"

"He has seen Miss Telfair?"

"No, but he has seen the jewels, the collection of Tudor era gems that now grace the back room of a disreputable pawn shop. Let us go shopping!"

We found the pawn shop in a seedy corner off Mitre Square. The place smelled of the desperation of its indigent clients who would pawn their last coat or pair of boots for a glass of gin. A lean man with a grizzled, unkempt patch of hair above both ears peered up at us through thick spectacles as we entered. In an instant, he recognized my friend and his manner became instantly obstinate.

"Here now, I have nothing you'd be interested in, Mr. Holmes. You may take your trade elsewhere!" He waved briskly. "Off with you!"

Holmes's smile was tight, with all the warmth of a cat about to pounce upon its prey. "My presence in the neighbourhood makes for speculation among the criminal classes, does it not? If your regular customers see you speaking with Sherlock Holmes, it might be bad for your business." Holmes turned to me, gesturing languidly at the array of dusty goods on the shelves. "These may look like everyday items, Watson, the pathetic debris pawned by paupers. But if we were to enter Mr. Kerwin's private showroom, the place where he entertains much wealthier and even less moral customers, I suspect we would find more intriguing items for purchase."

Kerwin bristled. "You have no right to utter such slanders. I am a respectable merchant!"

"As respectable as ten years at Dartmoor Prison can make you," Holmes parried. "I suggest you answer my questions, Mr. Kerwin, unless you would like an unscheduled visit from the regular forces of the law."

The man's eyes narrowed. "You can make all the threats you like! I've done nothing wrong and---"

"I would also suggest you take your hand off that gun beneath this counter," Holmes interrupted, his voice cool and smooth. "It is dangerous to toy with hair-triggers when one is so distraught."

Instinctively, I stepped back, and saw what Holmes had observed. There was something like a porthole worked into the greasy wood of the counter, at the level of our waists. The slender barrel of a firearm protruded through it.

Kerwin swallowed tightly and stepped back from the counter. He withdrew the oddly-designed gun and placed it between us. Holmes traced a fingertip over ornate engravings on the wooden stock.

"Another one of Von Herder's work. Interesting. Did you acquire it at a discount from Colonel Sebastian Moran's heirs?"

"Ask your questions," Kerwin snapped. "I want you out of here."

"And I wish to leave," Holmes replied pleasantly. "The air in here is decidedly noxious." He tapped a quick rhythm on the gun barrel. "Tell me about the woman who pawned the jewels."

"Which jewels? I have quite a collection!"

"The only real gems, not the paste diamonds you pass off on ignorant fools who are taken by their sparkle. I mean the dark emeralds and rubies, the ones set in the Tudor necklace and earrings."

Kerwin exhaled loudly. "The lady never gave me her name. She had no interest in pawning the necklace, only in how much I would give her for it. We settled on three hundred pounds."

Holmes nodded. "A mere fraction of the piece's value; it was worth three times that for the stones alone, not to mention the gold setting and its historical significance." His lip curled as Kerwin nodded, clearly pleased with having defrauded his client. "Was the lady in distress?"

"No. She was quite calm and business-like."

"Did she give you any reason why she needed the money?"

Kerwin harrumphed. "I'm not in the business of asking such questions. Now if you don't mind---"

Holmes caught his wrist. "I do mind. Who pawned the earrings?"

119

Kerwin seemed poised to deny any knowledge of them, but something in my friend's eyes and fierce hold encouraged him to be honest. He nodded his acquiescence. Holmes released his grip.

"It was another lady. She came that same day, just as I was closing. She was a sizable old dolly, all black skirts and bonnet. It was raining, and her veil was sodden, so she pulled it back and..."

The man hesitated. He lowered his head and took several deep breaths, as if suddenly stricken by intense nausea. Holmes leaned forward, almost whispering his words.

"Her appearance was horrific?" my friend gently prodded. "Was she deformed, or badly scarred?"

"No...no, she had a perfectly plain face. Wide and flat, with little piggish grey eyes sunk deep in her head and a bit of grey hair come down on her brow. But something about it---something in her gaze---it was unnatural. As if she didn't have a soul behind those eyes."

"Are you sure it was a woman?" I asked. "Not a man in some disguise?"

Kerwin favoured me with a look of disgust. "I believe I know the difference between a male and a female! This was a woman, not elderly or especially hideous, but she was wrong. Wrong in every way!"

Holmes frowned. "What did she tell you?"

"Nothing of consequence, only that she wanted to sell the earrings. I noticed the similarity, of course, understood they were part of a set. I figured the pair of sweet <u>ladies</u> had nicked them!"

"And you were willing to purchase stolen goods?" Holmes asked, sarcasm dripping from every syllable. "How shocking!"

Kerwin snorted. "Why would I hesitate? The fool never even tried to bargain, and I only gave her two hundred for what is easily worth seven. Good business all around." He paused, then shuddered. "If only the old bat hadn't make my skin crawl. Just like you do."

This last bit was directed at Holmes, who merely favoured Kerwin with an arch smile. "I am happy to have such an effect on my admirers. Thank you for your time."

Holmes turned and began moving toward the door. For a moment I lingered, not wanting to expose my spine to the powerful weapon the man was now returning to its place beneath the counter. Then I gathered my nerve and followed Holmes onto the street, where he was lighting a cigarette.

"He was rather unhelpful," I muttered.

"On the contrary, Watson, he was a font of information. We now know how Miss Telfair will fund her travels."

"And we know her disguise!" I replied. "She is posing as an old woman."

"Watson," Holmes said, with the air of a disappointed professor, "you are letting your assumptions run ahead of your facts. Alice Telfair could merely have employed a surrogate, thinking to get more for the jewels by selling them individually rather than as a set. However, I will admit the proprietor's reaction to the second lady is intriguing. I have known Kerwin for some time; he is a hard-bitten rascal to his core and not a man prone to fits of imagination. Yet the woman's appearance clearly unnerved him."

I was unwilling to abandon my pet theory so quickly. "Do you think he could be reacting to a disguise? Maybe it was a very bad one, and that is why the woman seemed strange." I thought back to my night in Pown's Music Hall and the startling effect of heavy makeup on the face of the girl who portrayed the virtuous maiden, in an act that was far from innocent. "Sometimes actors are quite frightful in their costumes. Maybe Miss Telfair was trying out her new role, to see if anyone would be taken in by it. I still say it was our lady!"

"I agree your speculation is very possible, though far from proven. It could have been Alice Telfair in disguise," Holmes said as he waved for a cab, "or another lady who was simply an exceptional example of homeliness. Good heavens, Watson, what are you guffawing about?" he asked, as we climbed up to share the hansom's seat.

"Holmes, you are the greatest misogynist who ever lived!"

"You err, Watson. I do not hate women; I merely do not trust them."

"Not even the Lady Hypatia?" I asked. Immediately, I regretted asking such an intimate question. Holmes flicked his cigarette away with great force. It required several more blocks of silent journeying before I felt returned enough to my friend's graces to pose another inquiry.

"Holmes...that weapon in Kerwin's possession: was it truly an air rifle?"

"As fine a gun as the blind German mechanic ever produced. But it is nothing more than a museum piece now."

"What do you mean?"

"Did you notice that I touched it?"

I nodded. Holmes turned, and I saw that unusual brightness slip into his eyes. It was the light of barely-suppressed magic.

"I neutralized it. Air is one of the easiest substances to manipulate, to ward away. He will never be able to prime it again."

Holmes settled back with a satisfied look on his face. His words, however, had a most unpleasant effect on me. I considered them for some length, and was almost startled when Holmes placed a hand on my arm.

"What is it, Watson? You look positively shaken."

"Holmes...if your powers are so subtle...then why not work your enchantments on recalcitrant witnesses? You could have forced Kerwin to tell you what you wanted. If by no other means, you could have stolen his air, tortured him into a confession!"

My friend's face was suddenly deep in shadow. "Do you really think I would do that, Watson?"

"I only mean, it seems possible that you could. Doctor Dee clearly tortured the devil."

"And I would have no hesitation to meet any element of the Shadows with equal force. Quite frankly, against the Shadows I have no intention of fighting fair. It is different with mortals."

"But if it were necessary---"

"It is never necessary to harm a human. There are always other ways." Holmes put his fingers to his lips, almost in the attitude of prayer. "It is true, I could have used my magic to coerce Kerwin. But that would make me no better than the Shadows from which I have sprung. I hope you will think, and find, me a better man than that."

The words stung. I coughed out my reply. "Of course. I never meant to imply---"

He did not let me finish. "If you ever see me use my magic against humanity, Watson, then do the sensible thing."

"And what would that be?"

Holmes lifted his cane and thumped the roof of the cab, waving for me to remain inside as he descended, embarking on some unknown errand. He leaned back in, his expression tense.

"If it comes to that, abandon me. And never look back."

CHAPTER SIXTEEN

I arrived in Baker Street to find Mrs. Hudson in a considerable state of annoyance. She barely gave me time to remove my hat before she was pushing me up the stairs.

"You must do something about him, Doctor Watson! He's going to wear out the carpet if he doesn't stop pacing about. He's been at it for almost an hour."

I paused and listened. Just as she had said, there was a steady clumping of heavy boots on the floor above us, a rhythm that did not vary in the slightest. I was certain I recognized the sound's creator.

"Is that Inspector Lestrade?" I asked.

"It is indeed. He arrived just after you left, said he'd wait for Mr. Holmes. He hasn't stopped that awful pounding since."

"I will see what I can do," I promised, and our landlady went back to her rooms, probably intending to calculate a new raise in our rent to cover the damage. When I opened the door to our chamber, Lestrade whirled around from our fireplace. I looked; a furrow had clearly been ploughed in the rug.

"Where's Holmes?" the officer barked, before I could even hazard a greeting.

"On a case. I left him in the vicinity of Whitechapel."

"You have no idea where he's gone, or when he will be back?"

"None," I assured Lestrade, insisting that he take a seat. I poured a libation as he dropped into our basket chair, a look of disgust and defeat on his ferret-like features. "Could I help you?" I asked as I passed him a glass. "I would be happy to relay a message."

"No, no, don't bother. It's too late. They will have cleaned the place up by now. Holmes would have no clues to go on."

I doubted such was true, as my friend had solved many puzzles long after the scene of the crime had been tidied. Lestrade downed his drink in one gulp.

"It's just that...well, dash it all, I might as well tell you as anyone. Anyone other than Gregson, that is. I'll not have him getting all the glory for this!"

I recalled my friend's assessment of the rival detectives, that they were as jealous as a pair of professional beauties. Holmes took a rather fiendish pleasure in helping one and then the other, merely to watch the fireworks explode between them. Without a doubt, setting Lestrade and Gregson to each other's throats was my friend's favourite pastime.

"Do tell me what it is," I encouraged. "And I will share it with Holmes the moment he returns."

"It's not that difficult a thing to unravel. How it was done is very clear. But it's the why that eludes me!" He gnawed on a knuckle that was already raw and inflamed. "Give me two blokes who bash each other's heads in over a girl, or thief who shoots his mate because he doesn't want to share his swag. That I can understand! Even the strange fellow from America, the cab driver, what was his name?"

I remembered it well. "Jefferson Hope."

126

"Right, that man! He saw himself as God's avenging angel, for what was done to his friend and his lover. Even the Ripper, he was 'down on whores' as he told us. But this---this is incomprehensible. Who kills an old couple in their own home and then walks away without a trace, not even taking the money or the jewels laid out in the very rooms in which they died?"

I nearly dropped my glass. "When did this happen?"

"Just this morning. Shall I give you the details?"

"Please do. Holmes would wish to know them."

Lestrade pulled a dog-eared notebook from his pocket. "Doctor and Mrs. Julian Sullivan. Is the name familiar to you?"

I shook my head. Lestrade cleared his throat and continued. "Residence on St. Anne's Street. The doctor was in his seventies, and his practice was small. His wife was also elderly and a rather stout woman. They employed just one servant, a girl who cooked and cleaned. She left them at nine a.m. to go to the market. Both were in good health and spirits, the doctor in his office, which was in the front of the house, and his wife upstairs tending to some mending. The girl found the front door ajar when she returned, which seemed out of place. Seeing no one in the kitchen or the parlour, she went to ask her master what he would like for luncheon. She found him slumped across his desk, his head chopped open."

"My God," I whispered.

Lestrade continued, never looking up at me, for which I was grateful. I had no doubt that my expression could have been deciphered even by the dullest of detectives. The inspector would have known that I had heard such a story before.

"The maid ran screaming into the street, and by good luck a constable was passing by. He went in and saw the doctor's body. After that, he climbed the stairs with his club at the ready, thinking the killer had remained inside the house. In the second bedroom he found Mrs. Sullivan on the floor, her head also shattered. She had been knocked from her chair. Her stitching was still in her hands."

"And nobody saw anything amiss?" I asked.

"No one. The girl was out of the house for less than an hour." Lestrade glanced back at his notes. "There was not a drop of blood on her, and a half-dozen witnesses will testify to the trip to the market. Apparently, the girl has a sweetheart in the grocer and all the boys who work for him are jealous, so they note her arrivals and departures with precision."

"You mentioned valuables?" I prodded.

"The physician had twenty pounds in his wallet and more in his unlocked desk. There was jewellery in the lady's room and on her person, not to mention a large number of Oriental curiosities made of jade and ivory that were displayed in a glass case in the consulting room. Yet the maid swears nothing is missing."

"Does the couple have children nearby?" I asked, even as I suspected I knew the answer.

"Their only son was killed in the Mutiny," he sighed. "They have no relations we can find record of." He threw the notebook to the floor. "That's what I do not understand. No one profited from this death! Why go to such lengths to kill a pair, if you stand nothing to gain?"

I knew the reason that eluded Lestrade. This killing fit the previous pattern of blood magic. Holmes had even predicted that it would come. But this was not information I could share with the inspector, despite the closeness of our friendship.

"Holmes drew my attention to a similar case in Prague," I said, in an effort to be helpful. At least Lestrade should know that he was not alone in his bafflement. "An old couple was murdered in their bed, for no reason. You know what Holmes says," I added, when Lestrade waved a hand dismissively. "It has all been done before."

"Well, Gregson thinks this is the work of a lunatic, that a madman with an axe is running helter-skelter in the suburbs. I ask you, how could a crazy man enter a house unseen, dispatch its occupants in such a brutal fashion, and leave no footprints behind, or be seen with blood on his clothing? It makes no sense to me." He leaned forward, motioning for me to do the same. His voice dropped to a conspiratorial whisper. "Do you know what I think is the only logical conclusion?"

"What?" I asked nervously.

"That this is sport. It is a dare, or perhaps a prank that has gone too far. Some of these coddled fops from the university, I'd wager, they've gone beyond all decency in their search for amusement. Do you know what their most recent entertainment is, the thing that half a dozen have been caught red handed at in Camford? Grave robbing!"

I wished I had some way to tell Lestrade how far he had gone off the track. Instead, I merely assured him I would alert Holmes to the situation. Lestrade took his leave, perhaps to journey to the university town and question fraternity brothers, while Gregson would follow his own leads and search for a blood-drenched madman on the city omnibuses.

Holmes returned late that evening, looking weary and unwilling to discuss his afternoon's work. I told him of Lestrade's visit, and the evening paper carried a concise summary of the atrocity. Holmes puffed on his pipe, shaking his head in dismay.

"Lestrade may well be right about one aspect of this crime, Watson. He strikes close to the bone when he dubs it an activity engaged in for thrill or sport."

I was stunned to hear Holmes advocate what I had immediately dismissed as a ludicrous theory. "What do you mean?"

"Magic can bring its user great pleasure, both mentally and physically. Indeed, for those of no discipline, it can be rather like a drug, a very powerful narcotic that transports the addict to a state of bliss. Miss Telfair has doubtless discovered that what is necessary to increase her power also brings her intense, if temporary, satisfaction."

This information unsettled me. I was more determined than ever that we must do something to stop such unholy actions. "Holmes, we must find her," I said.

"And we will. Can you be prepared to travel in the morning?"

"Of course. Where are we going?"

"To the same place Miss Telfair is going. Watson, we will seek the Fountain of Youth."

CHAPTER SEVENTEEN

It has often occurred to me that Holmes would have had a much less successful career if he had chosen a companion with no military background. As an old campaigner, I have always been ready and willing to shift my camp at a moment's notice, and I have never questioned my commander's orders. I will confess, however, a vigorous annoyance with the man for not telling me of our journey earlier in the day, so that I might have packed well before bedtime. Once again it seemed I had only just closed my eyes when Holmes was roughly shaking my shoulder and giving me a sharp slap to the chin.

"Up, Watson! The game is not only afoot, but on the waves, and you will be left behind if you tarry."

There was not even time for coffee. Holmes thrust me into a waiting growler, and I rubbed my bleary eyes as the vehicle lurched away from our home.

"Holmes, you are a most exasperating companion at times," I muttered. "Do tell me why it is necessary that we leave so early in the morning."

"Because late yesterday, my brother's agents spotted our prey in Southampton. They were disembarking from a carriage at the slip of the liner *Andromeda*, which is bound for New York, and will arrive hence in seven days. Both Miss Telfair and a female companion were sighted, so it seems that I was correct in stating the lady was not merely trying out a disguise for the pawnbroker."

"We assumed her assistant, the murderer, was a man," I muttered.

"And for all we know, it may well be," Holmes countered. "We are playing a game of veiled identities. Miss Telfair may have hired a man to handle the bloody work, and a woman to serve as an appropriate chaperone, so that no eyebrows will lift at her travels. Either or neither person could be the Boston-acquired companion."

It was too early for my brain to work out all the possibilities that Holmes was suggesting. I decided to focus on something more concrete. "What vessel are we taking?" I asked, with a barely-suppressed yawn.

Despite the pre-dawn gloom, I could see a spark of humour in Holmes' eyes. "She is called the *Friesland*, Watson. She is my brother's newest toy, as well as Her Majesty's best kept secret."

I swallowed nervously. "I fear I did not pack my best dinner jacket."

Holmes gave way to a rare fit of outright laughter. "I do not think her captain will stand on ceremony."

"But why are we even sailing? Could you not open a pathway through the Shadows, as you did before?"

My question erased his good humour. "It is out of concern for you, old friend. You did not find the Shadows a very hospitable place, as you will recall."

That was true. Just the memory of walking through that ebony world, where I could see nothing and was forced to guide my steps blindly, as vile and horrible things flitted around me, was enough to roil my stomach. My head swam for a moment. I struggled to speak calmly.

"It was unpleasant, but I trust you, Holmes. I would venture into it again, at your side."

"I know you would, Watson. But your courage would lead to unnecessary sacrifice. You still do not comprehend what a shock you suffered and how close to the edge of sanity you trod. Another trip through those infernal regions, with your recovery so brief, would be tempting fate."

His words made my blood run cold. "It would kill me?"

"No. But it would very likely drive you mad."

"In that case," I agreed, with a loud harrumph, "I would much prefer to sail to America!"

Holmes smiled and said no more. A short time later, we arrived at the grim area of the docks, where boats of undistinguished pedigree and accomplishments took on cargo. Upon sighting the *Friesland*, my heart sank. She looked to be a tramp steamer, dull and decrepit, her hull caked in barnacles and her paint cracked and faded. I could not imagine how such a poor excuse for a boat could hope to put us ahead of a sleek liner. Holmes leaned over my shoulder and whispered in my ear.

"Appearances are deceiving, Watson. Recall what I said about the most winning woman and the most repellent man."

I was in no mood for his cryptic lessons. I took hold of my medical satchel and carpetbag, making ready to trudge up the gangplank in Holmes's wake. But we had gone only a few steps when a soft yet determined voice called out to us. It was a woman's tone, so incongruous in this place and hour.

"Master Sherlock! Doctor Watson! Would you leave without saying goodbye?"

I turned, astonished at the figure who stood by a low pile of baggage. She was tall and slender, dressed simply in a white blouse and grey skirt, her hair pinned under a wide, delightfully tilted hat trimmed with a peacock feather. Gloves covered her hands and a high collar hid the scars on her neck. I remembered her so vividly from our former adventure, when we fought together against the darkest minions of the Shadows. Now the Lady Hypatia, mistress of the great Library of the Arcane, favoured Holmes with the look a schoolmistress would level upon an exceptionally naughty pupil.

"My Lady," Holmes said, sweeping off his hat to her. "I thought you disliked modern attire."

"This damnable corset is torturing me," she hissed, with no false modesty. "If Torquemada had possessed such a device, he would have found far more witches and heretics ready to confess!" She turned to me, her expression softening. "Doctor Watson, I have read your manuscript which tells the tale of our recent encounter with certain unsavoury elements."

Blood rushed to my face. I had lain senseless for almost a month, but before that time, before I drank down my soul, I had written up the case and, at its conclusion, expressed my deep admiration and fondness for the Lady Hypatia. When I penned those words, I had no real hope of ever being in her presence again. Though I meant them with all my heart, and had longed to speak with her once more, at this moment, exposed to her regal, fierce intelligence without any preparation, I felt shamed. I was certain I was unworthy of having any romantic regard for such a woman, especially one possessed of immortality.

"I hope you found it...interesting," I stammered.

"Perhaps we should discuss it when you return," the Lady said. As she spoke, I dared to lift my face and meet her eyes. There was no mockery in her expression, only a serene coolness that I was unsure how to interpret. "I would very much like to ask you a few questions on certain points in your plot."

I spoke bashfully, barely able to get the words past my lips. "Yes, yes, of course. I would be delighted to---"

A sharp whistle from the ship cut off my reply. Holmes stepped between us, obviously annoyed by our conversation.

"There is no time for this. My Lady, why are you here?"

"Because you are being followed," she answered, with no sign that his brusqueness in any way affected her. "You should know that other parties are interested in your pursuit of the map."

"I am aware of that," Holmes said. "I have been for some time. However---what have you heard?"

"That you should be careful," the Lady continued, "and beware of a small man with a box. He is a man who can change his appearance and travel in the Shadows. But he will always be short of stature and he will forever have with him a type of box or casket. This container is very important to him and he is never seen without it."

"Who is he?" Holmes asked. "Does he have a name?"

"That information has been lost. But he has been seen many times over the centuries. He seeks the map."

"Who wouldn't?" I asked, in an attempt to add some levity, for her simple statement had the effect of drawing a dark cloud around us. My friend's face had grown solemn and thoughtful. "Even a hideous dwarf would want a passage to the Fountain of Youth."

I cursed myself the moment my flippant words were spoken, for the Lady Hypatia turned and favoured me with a look of such infinite sadness that I was certain I had wounded her deeply. I tried to summon a proper apology, but Holmes was already striding up the gangplank, one strong hand on my arm.

"Holmes! Stop!" I disentangled myself from his grasp. "We must take our leave of her properly."

My friend halted and tilted his head. I swung around, hoping to make amends for his rudeness.

Fog swirled in the place where the Lady Hypatia had been. There was no sign of her anywhere on the docks.

An hour later, we were ensconced in the small stateroom we would share. Holmes informed me that there were no porters or servants aboard, and that we would have to shift for ourselves over the next five days. I paid him little attention. As he unpacked his trunk and settled his things about the cabin, I could not banish the lady or her words from my mind. Her warning made me think harder on my previous encounters with the strange figure of the grinning dwarf.

"Holmes?"

"Yes, Watson?"

"The man she described, there is something more that I recall about him."

There was a sudden silence. I looked up, and found Holmes frozen in the act of hanging his coat.

"Go on," he said.

"In the country, the night before you arrived at Haven House, I saw what it was the man carried much more clearly than I have seen it since. It was a coffin, one with a large cross on the lid. And now, as I recall, each time I have seen the man, no matter what the general shape or appearance of that box, the same cross remains atop it."

"You are certain it was a cross and not some other symbol?"

"Yes. It was golden and heavy, very ornate. My instinctive thought was that it appeared Spanish in design."

Holmes nodded. Much to my horror, he fished out his pipe out of his coat. Surely I would suffocate if he kept up his usual routines in such a small space. A three or even a two pipe problem would be the death of me!

"Intriguing, Watson. It opens new possibilities."

He explained no further. Much to my relief, he exited without a word, taking his malodorous tobacco to other regions. A short time later, I went on deck to witness our departure. No one on the docks waved goodbye; there was no festivity as there would be for the embarkation of an ocean liner.

One fair face would have been enough for me, but I feared that, in ignorance and insensitivity, I had said something that might have driven its owner away forever.

CHAPTER EIGHTEEN

For two days our journey was uneventful. The *Friesland* was, as Holmes had hinted, no mere steamer. Once we were clear of shore, at a distance no telescope could penetrate, her appearance began to change. The *Friesland* ceased to be a thick, clumsy freighter. I watched in amazement as fake sides and masts were pulled away, lowered and tucked into more spacious compartments than I had ever suspected existed. Nor could I find these compartments when I went in search of them. As if escaping from a nautical cocoon, the *Friesland* emerged as a sleek and elegant steam-powered yacht, fantastically bigger on the inside than the outside. She cut through the water like a clipper, her progress so fast and smooth we seemed to be skimming the waves. From time to time, awed by the ship's abilities, I would ask questions of the sailors. But their replies were generally stony silences.

"Watson, you must understand," Holmes said, with a touch of amusement, when I expressed my opinion that the sailors were exceptionally rude men, "that this vessel officially does not exist. It is a closely-guarded state secret. To speak of anything more than the mundane---'pleasant weather we're having, the sea is calm today'---would be treason."

"Yet your brother was willing to lend it to you," I noted. "I would hardly think that such an important ship would be surrendered for such a minor errand."

Holmes gave me a hard look. "You now think this investigation is insignificant?"

"Not to me, or for the sake of the soul of Miss Telfair," I defended. "But I will admit that, compared to your other cases, it hardly seems that the fate of the British Empire is at stake."

"And in that you are correct. Britain is not in play. But perhaps something greater is."

We were standing at the bow, watching dolphins leap and play in our churning wake. My friend's dark and ominous words took me completely by surprise. "What? Holmes, you are not generally given to melodramatic exaggeration!"

"Indeed. But, Watson, consider this scenario, which further reflection---and a long conversation with my brother the afternoon before our departure---has created in my mind. The girl and her partner-in-crime find the Fountain of Youth. Unlike her father, who selfishly kept the secret for himself, they decide to make the water available to the world for a price. What would happen?"

I shrugged. "Wealthy people would buy it, as they buy other things that the poor can not afford: art, carriages, fine houses."

"None of which is generally thought to cause rioting, except perhaps among our socialist friends," Holmes said, with a wry chuckle. "But consider the difference between owning a great manor and living forever, or at least until some assassin or accident overtakes you. Why, our unwashed masses might ask, do wealthy citizens have the right to be eternally youthful while the poor people must labour and sweat and die before even reaching their prime? Think of the social discontent, the brewing rebellions the introduction of this formula would cause."

"I confess it likely."

"More than likely, Watson, inevitable! And next, muse over the greed and envy of other nations. Alice Telfair would certainly offer her elixir to the highest bidders, regardless of nationality. But does it not also stand to reason that as time passes and the benefits of the water become obvious, nations will go to war to possess it? The Fountain of Youth flows in America; soon that country will forbid its water to be exported. When that embargo is enforced, other nations will band together in unholy alliances to steal the water from its source." My friend dropped his head, studying the ocean below us. "Watson, I tell you this in strictest confidence---a war is coming. A Great War, which all of mankind's magic and faith can do nothing to prevent. The east wind will bring with it horrors that the world has never known. But if my brother's speculations are correct, another war could precede it. That is what we must prevent."

He left me with that pronouncement. For almost an hour I stood there, staring out to the western horizon and pondering his words and the possibilities of the evils he had outlined. I had never thought of the Fountain of Youth as anything but a gentle fairy tale, an amusing and wistful illusion that all humans aspire to once they realize the brevity of life, the fragile nature of health. Who would not wish to be young again?

And who would not kill in order to be immortal?

I recalled the words that Holmes had said to me, in the aftermath of our defeat of Marie Laveau and her legions. Immortality was a curse, for if all humans attained it they would soon strip the planet of its resources. What further wars and suffering could come from this unnatural order of things was too hideous to even imagine! At last I understood that Edgar Telfair's secretive greed had been a blessing.

I looked back to the waves. Something was amiss in the churning waters. I worked it out; the dolphins were gone.

I turned away from the railing. It was almost noon, yet the sky was growing increasingly dark, with the threat of storms. I dreaded taking our simple repast on ugly seas, for it had been many years since my passage out of India, and I confess that I was more than a little indisposed by the motion of the ship. Something rumbled overhead. I looked up and found that the clouds were not merely gathering, but racing together, boiling and angry, darker at their edges than in the middle. Members of the crew were pouring up from the hatches, wielding telescopes and odd nautical devices. The weather alarmed them; that much was clear on their faces and in their rushed, clipped speech. They spoke some kind of technical code, from which I gained no intelligence. I decided to go to the stern, to not be in their way as they worked.

There was a pile of boxes and ropes to one side. I had seen it a hundred times, to the point that this collection was almost invisible to me. Yet something moved from that pile, just as I approached. It was something dark and small.

I halted, choking on a cry of surprise and horror. Before me stood the vile man of my previous encounter. He was no longer dressed as a peasant, or clad in a uniform, but was wrapped in a heavy pea coat, with a greasy cap on his misshapen head. Still, his wart-covered chin was visible to me, and he slowly lifted his face, obviously enjoying my astonishment and mortification. Malevolence glittered in his sickly, mismatched eyes. His mouth opened, revealing broken, slime-coated teeth.

Then I saw the box. It was in a different shape, longer and narrower, as if containing whaling harpoons. Yet the ornate cross was still in place, glimmering as the air around it became thicker and more oppressive.

"You!" I sputtered, jabbing a finger at him. "What is your name?"

The wretch laughed at me.

And then he was gone.

"Watson!"

I nearly screamed when Holmes's hand slapped hard upon my shoulder. My friend spun me around. His face was pale and agitated.

"You had best go below. It is not safe here."

"Holmes, what is happening? I saw the dwarf and the box!"

His brows met. He was poised to ask a question, but at that moment a great noise enveloped us. It sounded like a massive groan, as if Poseidon himself was in agony. There were shouts and the men began to run, many of them dropping their devices. Bells clanged, horns bleated.

"Battle stations! Battle stations!" the men shrieked. I looked around and saw nothing.

"Who are we fighting?" I shouted, over the din.

"Not who," Holmes corrected, "but what. Look there!"

I turned. The image I beheld was something from a nightmare. Great tentacles were shooting from the churning sea, slashing out at the sky. Bolts of lightning flashed down around them, illuminating the spectacle as slowly, majestically, a fantastic head arose from the foam. Larger than even a cathedral dome it loomed over us, its scaly flesh a sickly colour of green. Its entire form was encrusted with barnacles and twisted with seaweed, as if it had been eons slumbering on the ocean floor. And then, drawn closer to the bow by morbid fascination, I noted that protruding from its corpulent body were the bones of men, arms and legs and even grinning skulls, all melted into the beast, half-absorbed.

It opened eyes the size of wagon wheels. Multiple eyes, in thick rows, all red and glowing, seemed to fix to every man on deck. A mouth, circular and flabby, crested the dark waters and emitted a shriek, exhaling a stench that caused two sailors to faint. Holmes yanked me back, pulling me behind a set of crates as the spiky appendages began to flail and beat at the waves.

"My God, what is it?"

"Many things," Holmes shouted. "It is the Kraken, the Leviathan, the great Iuk-Turso and the Hydra! It is every evil that dwells in the ocean!"

Before I could speak, one of the tentacles descended and snatched a sailor from the deck. His fellows fired guns at the monster, and one flung a harpoon. No weapon was effective. The poor man was thrust down into the deep, and the great creature began pawing for another victim.

It was then that I heard a grinding. Large guns, as big as those on battleships, were being freed from hiding. Where pleasure decks had once stood, now the greatest array of firepower in the fleet was revealed, magnificent and fearsome. Holmes tugged me down, and instinctively I covered my ears as the glistening cannons began to fire. It was louder than any salute. The entire vessel rocked from the force of the expelled shells.

I risked a glance. The thing before us was unaffected by the assault. To my horror, it seemed to merely absorb the missiles, sucking them into its spongy torso. Another seaman was snatched away and devoured by the vicious jaws.

His scream still echoes. I fear I will never stop hearing it in my nightmares.

The vessel shuddered. Holmes twisted, looking to the bridge. Our bold captain was spinning the wheel around, and the angry pounding of the engines told me he was reversing our course, with the goal of fleeing from this apparition. The water churned, men ran for cover as the ghastly tentacles became more adept in their searches. The evil thing was rising ever higher above us, blotting out what little remained of the sky. In only a few moments it would be substantial enough to snatch up the entire ship and crush it to kindling.

"No!" Holmes shouted, standing and waving at the captain. "No! We must charge it!"

I saw the captain's eyes widen. "Are you mad?" he yelled back. "We must run."

Holmes was at his most commanding. "Ram it! It is our only chance!"

In a heartbeat of decision, the captain saw the reason in my friend's words. Even the fastest ship had no hope of outrunning this creature. All the vessel's weapons were ineffective; its firepower was impotent. Only the ship itself might be capable of doing fatal damage to the monster.

145

The captain spun the wheel and worked a lever. The ship shook as if it would be pulled apart, and then, to the accompaniment of despairing cries from the men, we shot forward like an arrow, aimed directly at the vile, noxious thing before us.

As the tentacles flailed, now too clumsy to make a sudden grab, I saw a moment of dawning intelligence on the monster's primeval features. For just a moment, the glowing eyes dulled. It drew back, as if pondering its next move. But it was too slow, too huge, too much a thing of bulk and fear to also be a thing of speed and stealth.

At the last second, as its great shadow overwhelmed us, I saw my friend grab the railing. A burst of blue light, crackling with unnatural energy, raced along the metal of the railing and spread wondrously along the entire frame of the ship. I felt it cover my being, sparking and pulsing, a living source of power. And then we crashed against the hulk of the beast, splitting it, passing through it like the blade of a tremendous axe.

There was a cry that rattled the heavens. We were enveloped by a hideous stench. I saw huge scales and greasy chunks of flesh falling around us, bouncing off the astonishing shield that Holmes's magic had created. Ragged and torn, the monstrous thing peeled aside, greenish blood spurting to the sky. Hissing rose from the waves as its remains sank back down. It looked like the combustive effects of acid causing a fiendish bubble and boil. Yet we, somehow, were unharmed, and once we had gained a clear distance Holmes released his grip. Instantly the light and the force his magic had generated disappeared. Men slowly pulled themselves to their feet, and with quiet dignity returned unquestioning to their posts. Holmes walked toward the captain.

"It would be best if you do not report this in your log."

The man nodded grimly. Holmes gestured for me to follow him. I moved as if in a dream, trailing him to our cabin. Holmes sat on his bunk and held out his hands.

"Your professional assistance will be required."

I turned up the light. Holmes's palms were covered in large, angry blisters.

"Magic meeting magic, Doctor," he said, as I hurriedly yanked my bag from beneath my bunk. "Such power is not always kind to the wielder, especially if one has little time to prepare."

"Good heavens---what was it? And why did it attack us?"

Holmes allowed me to work, for once proving to be a good patient. "It was something mankind has known for as long as he sailed, the great sea monster of a thousand names. The creature is an escapee of sorts, a refugee from the Shadow Oceans."

"There are oceans in the Shadows?" I asked, feeling foolish even as I said it. Holmes merely smiled.

"Of course. There are seas and mountains and forests. There are even cities, Watson, though they would hardly be recognizable as such. And there are gates, places were the walls between that world and ours are unusually weak. Sometimes, things cross through."

Those final words chilled me to my soul. "But was this attack a random thing? Was the creature only hungry?"

"Perhaps. But I would find such a coincidence---its hunger and our presence---difficult to believe."

I finished applying the dressing and gave Holmes a surely-to-be-unheeded prescription to rest. "At least you have killed it," I added. "It will trouble sailors no more."

"Killed it?" Holmes' laugh was frightening. "Doctor, I have merely *inconvenienced* it."

CHAPTER NINETEEN

Mercifully, the rest of our journey passed without incident. The creature did not return, and the weather was blessedly calm, as if nature herself were offering an apology for our previous terrors. A short time later, we arrived in New York. We docked just after a grey, cold dawn and took our leave of the *Friesland* quietly, with no ceremony, as a heavy snowfall began. Rooms awaited us at the Waldorf Astoria, and for a few hours we were able to relax in one of hotel's magnificent suites.

"The *Andromeda* should put into port this afternoon," Holmes said, as we sipped coffee at the conclusion of our luncheon. "We shall present our papers and affect an arrest of Miss Telfair as quietly as possible. Perhaps we shall be able to resolve this entire investigation without unnecessary unpleasantness."

"Holmes, we have been attacked by a sea monster," I reminded him. "I would say the unpleasantness has already occurred." I settled my cup, thinking once again of the man I had spotted aboard our vessel. A thorough search had revealed no trace of him, and his connection to us remained a mystery. Or rather, I realized, his connection to me. Holmes had never seen the fellow and had only my word to go upon. I told myself sternly to dismiss the hideous dwarf from my thoughts and apply myself to the more urgent problem at hand. "What crime is Miss Telfair officially accused of?" I inquired, thinking that not even Mycroft could completely suborn British justice for his own ends.

"Theft," Holmes said. "Of books from the Sorbonne."

"So the French government is involved."

Holmes gave me a look that indicated I was either stupid or hopelessly naïve, so I decided to drop the subject. Even if we were breaking international laws, it would hardly be the first time I had helped my friend commit a crime.

We settled our bill and hired a cab, timing our arrival so we could watch the sleek liner's approach. Holmes presented his false credentials to the authorities. They never questioned the warrant's authenticity, and I suspected Holmes's magic was behind the American officials' complete acquiescence. I remained behind in the vast reception hall where people waited for their loved ones and friends to arrive after clearing customs. Some ten minutes later, a messenger boy galloped up with a note from Holmes. I could tell by my friend's handwriting that he was agitated.

<u>Observe passengers closely. Captain claims Telfair and companion not aboard</u>.

I scribbled a reply and sent it back with the lad. For the next two hours, I watched as the ship discharged its passengers. The trickle became a flood, and it was difficult to make observations amid the increasingly frantic pace of the greetings. I speculated on what type of disguise our prey might adopt. Would she have dyed her hair or painted her face? Was she wearing the clothing of a steerage passenger, rather than a proper British lady? Would there be someone waiting to meet her, perhaps a friend or a lover whose exuberance might give her away? All of these thoughts scampered through my brain like crazed mice. I darted hither and yon, looking boldly into every woman's face, making a great nuisance of myself in the process. I had hoped that if I did not recognize Miss Telfair, I might spy the companion the pawnbroker had described. But by wretched luck it seemed that half the women who emerged were stout and dressed in black, with heavy veils obscuring their countenances. I could hardly demand that every widow reveal her face to me; I would be no aid to Holmes if I were arrested as a molester of women! Finally, as the last of the passengers slipped away from the great shed, Holmes reappeared.

"What happened?" I asked.

"They claimed she never boarded the ship, and her name was not on the passenger list, or assigned to any cabin." Holmes ground his teeth together. "It was Mycroft's agents who saw their carriage arrive at the dock, not my Irregulars, and quite frankly I would have trusted my little urchins to do a better job of surveillance." He shook his head. "This trip across the ocean may well have been in vain. It will be a low point in my career." Holmes's expression mingled disappointment and exasperation as he turned to me. "I take it you spotted no obvious disguises."

"None," I confessed.

"Then let us return to the hotel. I have done all I can do here, but perhaps Mycroft can be finessed into being my representative in London. I will need to speak to him."

"You could send a telegram before we depart," I noted. "There is an office just across the street."

Holmes shook his head. "This requires more direct communication."

"The mirror?" I asked.

He looked pleased. "So you remember our private form of distant conversation. I feared some details of my magic might be lost to you," he explained.

"Seeing your brother inside a looking glass, as if viewing him through a portal, is not something I would ever forget," I huffed, to his wry amusement. But, as fate would have it, I was not destined to witness the conversation between the siblings. As we entered the hotel, the desk clerk raced toward me, drawing me away into the ladies' lounge. A woman had come in from the street, complaining of heart palpitations, the nervous young man explained. He had been ready to sally forth in search of a physician when my appearance in the doorway saved him.

The woman resting on the sofa was a substantial dame, dressed in a walking outfit of grey wool. A stylish hat crowned with ostrich plumes was tossed atop a massive fur coat, which in turn had been flung carelessly on the carpet. A little girl sat on a stool beside the lady, fanning her vigorously. A moist cloth had been laid across the sufferer's face. My gaze was drawn to the unusual brawniness of the hand that held the towel in place. Despite the woman's fashionable attire, her hand was muscular and covered in calluses, like a common workman's would be.

"Mrs. Maplecroft," the clerk coaxed. "A very fine English doctor is here."

Her reply was a rough grunt. She refused to remove the cloth from her face, despite my plea that I could hardly diagnose her without checking her colour. Unable to win her trust, I made as much of an examination as her stiff bodice and modesty would allow. Her heartbeat was strong and her breathing was unlaboured. Clearly, she had succumbed to nothing more than exertion and tight lacing of her corset, and would be fine once a glass of water, which the child had fetched, did its restorative work.

"We are supposed to catch a train in two hours," the youngster said, in a soft, embarrassed voice. "Will my mother be able to travel?"

"Oh yes, just give her a few moments to rest. And she should take a cab to the station. She must not tax herself further."

The girl nodded eagerly, nearly dislodging the sweet little sailor cap that she wore. She was a startling contrast to the substantial matron, as delicate as a doll, with golden ringlets falling almost to her waist. "I told Mother she did not need to take exercise, but she insisted. We will soon be in a place where we can walk every day, because there will be no snow."

"Indeed? Where are you bound?" I asked, but at that moment the woman gave a loud groan and gruffly dismissed me with an imperious wave of her muscle-defined hand. I gathered up my things and exited with as much dignity as I could summon.

Holmes had concluded his conversation with Mycroft, but I found him in nearly as foul a mood as my patient. He was striding up and down the carpet, puffing on a cigarette, dark brows drawn together. It would not have surprised me to see sparks fly from his heels as he was in such a barely restrained temper.

"Mycroft claims that our prey did board that vessel. His sources assure him the profiles were unmistakable, despite the long cloaks they were wrapped in." Holmes threw open the windows, staring down into the street, impervious to the blast of cold air that now howled through our rooms. The snowy lane below, with its crush of people, did nothing to improve his humour. "And there is more, Watson. The captain permitted me to board and search the *Andromeda*. A certain odour lingered there. It was nothing you or any mere human could smell---it was the last vestiges of ancient, but very foul, magic."

"The presence of the map generates the smell?" I inquired, schooling my features not to show how much the phrase 'mere human' distressed me.

Holmes nodded. Slowly, his temper faded, and his features took on the more relaxed nature of deep thought. "Perhaps that is how the unnamed thing, the shadow that Telfair feared, tracks the map. One wonders if the map's previous containers have somehow impeded the scent, and kept the shadow fiend at bay for decades. But now..."

I waited for long moments, respectful of my friend's musings. At last, I felt the need to pose the obvious question. "What will you do?"

"I must anticipate our prey's next move. However Miss Alice Telfair managed to elude us, the ancient city of St. Augustine, where her father camped while in search of the Fountain, seems her most likely destination. A consultation of an American Bradshaw would be in order."

Someone tapped on our door before either of us could examine the train schedule. I opened the door to find a tall, thin man on the threshold. Silver-haired, he was dressed sedately in black, with a fine watch on his vest and a golden-headed cane beneath one hand. Everything about him projected the air of an American businessman, a captain of industry. His speech emerged with a crisp Yankee accent.

"Which of you is Mr. Sherlock Holmes?" he demanded, his immense white moustache shivering with what I took to be tightly controlled, indecipherable emotion.

"I generally answer to that name," my friend said, stepping into view. For a moment the men considered each other. The American finally huffed out loud.

"Well, you're not exactly what I expected! You don't look a thing like a policeman!"

"For which I am grateful, Mr. Flagler."

The man gave a start. "How do you know who I am?"

"There is no great mystery, sir. You look exactly like your pictures. Please, do come in."

The man accepted Holmes's invitation, shoving his hat and cane at me as if he mistook me for a valet. Holmes attempted to make an introduction, but Flagler was already pumping his hand. In an instant, the man's manner had changed, and he was as profuse in his praise as he had been close-lipped in his coolness just moments before.

"You've saved me a million or more, Mr. Holmes. If not for your intervention, I might well have lost my company. What rascals they were, what perfect scoundrels! God will deal with them, no doubt. Providence always punishes the wicked!"

Holmes finally freed himself long enough to gesture to me. "Doctor Watson, may I present Mr. Henry Flagler, a bastion of American industry and the co-founder of Standard Oil. Though we have never met in person, I had the opportunity to provide a small service for Mr. Flagler some months ago."

I knew instantly that Holmes was referring to the period in which I had been so very ill. He had claimed his cases were small and unimportant, but it was clear from the businessman's fulsomeness that whatever problem Holmes had solved for him had been a most important one. He continued to offer his personal thanks, chiding Holmes only for not mentioning that he was in town.

"Had one of my men not recognized you in the dining room, I would have missed you completely," Flagler said. I quickly inferred that the business baron had something of a private army of detectives, and that Holmes had bested them all by his trans-Atlantic deductions. "But I am afraid I have little time to chat. I must finish my business in the city as I am bound for Florida this evening," Flagler continued, waving aside our offer of cigars and brandy. "I have been selected to represent the state of New York in a conference on coastal defence, down in Tampa."

"Will you be staying in one of your own hotels?" Holmes asked, turning toward me as he spoke. "Mr. Flagler is building a new empire of hotels and railroads in the southernmost state," my friend informed me. "There is no gentleman more interested in the development of that region."

The millionaire shook his head. "Unfortunately, I will have to stay at my rival's hotel! Perhaps you have not heard of that other Henry?" He chuckled softly. "My colleague, Henry Plant, has a spectacular lodge, the Tampa Bay Hotel! He had the cheek to send me an invitation to its opening, to which I replied 'where is Tampa' and he, the sly old devil, answered 'follow the crowds.'"

"Between such Henrys, Florida will be opened to the world," Holmes agreed.

"But only in the winter," Flagler demurred. "It's too cursed hot down there the rest of the year. Truly, I don't know how the natives of the place bear it! But in the winter it is paradise on earth.

My latest venture, the Royal Palm, has just opened in Miami, where there is never a frost."

"We are likewise on our way to Florida," Holmes informed him. "We are travelling to St. Augustine, on a confidential matter."

Flagler brightened at the mention of the city. "Then you must stay in the Hotel Ponce de Leon. It is the jewel in my crown, my masterpiece! No, Mr. Holmes, I will not hear of anything else. You will have the finest suite and the best waiter. It is the least I can do. I'd be begging my bread on the street if you hadn't fingered those swindlers so easily. Yes indeed, Mr. Holmes, whatever your business is---and I won't ask, one businessman to another, I respect your privacy!---you will at least conduct it in the finest style." He snatched back his hat and cane, promising to speak with his agents and insure that our arrangements were first class. "You'll never regret your journey, Mr. Holmes! It may be winter here, but it is summer there, and you'll depart as happy as Ponce de Leon was after drinking deep from the Fountain of Youth."

He took his leave with a flourish. Holmes closed the door and considered me with one of his arch little smiles.

"Let us hope the old conquistador did not actually drink the magical waters," Holmes said. "We have enough trouble as it is!"

CHAPTER TWENTY

The following morning we boarded a train for St. Augustine. Our journey on the Southern Railway was scheduled to take twenty-seven hours, with stops in Washington, Charleston, and Savannah. For the most part, the trip was uneventful. I wished we had possessed the leisure to tour the American capitol, but Holmes quickly nixed any thought of a diversion. I could see that Miss Telfair's evasion continued to torment him. He was not a man who took being bested gracefully, especially when his opponent was female.

We were seated in the smoking car that evening when a heavy-set man with an impressive pair of bright red side-whiskers approached us. His green eyes were sharp and quick, his face well-tanned. He scowled at us both for a second and then offered a hand.

"Mr. Holmes, Doctor Watson? My name is Hanscom. Mr. Flagler said that I should introduce myself to you, and let you know that should you need any assistance while you are in St. Augustine, you must not hesitate to call on me."

"So you are Mr. Flagler's parlour man at the Hotel Ponce de Leon," Holmes said. The gentleman's jaw sagged, and he dropped into the seat beside me without invitation.

"It's true then, everything I've read about you! Tell me more about myself, Mr. Holmes, if you can."

My friend smiled languidly. "You are an enigma, Mr. Hanscom. Besides the fact that you are Flagler's private agent of law enforcement at his flagship hotel, and that you are a retired Pinkerton detective, a former boxer, recently widowed, of Irish extraction, of the Catholic faith, and a native of Boston, I can say no more."

Our new companion nodded. "It's all true. Let me see if I can work out how you did it. My accent gives me away as Boston-born and of Irish extraction, I suppose, and my ginger hair confirms it. You'll rarely meet an Irishman who isn't a son of the Roman Church, so that was an easy call. I'd wager you got the boxer from my hands," he added, displaying two huge, much scarred mitts. "Or maybe it was my snout," he corrected, touching a nose that had been broken and was now piggish in his features. He pulled back his hand and studied a line around his ring finger, where the skin was still fair. "I lost my wife just a month ago, and I buried my ring with her; now I see my skin is pale where my wedding band was, so I can tell how you worked that out." He nodded in admiration then gave a quick tug to his whiskers. "I told you Flagler sent me, but how you got that I was his parlour man, and a former Pinkerton, is beyond me."

Holmes answered like a tutor conducting a review with a student preparing for exams. "Your accent is very distinctive; I would wager I could place your home within five blocks in Boston. Your hair speaks of Irish roots as well, but the St. Christopher medal that you wear on your watch chain serves as confirmation to your Catholic faith. As for the boxing, your ears are a better signal than either your nose or hands, though I assure you that no feature went unnoticed. You walk with authority, which indicates a higher position in Mr. Flagler's private service. The unnatural darkening of your fair Celtic complexion tells me that you have worked for him for some time in Florida; you knew of our destination and offered your services in that city. It stands to reason that you are the 'parlour man.'"

"What does that mean?" I asked Hanscom, who was silently applauding Holmes's recitation. "What does a parlour man do, exactly?"

"I'm the head hotel detective," he explained. "My job is to loll around dressed like one of the swells and keep an eye out for the con men who like to prey on Mr. Flagler's guests. You wouldn't believe how they crawl out of the woodwork down in Florida, with their grand schemes and their 'safe investments.' And there are worse things as well! Just last season I had to toss out an old faker from New Jersey who was offering the young men tours of his 'convent' where they could go and make a 'donation to the sisterhood.'" He shook his head and pulled out a cigar. "There was no Saint Voluptuous where I went to school, I'll tell you that."

"Your job must require some physicality," Holmes said.

"From time to time," Hanscom agreed, flexing his pugilist's fingers. "But I only pummel a man when I absolutely have to. I have carte blanche from Mr. Flagler, and the city police look the other way." Holmes urged him to tell us more, and I sensed that our new companion would be a font of information. He struck a Vesta to his boot, lighting his cigar.

"It's a strange town, St. Augustine. Over three hundred years old, much older than this country, and it sleeps seven months out of the year, like one of those princesses in a fairy tale. It's only when the rich people come for the winter season that it wakes up, for good and for bad." He puffed on his cigar, and as he spoke I sensed his deep pride in his adoptive city. "The city is full of quaint old houses, half falling down and unpainted, some of them relics of the Spanish days. Only a few of the streets are paved and larger buildings use coquina, a rocky material made of crushed shells. The old fort pushes out in the harbour, and sometimes in the evenings you'd take an oath that you are back in time, transported to the days before newspapers and streetcars and telegraph lines." He winked at us. "It's said to be a haunted city, full of ghosts, but I've yet to see one myself. Though...I can't quite explain why every morning the door to my armoire is open, even though I know I closed it quite firmly the night before." He chuckled. "Maybe it's the wee folk, the fairies who are up to no good!"

One dark eyebrow rose on my friend's face. It took all of my self-control not to expel the sip of brandy I had just taken.

"An intriguing theory," Holmes said, his tone at its driest. "I find myself more interested in the living than the dead, however. Tell me about the mortal residents of St. Augustine. I assure you I have no interest in fairies."

Hanscom nodded. "It's a strange mix of folks in that town. There's some descended from the Spanish, of course. All the exceptionally lovely girls have that blood in their veins. There's a small group of folks who came from Minorca as well, and plenty of Negroes who used to be slaves. But most of the city's residents are plain Americans, Southerners with a dash of Yankee entrepreneurs. During the Rebellion, the city was under a Union flag, and a fair number of the gents who took their turns guarding the place decided to move south and marry their Confederate sweethearts. But it wasn't until Mr. Flagler built his hotels that anyone really cared about the place or tried to make anything of it. Before Mr. Flagler, no one came in the wintertime except for invalids and people with bad lungs. I'm told, back then, the most exciting thing to do in St. Augustine was lie on the seawall and yawn."

"It sounds like a very unique city," Holmes offered. "Are there any colourful characters we should meet?"

"You'd do better to avoid them!" Hanscom chuckled. "Half the men in town are proposing some type of scheme and trying to get people to invest in their hotels and stores and broken-down old plantations. Those are some of the ones I have to toss out morning, noon, and night! But one you can't avoid is a gentleman named David Miller. He's the king of the St. Augustine promoters. He believes that the entire state will belong to tourists someday, and the fellow who can squire them around and keep them entertained will be the greatest man in history."

I shook my head. "That is mere illusion. He must live in some kind of fantasyland."

Holmes countered my dismissal. "Watson, consider the fortunes amassed by our British promoters. The man who invented the package tour retired with more money than an earl."

"I guarantee you'll be accosted by Miller, but he's not a bad sort for all his bluster. He does offer the best tour in town, and even takes people on boat rides along the San Sebastian River." Hanscom chewed on his cigar. "But, Mr. Holmes, before I wax eloquent any longer, it occurs to me that you never said how you knew I was a former Pinkerton man."

Holmes considered our guest through the narrowing slits of his eyelids. "I am aware, of course, that Mr. Flagler prefers to hire former agents of the Unsleeping Eye. But I will also confess that I held an unfair advantage---I recognized your name."

Hanscom drew back, suddenly wary. "You did?"

"Yes. I would be much obliged if you would tell me about the Fall River Tragedy. I have always been curious as to the events surrounding the case of the notorious Lizzie Borden."

I could tell my friend had touched a sensitive nerve. Hanscom puffed on his cigar. It was clear from his expression that he was considering abandoning our company as brusquely as he had joined us. At last he tapped his cigar against the bronze tray in the centre of the table.

"You are Sherlock Holmes. Do you think you could have solved it?"

"I already have," Holmes answered, and even I, who knew him so well, was stunned by this bold assertion. "As have you, Mr. Hanscom. That is why you went back to Boston, after spending only two days in Fall River. It is why you could no longer work in Miss Borden's interests, because you knew the truth."

Hanscom rose. His expression was one of disgust. "I did, and no one would believe me. If you know the truth, you who have never been to Fall River, or seen that house, or gazed into those soulless eyes, then you are welcome to it."

He stalked away from us, departing the car. I turned back to Holmes with some dismay. "You have a fine knack for losing friends," I said.

"I did not anticipate the case would be so raw in his memory," Holmes admitted. "I will offer an apology, should we encounter him again in our travels."

"What was the tragedy?" I asked. Unlike Holmes, I was no walking compendium of crime. My friend fished out a short pipe and spoke as he lit it. His expression took on the far-off look of a man lost in a dream.

"On August 4, 1892, in the town of Fall River, Massachusetts, a wealthy man named Andrew Borden and his wife, Abby Borden, were viciously murdered in the middle of the day. Andrew's daughter Elizabeth---better known as Lizzie---discovered her father's corpse in the parlour, stretched out on a sofa, his head brutally shattered. The police soon found Abby Borden's body upstairs, behind a bed, her skull broken with similar wounds. The murderer had entered the home, done his work, and disappeared without ever leaving a trace. Despite the blood, no footprints or fingerprints were discovered. As you can imagine, this prim American community was in a great state of shock."

I nodded. "Were there any suspects?"

"A number, but all of them were quickly dismissed. The maid had no motive to kill her employers, and an uncle and an older daughter had been away from the home at the time of the murder. No intruder or suspicious person was sighted in the area by a neighbour. You recall my maxim, Watson?"

It was not one I was ever likely to forget. "When you have eliminated the impossible, whatever remains, however improbable, must be the truth."

"Therefore the murderer was the younger daughter, the aforementioned Lizzie: a spinster, a Christian woman, and a most devoted child."

I shook my head. "Holmes, that cannot be!"

"And why not, Watson?"

"Because this is not some fishwife, or a hardened woman of the streets. By your own words, she was a genteel lady." I scowled. "Was there blood on her?"

"Not a drop," Holmes answered.

"Then how could she have done it?"

"Simplicity itself, Watson. If you wished to do murder and have no evidence upon your clothing, how would you accomplish the thing?"

I knew Holmes was enjoying himself by posing such riddles to me. Perhaps they were even necessary for him to escape back into the world of mundane crime and mystery, to elude the Shadows for at least one evening.

"Well, I suppose the easiest thing to do would be strip naked before picking up the axe," I finally offered. "Oh, good Lord!" I gasped, when Holmes offered a silently mouthed 'bravo' to my statement. "Not a lady!"

"Are genteel ladies never nude?" Holmes asked. "You will have to tell me, Watson, for I have never been married."

"Holmes, this is not a thing to make light of!"

"Indeed it is not," he agreed. Blue vapours wreathed his head, and our conversation was once more a solemn one. "Lizzie Borden was arrested and tried for the murder of her parents. But, like you, the jury of twelve good and honest men could not imagine a sweet spinster lady, especially one who carried bouquets of pansies into the courtroom and fainted when the skulls of the victims were produced, as being culpable of such an unspeakable deed. Miss Lizzie Borden was easily acquitted."

"What has become of her since?"

"Her name is now infamous," Holmes said. "But that has not stopped her from claiming her sizable inheritance and purchasing a manor in Fall River. But I suspect she is a very lonely woman...am I correct in that deduction, Mr. Hanscom?"

I started. While Holmes had been speaking, the former Pinkerton agent had returned to the smoking car and crept up behind me, so silent I had not hint of his presence until Holmes uttered his name.

"That she is, Mr. Holmes," the man rumbled. "No one will speak to her on the streets, her own family has shunned her, and when she comes to church the pew beside her is vacant. All the money in the world can not buy back her respectability, nor clean the taint of suspicion." He stepped between us, offering Holmes his hand. "I am sorry for my rudeness, sir. I surely would not wish to offend such a celebrated agent of justice."

"Nor I a man willing to speak the truth that others would prefer to ignore in favour of more comfortable lies," Holmes said, accepting his grip. "Do have a seat, Mr. Hanscom. I would be delighted to hear of some of your other cases."

CHAPTER TWENTY-ONE

Upon our arrival in St. Augustine one of Flagler's men met us to take us to our rooms at the Hotel Ponce de Leon. Before we even reached them I was certain of one thing: I required new attire.

"This warm in January!" I exclaimed, as we were loaded, along with two large families and multiple entourages of servants, into a pair of open carriages for the short ride to the hotel. "It reminds me of India."

"You'll be---what were the words Stamford used---as 'brown as a nut' in a few days," Holmes chuckled. "But you are correct, Watson. Residing in this sub-tropical region while clad in the garments of cold and dreary London will be somewhat of a challenge for me."

And so, as soon as we were registered in the hotel, I asked for directions to a respectable tailor on a nearby street. The man's coffee-hued skin hinted at the mixed ancestry common to the class of Southerners who had been freed from slavery before the war that liberated their kin. A most efficient worker, he soon had me attired in linen rather than wool, with a straw hat and a light jacket that seemed to breathe. Upon his return to our rooms that evening, Holmes informed me that I appeared ridiculous. Yet by the next morning he had abandoned his chequered cape and was similarly turned out in a more practical wardrobe.

That second afternoon, as we took luncheon in the grand dining hall of the hotel, beneath allegorical figures of the seasons and to the sweet music of a small orchestra tucked away in the balcony, Holmes brought me up to speed on his inquiries. He had made the rounds of all the hotels, claiming to be a distant relative of

Alice Telfair, a benevolent uncle who wished her to make the acquaintance of his wealthy new business partner. St. Augustine was a virtual happy hunting ground for Cupid, and it was not uncommon for lovely ladies on holiday to catch the eye of lonely businessmen. Holmes's pose as a matchmaker was calculated to elicit the most information, as he hinted that the grateful swain was sure to be generous to the hotel clerk who had made his wooing possible.

"She is not in residence, Watson. Or, she is not in residence under her given name. The number of maiden aunts escorting young women is incalculable! We would be better served if we knew the moniker of her accomplice, or at least had a decent description of her. We could then..." Holmes's speech trailed away as his eyes narrowed. I followed his gaze across the room.

A man had just entered, and was making conversation with the headwaiter. He was tall and broad-shouldered, stout but not fat, with a bald scalp and a sharp salt and pepper goatee. A monocle was held in place against tanned skin. Prosperity radiated from the fellow, as well as confidence. I saw him boldly place a silver coin in the hand of the headwaiter. The server at last nodded toward Holmes.

Holmes uncharacteristically swore.

"Who is he?" I asked, as the man began to make his way around the crowded tables, whose chairs had been designed by no less a personage than Louis Comfort Tiffany.

"He is David Miller, the man Mr. Hanscom warned us about, the tourism promoter with a reputation for accosting wealthy visitors and encouraging them to invest in his schemes."

I almost chuckled at my friend's discomfort. Holmes continued to speak, but signalled that if I wished to finish my dessert, I had better hurry.

"From what I have learned in the last day, he is a legitimate, if tedious businessman. Mr. Flagler has some shares in his tourism ventures, though I suspect he purchased them more to be left alone than because of any belief in their merits."

The gentleman ploughed across the room and hailed Holmes as cheerfully as if they had been old army chums. Holmes retained his usual measure of calmness and detachment, even as Miller announced Holmes's accomplishments to the entire assembly. Any hopes my friend had entertained of remaining relatively inconspicuous on this mission were instantly dashed.

"Such an honour, sir, to have you here in our sunny climes. We have all read of your adventures, of course. Just marvellous they are, better than any dime novel! Tell me, sir, does some mystery bring you to St. Augustine? Has here been a theft of diamonds or the murder of a potentate?"

Holmes reluctantly allowed Miller to join us. "I assure you, Mr. Miller, we are merely on holiday. My friend has recently suffered from a pulmonary attack-" at this cue I coughed loudly, "-and was advised to recuperate in a region with more salubrious air than London possesses."

Miller grinned. "Ah, you do not wish to discuss matters, eh? Say no more." He winked boldly and jabbed his elbow into my friend's ribs. "I am discretion personified!"

I could sense that Holmes was regretting his promise never to work magic against humanity. The temptation to hex the obnoxious man must have been overwhelming.

"But if you are here on a vacation, then you must see the sights! Please, Mr. Holmes, allow me to be your guide. I have resided in the Oldest City for over thirty years, since the end of the Rebellion. No one is more knowledgeable about this little piece of paradise, and I have vehicles that will make your tour more comfortable."

I expected Holmes to put the man off, but to my surprise he accepted the invitation, claiming we had made no plans for the afternoon. During a final stop by the washroom, Holmes confided to me that Miller's tour would at least serve the purpose of familiarizing us with the city. If Miss Telfair and her companion were posing as common tourists, we might spot them in the crowds, which Holmes feared would be swelling by the day as the winter season advanced.

For two hours Miller led us on a walking tour of the tiny town, which had been first settled in 1565. He pointed out the old slave market, the cathedral, and the grim grey walls of the fortress at the edge of the harbour. The Spanish had christened it the Castillo de San Marcos, and for hundreds of years it had guarded the city against attack by pirates and Englishmen. Miller thrilled me with legends from the castle's murky past, of how unfortunate wretches were starved and tortured to death in its dungeons, and of how, in more recent decades, Indian braves had engineered daring escapes over the ramparts, fleeing into the swamps after collecting the scalps of their guards. I could tell from the expression on my friend's face that he found many of these tales rather suspicious, but he held his peace and played the part of a bored visitor with aplomb. On exiting the Castillo, which the Americans had unimaginably renamed Fort Marion, Miller put his fingers to his lips and whistled.

A strange buggy answered his summons. It was driven by a Negro man in a smart white uniform and was decorated with all manner of flowers and palmetto leaves. Of unusual size, it featured five rows of seats and could transport up to ten people. A painted broadside announced 'Miller's Historical and Novelty Tours: Authentic and Exciting.' Even more ludicrous was the headgear of the two dun-coloured mules that pulled the buggy. Each was crowned with a straw hat covered in bright yellow daisies. Holmes grimaced.

"Do climb aboard, gentlemen," Miller coaxed. "We are going to cross over the bridge to Anastasia Island, and that might require more legwork than would be beneficial for you, Doctor."

As the day was unseasonably warm, I was grateful for the transportation, even if Holmes was not. We rattled over the narrow bridge, crossing an inlet where dolphins played merrily amid the sailboats. The land just beyond the bridge was wild and green, a tangle of vines that suggested an American jungle, but our driver stuck to a shell-covered path. We passed a number of pedestrians, many with small children. The youngsters were galloping ahead of their parents and nurses, faces flushed with excitement.

In a short time, we pulled up before a walled enclosure that greatly resembled the frontage of a saloon. A bright green creature was sketched across the wall above the awning, and a large fence ran completely around the building. Several children were pressed to the boards, seeking peepholes to view whatever wonder lay within.

"The St. Augustine Alligator Farm and Burning Spring Museum," Miller announced as we climbed out of the buggy. "There is no other attraction in America like it! Entertaining, educational, thrilling! Everyone who comes to visit our fair city spends an afternoon here at least once, and some of our guests visit every day."

I buried my amusement in a cough, and caught Holmes giving me a knowing look. He waited as Miller gave orders to the driver, who saluted sharply before turning the buggy around.

"I was not aware that alligators were cultivated like crops," I said.

The promoter chortled. "It is perhaps more of a ranch than a true farm. Our men have scoured the swamps and harvested the largest and fiercest of the reptiles. Why, we have specimens here that have amazed, astonished, and even baffled men of science! Not to mention small boys," he added, with a benevolent chuckle, as two barefoot urchins cut to the front of the line that was forming at the door. While Miller was prone to exaggeration, he had not misled us as to the attraction's popularity. Already a crowd had assembled before the box office. Even at pennies per head, the Alligator Farm was certain to show a profit. Miller waved to the usher at a gate in the fence. The man nodded and motioned us along, *sans* tickets.

"You must be familiar with all of the local diversions," Holmes said, as we began to walk inside the strange farm. I was reminded of a cattle market, except that instead of livestock pens, there were all manner of deep pits, filled with specimens of alligators, crocodiles, iguanas, and a number of other lizards I could not put names to. Another deep hole writhed with a tangled knot of snakes. A thousand vipers were woven together, slithering and caressing each other. I turned away from the sight with a shudder.

"That I am," Miller answered proudly. "I am convinced, Mr. Holmes, that Florida's future lies in the steady promotion of these attractions. Our soil here is poor, our interior is uninteresting. But along these balmy coasts we can create lands of fantasy and amusement, something for every class of traveller."

"Including those who are very easily duped," Holmes replied. He pointed to a low well, which seemed to be belching fire. A dapper gentleman in the long white coat of a scientific researcher was giving a presentation to a half dozen awed visitors. He stepped away from the well and the flame extinguished. A second later, he returned to close proximity to the brick foundation, and combustion leapt skyward, nearly igniting his handlebar moustache. "The burning spring, I presume?" Holmes posed to Miller.

"Why yes! Its waters are such a bizarre mix of chemicals that it bursts into flame on regular intervals, rather like a geyser. Scientists have yet to determine the exact reason for this unique phenomenon."

"Then perhaps they should inspect the gas line that runs into the well, and the switch which the professor over there is clearly tripping, in order to ignite the flame. Really, Mr. Miller, Florida must do better than mere humbuggery if it wishes to become the world's holiday resort."

Two bright spots of colour bloomed on the promoter's cheeks, but he refused to be cowed by my friend's quick dismissal of the attraction's fraudulent claims. "I will show you something even you can not explain, sir," he promised. "Something so astonishing and horrifying I hope your nerves can bear it." He grinned at us fiendishly. "Right this way."

CHAPTER TWENTY-TWO

Miller led us to an arbour formed by the heavy branches of oak trees that must have been ancient when the conquistadors arrived. Wooden benches were assembled in a rough-hewn grandstand overlooking a deep circular pit. The crowd filled in around us, as Miller bragged at length about the new hotels Mr. Flagler had constructed along the state's eastern coast. As the promoter waxed eloquent on suites, casinos, and swimming pools, I could tell that Holmes's attention was elsewhere. I directed my gaze to the pit and understood at last what held him entranced.

The hard-packed dirt in the centre of the ring was surrounded by a murky moat. Though the waters were dark and cloudy, I could make out sharp ridges on the surface and catch the reflection of onyx eyes. The water was filled with the alligators (or 'gators', as the locals called these beasts), and judging the distance from the bumps of their snouts to the tips of their tails, I realized the creatures were of exceptional size, larger than any we had seen in the other pens. As the last of the spectators packed into the benches around us, a gong sounded. A door opened in the far wall of the pit, and with a noisy clatter a gangplank was laid down over the water. The people, many of whom were surely regular attendees, began to applaud.

A performer walked out across the planking. He was a man with a slender but powerful physique, and he strolled barefoot onto his stage. His skin was a shade of mahogany, with a reddish sheen, while his long hair was black and shiny, tied into a plait that fell down his back. He wore dark cotton breeches and a bright yellow shirt decorated with intricate bands of quilted patches. It was open nearly to his waist, and a leather cord with a large arrowhead attached was his only adornment. His features were strong, showing a clear blending of Indian and Negro blood, which made it difficult to estimate his age. A barker with a bullhorn introduced the man as Tiger Tail, a grandson of the great warrior Osceola. The man in the pit bowed with regal dignity.

"Before the white man came to this land," the barker continued, "the Seminole people lived in vast numbers in our swamps and prairies. There was no fiercer tribe on the continent, for while other Indians hunted bear and bison, the red men of Florida hunted alligators, the most dangerous creature ever encountered by the human race. Tiger Tail will now show us the skills that were required to track and kill these monsters."

Two white men, rather scrawny and dressed in denim overalls, chequered shirts, and straw hats, emerged from the backstage area and brought out a set of targets and a cache of weapons, placing them in the middle of the circle at Tiger Tail's feet. Abruptly, one of the alligators lunged from the water, his massive jaws opening wide. Both men screamed with the shrillness of young girls, and one leapt into his companion's arms. Untroubled by the aggression, Tiger Tail walked toward the reptile, holding out an arm and giving a signal with spread fingers. As if intimidated by nothing more than the gesture, the alligator slunk back into the murk. The stooges hurried out of the pit so rapidly that their hats were left behind.

Tiger Tail picked up one of the hats and flung it into the air. Before it could fall, he drew a knife from his belt and hurled it at the straw chapeau. It sliced the hat cleanly in two before landing, blade-first, in the ground. The audience clapped and cheered.

"No showing off now," the barker scolded. "Get to work and teach our guests how to hunt gators!"

For the next several minutes Tiger Tail performed a series of exercises in the pit, demonstrating his adeptness at hitting targets with knives and tomahawks and his elegant mastery of a bow and arrow. He also used a rope, tossing it easily around a series of stumps that were brought out for that purpose, catching each target while blindfolded. At the climax, he whirled around and tossed the rope into the audience, where he succeeded in snaring a rather pale woman who wore glasses with darkened lens. The audience laughed even louder when the lady freed herself and threw the lasso back to him with an annoyed huff.

"And now, the moment has come!" the barker announced, following a short interlude where Tiger Tail handled a number of lizards and deadly snakes while the barker described their attributes for the crowd. "Every Seminole youth, to prove his manhood, was required to complete a strange and bizarre ritual. It required nerve and skill to kill an alligator, but a Seminole was not considered a warrior of true courage unless he could coax a gator from its lair and wrestle it into submission!"

I shook my head. Surely the announcer was joking.

Tiger Tail pushed up his sleeves. He walked a circuit of the pit, as if selecting a victim. Then he crouched and began a low chant in his native tongue. His hands beckoned, strong fingers pulling and tugging as if working an invisible line. To my amazement, an alligator began to slowly emerge from the depths, oozing languidly across the sand in answer to the magical summons. The crowd gasped as it became obvious that this was a truly monstrous beast, nearly twelve feet in length, of significant girth, many times heavier than the slender man who lured it. As Tiger Tail rose, the spell seemed to snap. The alligator threw open its jaws, its massive tail lifting and swinging. People screamed, yelled for him to look out, tried to warn him of his peril.

Tiger Tail was oblivious to their concerns. He vaulted the tail with ease, dancing around the alligator as if they were partners at a society ball, rather than opponents in a life and death struggle. He lured the alligator through many paces, working him with the ease of a matador to a bull. The animal's bellows and hisses were fierce and real. The least stumble or misstep, and the man would be devoured.

With a motion almost too swift to comprehend, Tiger tail abruptly pounced on the alligator's spine and caught the creature at the tip of his jaw, forcing his teeth together. The beast was pinned, and with a show of unsurpassed bravo, Tiger Tail held the lord of the swamp in check. Tiger Tail threw out his arms, keeping the alligator still, its jaws of death firmly tucked in against his chin. The crowd roared its approval.

I thought surely his helpers would now rush out to restrain the foe. Instead, with another deft move, Tiger Tail flipped the alligator onto its back. It writhed for a moment, its tail once again thrashing about, anxious to deliver a deadly blow. Tiger Tail placed his left hand on the animal's gray-green belly. To the crowd's astonishment, the native began to sing to the creature, his words some form of Indian lullaby. In less than a minute, the alligator was still, its eyes closed and its legs going limp. It had fallen asleep.

Tiger Tail bowed again before exiting over the planking. The audience applauded, laughing heartily as the performer's assistants returned to roll the alligator over. The beast awoke immediately and nearly made a meal of his unfortunate rescuers.

Miller beamed at us as the throng began to disperse. "There is nothing like this in jolly old England, I'll wager!"

Holmes met Miller's pride with a patronizing smile. "I confess there is not. However, the Hindus of our empire are no doubt similarly skilled, from confronting crocodiles in the Ganges."

I was pleased to see Holmes's reminder of British superiority take a bit of the starch out of Miller's high American collar. "Well, I suppose that could be---excuse me for a bit. I see an investor! Mr. Vanderbilt, a moment if you please!"

He clattered down the boards, hailing a well-dressed gentleman. The man gave an audible groan when Miller caught up with him and began pumping his hand like a politician eager for votes. Holmes tugged at my jacket sleeve.

"Quickly, Watson. Miller won't be distracted for long, and I would like a word with the star of this show."

I followed Holmes around the end of the pit, to a kind of backstage area where the showmen were gathered with their props. The two assistants sat on stools, smoking cheap cigars and playing cards with one of the target stumps serving as a low table. Tiger Tail, however, was mobbed by his adoring public, which consisted of a half dozen young boys.

"He has his own Irregulars," I said to Holmes. My friend nodded, his expression softening. Many people have, in the long years of our association, spoken of Holmes as cold and calculating, lacking normal human emotions. Perhaps to some degree it was a factor of the magic that ran in his blood, this habit of maintaining a detached demeanour. Yet I never saw him speak of the street urchins who served as his eyes and ears with anything other than sincere affection. Even the comparison of these children to those drew a hint of a smile.

Tiger Tail looked up, locking eyes with Holmes. Something passed between them, some odd understanding. The performer finished scribbling his signature and gently shooed the little crowd away. As the children ran past me, I noticed they were clutching stiff cards with double pictures on them. Tiger Tail had been signing stereoscopic photographs.

Holmes inclined his head politely. "That was a most impressive act, sir. Your courage is unsurpassed."

Tiger Tail merely continued to study him. Then, to my puzzlement, he removed the leather cord from his neck and settled the ornamental arrowhead in the hollow of his palm, with the point toward his chest. Tiger Tail whispered a word, and the artefact began to vibrate. It turned slowly, so that the tip now pointed toward Holmes.

"One hoodoo man knows another," Tiger Tail said, so low I had to strain my ears to hear. "What do you want?"

I was amazed, not only by the small display of magic, but also by the undercurrent of hostility in his tone. Holmes showed no reaction. He folded his hands on the head of his cane, chatting easily. If anyone had observed us, they would have assumed we were merely lavishing praise on the star.

"I need your assistance. The map to the Fountain of Youth is here. I must find it and destroy it."

If this news was startling to Tiger Tail, he gave no sign. "Many men have sought that map. It is a cursed thing. One day, it is said, its true owner will take it back and avenge its theft in blood."

"That is what I am trying to prevent," Holmes said. "I have reason to believe that its newest owner will be searching for native practitioners of magic, wizards who have the power to lift the mist that surrounds the Fountain. You are the only wizard of any variety that I have sensed in this town." Holmes's eyes narrowed. "Whoever assists this person will be in great danger."

Tiger Tail folded his arms. "Why should I believe you?"

"Because the last hoodoo man to find the Fountain was killed."

The native man's face darkened. He stepped back, scowling fiercely at Holmes. I suddenly understood why the American soldiers had been terrified to fight with his ancestors.

"This I know, all too well." He slid sideways, looking around Holmes. I glanced back and saw that Miller was coming toward us, mopping his bald dome with a handkerchief and fanning his face with his straw hat. Tiger Tail reached into his shirt and withdrew one of the stereoscopic cards. He flipped it over, indicating an address on the back. "Meet me here, at sundown, and we will discuss it."

Holmes nodded and slipped the card into his pocket. He allowed Miller to pull us away, feigning interest in his description of the newest golf course near a town called Ormand. As we departed from the arena, I noticed one of the little boys was still there, leaning over the wall and watching the alligators in the murk below.

There was something about this child that caught my eye. He was dressed in unseasonably dark clothing, which only accented his frailty and his pallor. His chin jutted forward and his eyes were sunk in his head. I guessed him to be less than ten, yet there was already something of an old man about him. He projected age and knowledge in a most unsettling way. I felt a chill as we passed.

I paused for a moment to look back at the lad. His gaze never left the monsters below him, and I heard him whispering to them in strange, unintelligible words, like something in an ancient language.

CHAPTER TWENTY-THREE

Escaping from Miller's clutches was a feat worthy of inclusion in an adventure novel; I felt like a prisoner who had leapt from a pirate ship as we finally dismounted from the ludicrous carriage and bid him good day. We had arrived at the Hotel Ponce de Leon, and from the collection of carriages and untidy mountains of luggage at the hotel's gate, it was clear that the train had just disgorged several cars filled with winter visitors. We entered the lobby, where heavy-set men sought to gain the attention of porters while ladies in frothy white dresses and massive hats mingled at the entrance to their special parlour. Nurses sighed wearily as they struggled to corral herds of children, and valets hurried behind their masters with fans and carafes of iced water. We climbed the stairs to escape the masses. Holmes paused at the rotunda balcony, surveying the scene below like a general inspecting the field of battle.

"Miller is more intelligent than his buff exterior and obnoxious bravado would allow one to believe," Holmes offered. "Look at this eager collection of guests and multiply it by a thousand-fold. Consider their needs, not only for lodgings but also for transportation, food, and most especially for amusement. A man who invests in such diversions is a wise one."

"But these crowds are limited to the winter season," I objected. "It is still, to my tastes, objectionably hot, and I can only imagine how stifling it must be in Florida between March and October. Your potential investor could hardly survive on only four months' profits!"

Holmes refused to concede the argument. "The sea breezes mitigate the heat to some degree, and it is clear that the new electric fans make housing conditions more tolerable. Who knows, perhaps before many years have passed some clever inventor will find a way to actually cool the air inside a dwelling rather than merely stir it into a tolerable wind." He beamed at my scowl of derision. "I hear that some notable experiments in that direction have already been made in this very state."

"Holmes, surely you are now venturing into the realm of magic," I warned.

"And heaven forbid that I should do that," he replied, in an excellent humour, before suggesting that we take a brief rest in our suite. Holmes was soon dozing on the divan, while I availed myself to some of the books and pamphlets our gracious tour guide had pressed upon me, insisting that I study the history of the ancient city.

I found the stories to be amusing, if somewhat trite and contrived. Most of them concerned the conquistador Ponce de Leon and his quest for the Fountain of Youth. I read how the noble Spaniard heard Indian tales while serving in the Caribbean and, convinced of their veracity, resolved to find the magical spring, discovering the land of 'La Florida' in the process. Unfortunately for the intrepid explorer, he always fell short of his goal, and vengeful natives drove him from his new territory. One particularly sanguinary version of the tale held that Ponce de Leon had been assassinated by Indian braves, whose arrows punctured him in so many places that an entire spring was stained red by his blood.

These stories naturally made me more curious about our own quest. When Holmes finally roused and stretched, I quizzed him in detail about the marvellous place that Telfair claimed to have found.

"In the Shadows, we have a different term for it," Holmes said. "We know it as the Broken Place."

"An odd name."

"But an accurate one. The water that fills the Fountain of Youth is water that originates in the Shadows. You have seen what that dark region produces, Watson, so you realize why this liquid could be both a blessing---for the astonishing preservation of life---but ultimately a curse, as it eats away at the only truly immortal aspect of a human, that being his soul. This spring is a place where the veil between the worlds is broken. Eons ago, to preserve the division of the worlds, great wizards spun the guardian mist. A map to the Fountain was never meant to be drawn, but somehow it was, and it fell into human hands."

"You do not know how? Or when?"

Holmes shook his head and looked about for his discarded boots. "That story was already ancient when I was a boy being raised by my fairy kin."

"So there may be some truth to this tale associated with Ponce de Leon."

"Legends have origins," Holmes agreed. "It is intriguing that the first known possessor of the map was a Spanish friar who had already achieved great age in the eighteenth century. Recall what Telfair said, of how he flippantly speculated that Olivarez had known a variety of European courts. Recall also Olivarez's reaction to this, how he almost ceased his friendship with Telfair over it. The padre had much to hide."

"And he was not the first owner," I said, thinking back on the tale. "He claimed to have stolen the map from someone else."

"Perhaps from that dark, unseen fiend who followed him and, we must presume, caused his death. Afterward, Telfair was similarly haunted and very similarly murdered."

I began to see the story as a circle. And then a new element entered into the picture. My heart picked up a faster pace.

"Holmes---the little man, that hideous dwarf that I saw the night before Telfair died. The same one I saw in Paris, and in the railroad station at Prague, and aboard the boat. How is he connected? Is he the murderer?"

"That is a possibility, but only a slight one. He seems more of a harbinger of death than the actual agent." Holmes rose and stretched. "And he does appear to be following us, though strangely only appearing to you."

As Holmes wandered off to splash water on his face and don a new collar, I returned to my historical tomes. I quickly devoured another sketch, this one of the notorious Don Pedro Menendez, who murdered fifty Frenchmen just downstream from the city of St. Augustine. His merciless act gave the river its name, Matanzas, which meant 'slaughter' in the Spanish tongue.

"It is time to go," Holmes said, and I was relieved to toss the book aside.

It was almost twilight when we walked through the inner courtyard of the hotel, skirting around the fountain where twelve frogs gushed water around an unusual pillar. I commented to Holmes that the fountain seemed peculiar to me, suggestive of something that I could not quite define. He halted and studied it for a moment, brows drawing together.

"You are right, Watson, it does hint at something in its fanciful design. One could almost imagine that it is the hilt of a sword. A conquistador's weapon, perhaps, plunged deep into a spring."

"Of course," I said. "It must be Ponce de Leon's sword!"

I began to walk toward the huge portcullis in the gate, only to realize I was alone. I looked back. Holmes was still considering the fountain, one hand slowly curling before his lips. I had seen that look before, recognized the countenance of my friend on the brink of revelation. I knew not to question; I dared not speak a word.

Music, however, knew no such restrictions. A song wafted on a breeze, a warm communal chanting in sweet harmony that reached all the way into the busy courtyard and began to grow louder. It was unlike anything I had ever heard produced by a choir or glee club. The other guests heard it as well and shushed to listen. I saw Mr. Hanscom hurrying by on some errand. Impulsively, I reached out to snag his sleeve.

"What is that singing?" I asked.

"Ah, it must be a river service," he said, gesturing westward, toward the sluggish San Sebastian, which cut the town from the mainland. "A Negro one. You should walk down and see it; it's not the kind of thing you'd witness in England."

Holmes offered a quick thanks to Hanscom and moved so rapidly that I nearly lost him in the crowd. In a few minutes we had reached an area near a dock. The scene before us was, as our friend had said, a rather unique one. A group of dark-skinned worshippers, all in long white robes, were standing in water up to their waists. The women were crowned with white turbans, and the men seemed transported in spiritual ecstasy as they clapped and sang. In the middle of the circle was a large man with a gleaming, shaved head, whose robes were so finely spun they floated on the surface of the water like magnificent wings. He held a youngster in his left arm, and as we watched he prayed loudly for the youth's soul, then swept him down fully into the dark river. He held him there for only a few seconds, but as he did a low moan swept the congregation, as if they collectively felt whatever sins were being driven from the young one in the water. Then the minister lifted him out of the river's depths, while the congregation erupted in great shouts of praise.

"A baptism," I said, recalling an article I had read about such practices among the descendants of Africans. In slavery days, these people had not had the privilege of taking the sacrament in their owners' churches before gilded fonts, but instead had snuck away to the rivers and streams, worshipping God in their own manner, in stealthy defiance of their masters' instructions. I smiled; the congregation's joy was contagious, and even at our respectful distance I could feel their great happiness. I wondered if it affected Holmes in the same way.

The look on his face was identical to the one he had worn at the fountain. His mind was hard at work, divorced from all emotions.

"Now I know," he whispered.

I barely dared to question. "What is it? What do you know?"

He seemed not to have heard me. I glanced back to the worshippers in the river. Another youth had come forward and was being prayed over by his people. I was certain, in that instant that if there was dark magic in the Shadows, there was much stronger, surer magic in the Light.

Holmes tapped his cane to the ground. "Come, Watson. We must not be late for our appointment."

CHAPTER TWENTY-FOUR

The shop was located on St. George Street, a short distance from the cathedral, in the very heart of the town. We passed knots of tourists returning from the Castillo de San Marcos, still marvelling over the fantastic tales their guides had told. Others paused to buy oranges and candies from vendors on the street, though several of these entrepreneurs quickly vanished when a policeman came in sight. Just beyond the last store offering strange trinkets for sale, including alligator bone whistles and small sculptures made of shells, was the placard for 'Rathburn's Photography.'

We paused for a moment at the shop's window, where samples were displayed. Even a cursory glance revealed that the photographer was skilful and artistic, able to capture the personality of his subjects in portraits. A man in a dapper stripped jacket looked poised to sing a joyful tune, while a bride with modestly downcast eyes radiated purity and innocence. A little boy knelt with his arms around his shaggy dog, his smile revealing several missing teeth. A nurse held a baby on her knee, keeping it amused by dangling a toy bird just out of reach. Finally, a set of group photographs spoke to the pride of brotherhood shared by firemen and constables, as well as brass bands, temperance societies, and even a merry collection of circus clowns.

"These are exceptional portraits," I said.

"I doubt that Alexander Gardner, Abraham Lincoln's photographer, could have done any better," Holmes agreed. "Let us go inside."

As we opened the glass door, the first thing I noticed was the room's exceptional coolness, so at odds with the intemperate conditions outside, which turned winter into late spring. The little room had been made into a comfortable salon, complete with a sofa and several ancient, ornately carved chairs that would not have been out of place in a palace. An album was open on a low table, revealing more samples of the owner's art. A counter ran across the back of the room, and behind it was a doorway, covered by a velvet curtain. A bell had jingled at our entrance, and now the curtain parted.

A slender woman stepped through. I recognized her instantly as the target of Tiger Tail's lasso, the one who had tossed it back with some indignation as the crowd laughed. She still wore the dark glasses, but had changed into a simple skirt and blouse, over which she wore a long apron.

"Do forgive me, gentlemen. We were working in the darkroom. How can I assist you?" She turned her head slightly, seeming to look in my direction. "Would you like your portrait taken, Doctor Watson?"

This was beyond even Holmes' remarkable and often frightening deductions. I had grown accustomed to having my mind read at inopportune moments, but I was hardly reconciled that perfect strangers could know my name and profession. I looked aside and noted that even Holmes appeared astonished.

"My dear lady, your powers of observation are phenomenal," he said.

"Especially for one without sight," she replied, removing her glasses as she spoke. Her eyes bore the watery white film I associated with congenital blindness. Holmes scowled for an instant then came very close to laughter.

"Tiger Tail informed you to expect us."

"That he did," she agreed with a laugh, returning her spectacles to their place. "But at least give me credit for some deductive powers. I knew you to be the Englishmen from your smell, and pinpointed Doctor Watson from the heavier nature of his tread."

Holmes smiled. "I was not aware that we were odiferous!"

"Your particular brand of cologne is only popular, I find, with British visitors," she said. She stretched out her hand. While her thin frame and brown hair made her a rather plain specimen of womanhood, her merry disposition made it a pleasure to greet her. "My name is Temperance Rathburn. As you can tell, I had the misfortune to be born to Methodist parents! Please, come into my studio. I will dismiss my helper, and Tiger Tail should be here at any moment."

We followed her past the curtain. She stepped into a darkroom to release her assistant from his duties while Holmes and I considered the arrangements. Like many of her profession, she possessed accoutrements for her clients: wicker chairs, plaster columns, artificial flowers, and a variety of exquisite drapes. A large trunk overflowed with other props and costumes, including musical instruments, swords, and helmets. Propped against a wall were fake, grotesquely large wooden fish and alligators, brightly painted with comical expressions of dismay on their faces. I attempted to divert Holmes's attention to them, only to find him fascinated by a large camera that stood ready before an overstuffed sofa. He poked his head inside the drape.

I was turning to go to his side when a hatchet split the floor between us. I froze. Holmes slowly pulled free of the drape, daring to look to the door that led from the outer room.

"Good evening, sir. Is Tiger Tail your true name or a stage persona?"

The man who had thrown the hatchet now crossed the room to retrieve it. He merely glared at Holmes. It was Miss Rathburn, just emerged from her darkroom, who answered the question.

"Jack Madison, for shame! Throwing that awful tomahawk at your own guests! And don't claim you didn't do it because I heard it hit the floor!"

"One hoodoo man should know better than to be too curious about another's philosophical instruments," the native said, speaking lowly. He had shed his colourful performer's attire and was dressed as a common labourer in dark denim trousers and a white shirt. His amulet still dangled from his throat. "Tempy, we have business to conduct."

"Then perhaps you should set up your own store, so you can receive clients properly," she huffed. "I'll lose the evening trade!"

Tiger Tail said nothing. I knew the lady could not read his solemn, almost hateful expression, but in the way of couples everywhere she seemed to know his thoughts. After a moment she surrendered.

"Oh, very well, I will close the shop." With impossible aim, she snagged my hand as she walked past. "Doctor Watson, perhaps you can assist me since I have already sent Sam home?"

I understood; presumably the 'hoodoo' men wished to discuss their dark profession in private. I followed my hostess to the front room, where I helped her lower the shades. She flipped the wooden sign that hung in her window, closing her business for the day.

"Do forgive me for asking," I said, hesitatingly, "but with your condition, I wonder how..."

"A blind woman can be a photographer? Do not worry, Doctor, I am not mortified by your question. You are certainly not the first to ask it. In fact, I am something of a local curiosity." She touched her hair and preened like a diva of the stage. "I am only surprised I am not included in the guidebooks!"

"You must have a remarkable talent."

She signalled for me to join her at the table. "I have a remarkable set of cameras. You noted how incensed Jack became when you friend dared inspect one---that had to have been the impetus for the hatchet toss, I know. I heard when Mr. Holmes pushed the drape back! Anyway, my cameras are thoroughly enchanted. When I place my gaze to the glass beneath the drape, I can see as well as any person with healthy eyes."

"So you see the world through your cameras."

"Indeed. I would not even know what Jack looked like, if not for them."

I tiptoed closer to the truth. "So are you magically gifted as well?"

"I fear not. I am a perfectly ordinary woman, trying to make a decent living. I was born to a plantation and wealth, but my father was killed in the war and my mother died of grief soon afterward. Everything was lost to the Yankees. My world disappeared, but perhaps it was for the best. I would have died all alone, starved to death in that wrecked house in the swamp, had Jack not found me while he was out searching for snakes, of all things!" Her expression softened. "I owe everything to Jack---or Tiger Tail, as the world knows him. I would marry him, if not for the abominable laws of this state." She touched the album, turning it to its last page. The final image was of Tiger Tail in his Indian regalia, arms crossed on his chest, his bare foot propped atop an alligator's spine. "He is a Seminole, and his blood is mixed with those of slaves. That makes him less than human to our government."

I was poised to inquire further, to ask how she had learned that her gentleman was a 'hoodoo man,' when the curtain was swept back and Holmes strode across the threshold. The expression on his face implied that the brief interview had not been a pleasant one. Tiger Tail stepped past him, pausing only long enough to lift his lady's hand and kiss it before walking out the door, slamming it in his wake.

"Goodness, what was that about?" our hostesses cried. "I've rarely felt such a mood from him. Mr. Holmes, what did you say to upset him so?"

"I only told him what I know about Alice Telfair and her quest for the Fountain of Youth. I had hoped to find a friend in him," Holmes continued. "But if he will not aid me, I trust, Miss Rathburn, that I might make an ally in you."

The lady registered shock. "Mr. Holmes, I am hardly equipped to assist a wizard! Jack told me that he had met another magic wielder. I could not possibly move in your elevated circles."

"On the contrary, Madame, you are uniquely poised to help me. And by helping me, I assure you that Mr. Madison's cause will benefit as well."

"What do you propose?"

Carefully, and with great detail, he described Alice Telfair. He told how she would most likely be travelling with an older female companion, and added the details that the pawnbroker had offered as to the appearance of the mysterious older lady.

"Should either or both of these women enter your studio, send for me at once," Holmes said, giving her our address at the Ponce de Leon. "Do nothing to let them know you are informing us about them. They are both, I fear, rather dangerous."

"I understand. Do you plan to capture them here?"

"No, but I intend to follow them and apprehend them for their crimes."

The woman's sandy brows met above the rim of her tinted spectacles. "And what exactly do you accuse them of?"

"They have the only map to the Fountain of Youth and are in pursuit of it. I also believe that they have killed in order to lend power to Miss Telfair's spells."

The lady photographer gasped. "Blood magic!"

Holmes placed a hand on the table. "You are more of an adept than I thought, Miss Rathburn. If you understand the principles of blood magic, then you understand why it is so important that Alice Telfair and anyone who assists her be captured."

The lady lifted one finger and laid it against the back of my friend's hand. "I will do this, but I will also tell Jack what I am doing. I cannot and will not hide anything from him. Are we agreed in that bargain?"

"We are agreed," Holmes said.

CHAPTER TWENTY-FIVE

The next two days proved fruitless. Holmes, feeling somewhat handicapped by being so far away from his network of spies and informers, began to recruit a new band of Irregulars from the hordes of children who swarmed around the hotel complaining of boredom. He sent them out with the charge to watch for any signs of the devious pair. He showed them the purloined picture of Alice Telfair and told them to also listen carefully, that the lady was probably in disguise but an unusual accent might give her away.

"Why do you think she would have an unusual accent?" I asked, as the youngsters hurried from our table to do my friend's bidding.

"It is a reasonable deduction," Holmes said, signalling to our waiter to bring more coffee. "While she was born and raised to young adulthood in America, Miss Telfair's vocal tone has doubtless been somewhat tempered by long years in England, as well as on the continent. It has been my experience that well-travelled persons often acquire rather unique ways of speaking and accents that vary according to the words chosen."

"Still," I muttered, thinking of the boys who had just clattered off in pursuit of mystery and the gold piece Holmes had offered as a reward, "I do not like you bringing these mere children into this. What if Alice Telfair learns she is being followed? What would prevent her from harming them!"

"They are not to confront her, only to report to me."

"Holmes, you go too far! If one of the boys should---"

My words were cut off by the appearance, belatedly, of the strange lad I had seen at the Alligator Farm. As he approached an unnatural chill seemed to swirl around our table. His pale skin was damp and his dark hair was plastered to his brow, giving him the look of a patient lost to a fever. He stepped close, his eyes locked to Holmes's with a gaze that was disturbingly adult.

"Ask her about the dead," he stated.

Holmes put down his napkin. "Whom should I ask about the dead?" he inquired.

"The lady who takes their pictures," the boy replied. Without awaiting further instructions, or demanding payment for his information, he turned and walked away. The air was suddenly warm again.

"That is the strangest child!" I said, barely suppressing a shudder. "Whatever did he mean?"

Holmes scowled. "I do not know. But the dead have no bearing on this case. I am much more concerned about the living." He set his cup down. "It is time for us to divide and conquer. I am going to return to the Alligator Farm and seek another interview with Jack Madison, also known as Tiger Tail."

"You think he knows more of this matter than he has said to you?"

"I am certain of it. And we should work together, not be at odds. I had the distinct impression that he has a particular reason for refusing to assist me; I would like to know more clearly what that reason is."

"And what should I do?" I asked.

"Walk and listen," Holmes said, "play the tourist and continue to look for Miss Telfair. I believe you have studied her picture long enough to recognize her in an instant even in the most ingenious disguise."

With only these vague instructions, I set off for the centre of town. I paused for a time on the square, near the bridge to Anastasia Island, where a group of old Negro women were gathered in the shadow of the former slave market. Their nimble fingers wove palmetto fronds together, forming the pliant material into baskets with fantastic whorls and bright patchwork patterns. As they worked they gossiped in a strange dialect that mixed together English, Spanish, and what I presumed to be African words. The magic of their peaceful occupation held me spellbound for some time. When I at last departed, I wondered if the Lady Hypatia would appreciate the gift of a basket, to add to her collection of unusual containers.

The thought of her amused smile warmed my cheek in a way the sun could not. I hoped our mission would soon be concluded, for I had begun to think of Alice Telfair less and the Lady Hypatia more. I resolved that once we returned to England I would give Holmes no option but to act as my escort to the Lady's mysterious residence beneath the streets of London.

I halted, suddenly inspired. I would present the lady with a further souvenir of our adventure by having my picture taken by Miss Rathburn. Holmes was correct in opining that I looked ludicrous in my white linen suit; the attire of a slim southern planter was hardly a match for my sturdy British frame. A portrait of me in this bizarre garb would make the Lady Hypatia laugh. Such a ridiculous token of our tropical quest would surely renew that lovely twinkle in her eyes and win me a measure of forgiveness for the insensitivity of my words on the London docks.

I travelled to the corner of St. George Street, only to find the studio locked. A loiterer on a bench noticed my dismay. In dirty clothes and with a mangy dog at his feet, he was surely a specimen of the 'Cracker' class of residents, who I had learned at the hotel were universally regarded as the lowest dregs of society. He jabbed his filthy thumb toward the ancient stone gates that had once marked the edge of the city.

"If yewr a'lookin fer that lady what makes the pic'turs, she done gone 'cross to dat dar cemetery."

Once I deciphered his speech, I thanked him. Following his directions, I walked between the dull gray gates and crossed the street to the old burying ground. A brass plaque informed me that the bodies within were the remains of yellow fever victims and of Protestants who had been denied rest within Catholic hallowed soil. Many odd tombstones and vaults marked the plots, but the little cemetery was rapidly succumbing to decay, being reclaimed by grass, vines, and moss-bearded trees. I leaned upon the stone wall, searching amid the markers until at last I saw Miss Rathburn walking between the graves. She used a long, slender stick to guide her, and carried a smaller version of the camera from her studio, one that she could hold without a tripod.

Perhaps she was using her special lens to simply view the world around her studio. I marvelled at the thought of always carrying a camera to find my footing. It would be a most inefficient way to get around London, though I supposed it would be better than being blind. But would even a magic lens be able to penetrate our city's fog?

Something flickered in the corner of my eye. At first I assumed it was one of the large mockingbirds that were so populous in the town. I turned and realized the motion was not the flight of a fowl or the swaying of a low branch, but the hobbling progress of a man who had entered the cemetery by its northern gate and was now following several paces behind the lady photographer.

The man was the wretched, hunchbacked dwarf who had appeared to me in England, in Paris, in Prague, and on the ocean. Now he was dressed in funereal garb, including a long black coat with a high silk hat trimmed in mourning ribbon. Each step was a lurch, because behind him, on a kind of sled, he dragged the coffin-like box. His face was distorted, his mouth held open as his tongue worked over his lips, giving him the appearance of a monster eagerly anticipating a warm meal.

I thought of the people in the elevator, the conductor crushed beneath the wheels of the train, and the sailors plucked from the decks of the *Friesland*. I shouted at the top of my lungs, and in a flash I was over the fence, charging at the man.

"You there! Stop! STOP!"

I had the impression that Miss Rathburn halted, dropping her cane in alarm. But I ploughed onward, dodging tombs, stumps, and vicious vines that seemed to lift up eagerly to bring me to heel. I waved my cane, determined that this time I would apply it to the villain's skull. He could not escape me in such a confined space. At last, I exulted, even as I charged, I would have some answers.

The man stopped and twisted his head to look at me. I saw no fear, no sudden expression of dismay or shock. Indeed, he merely smiled and made a short bow. He could mock all he wanted; I was but a few strides away, and he would soon know not to trifle with me. Nothing except a crumbling brick vault kept me from him. With a hero's cry, I put my free hand to the tomb and leapt over the impediment like a champion gymnast.

But when my feet hit the ground, disaster struck. I felt myself topple and fall, plunging into soft, spongy earth. The grave on the other side of the vault was rotten, and my weight had broken through it. I sank down to the sound of splintering. Wet dirt pelted me, and I felt sharp pains stab my legs.

I gasped for breath. In a dazed instant, I realized I was inside the grave and that all around me was the broken debris of a coffin. Long bones poked through the splintered wood, dead fingers crabbed and grabbed at my body. A smell, charnel and vile, puffed up to assail my senses.

Madness beckoned. I fought not to scream.

"Doctor Watson! Doctor, are you hurt?"

I seized control of my thoughts. I clamped down on all my instinctive urges to fight, lest any struggle drive me further into the earth. Looking up, I saw Miss Rathburn standing over me. Her assistant, a robust young man, was at her side.

"This cemetery is so dangerous. It is full of collapsing graves! Sam, help him."

The youth knelt down, and by grasping his hand and using my cane as a tool, I was able to climb out of the pit. My white suit was smeared with dark soil and ripped at the knees. Doubtless, I reeked of the decay I had fallen into. I must have been a sorry sight. I looked around as Miss Rathburn peppered me with questions, but the vile dwarf was nowhere to be seen. At least my theatrics, my abortive rescue, had served its purpose.

"My dear Doctor, whatever possessed you?" the lady demanded. "Our cemetery is not exactly suited for a steeplechase."

"I was alarmed. I saw...well, I thought I saw a rabid dog stalking you." I did not like to lie, but I feared that any attempt at a true explanation would give her concern for my sanity. I knew what I had seen, but how could I tell her without sounding like a crazed fool when there was no trace of either the man or his burden in the small confines of the burying ground?

"Then you are my hero," Miss Rathburn said. "There are far too many unloosed hounds in this town. Someone should do something more than shake broomsticks at them. But I am sorry that you have suffered on my account."

"Think nothing of it," I said, grateful that she could not witness the expression on her assistant's face. He no doubt thought me a clumsy oaf who had embarrassed myself in an awkward effort to impress the lady. He was certainly having difficulty restraining his laughter. His entire body shook from the effort of holding in guffaws.

"Let us take you back to the studio and tidy you up," Miss Rathburn insisted, "and I will take your photograph, free of charge. It is the least I can do to reward you."

"I am hardly fit to be immortalized," I muttered, silently cursing my foul luck as we walked back to the studio. The lady slipped a hand into the crook of my elbow.

"Consider it the portrait of the warrior on the field of battle, Doctor Watson."

Her good humour lifted my spirits. I availed myself to the washroom, cleaning up as best I could. Once I emerged, Miss Rathburn insisted that I sit in the large wicker chair with the velvet curtain behind me.

"Let us make this a very special picture," she said. "Do you own a stereo viewer?"

I allowed that I did not, but that our landlady did. Miss Rathburn moved behind her camera.

"Then when you return to London, you must borrow her device. You will want to see yourself as if you are living inside the viewer. It is far more realistic than anything another medium can achieve. Now hold very still!"

I sat frozen while she snapped two pictures, making a small adjustment to her equipment between the shots. She removed the plates from the back of the camera, passing them to her helper.

"Henry, take these to the darkroom. And is the print from last night finished?"

I noted that at the question all the amusement seeped from the young man's expression and the ruddy colour leached from his face. He took the plates and reached into his apron pocket, passing a stiff stereographic card to his employer.

"Yes, Ma'am, in fact, that's what I was running out to the cemetery to show you. The picture is done but....well, it's an odd one." The youth coughed. "The lady brought some friends with her, from the look of it."

Miss Rathburn took the card and deftly placed it in a viewer that rested on a small table. It was remarkable how well she knew her limited world and did not need her cane to find the things in her studio. She removed her glasses and raised the viewer to her eyes. I deduced that her viewer, like her cameras, bore a special enchantment.

She gave a sharp gasp, nearly dropping the device. Sam was dismissed with wave. Miss Rathburn turned, holding the viewer out to me.

"Doctor Watson, please believe me when I tell you that I am not a charlatan. I do not use the double exposure or any other dishonest technique. But it is the nature of Jack's enchantment that sometimes my camera sees beyond the image presented to it and translates the truth into forms of light and shadow."

"What do you mean?"

"Put more plainly, I sometimes capture ghosts in my pictures. You have no doubt seen examples of 'spirit photography'? Those portraits are achieved by devious means. Mine, I assure you, are done without effects." She smiled tightly and nervously. "Some people simply trail ghosts behind them, like perfume fragrance or cigar smoke. This lady, for example."

She pressed the viewer into my hands. Carefully, I lifted it and put it to my face, bringing the images on the card into a special focus.

What I saw froze my blood.

A large, matronly woman sat in the same chair I had just vacated. She wore a fashionable suit, with a jaunty straw boater at an angle on her tightly curled hair. She had a ponderous double chin, and a vapid, cow-like expression on her face. There was something singularly empty about her. The pawnbroker's words came back to me---as if she lacked a soul.

But the woman was not the most hideous thing in the picture. Surrounding her, floating about, seeming to move in a gelatinous way, as if suspended underwater, were forms of men and women. Detached half-bodies, unfinished and vague, they were like the brush strokes of a crazed artist. Only their wounds were clear. With their smashed faces, blood-smeared throats, and heads battered into pulps, these spirits swirled around the sitter, glaring at her, radiating an impotent fury that they could not touch her. Even as I watched, one of the forms, of a man in a black coat, turned his maimed head and looked to me with an eyeball that had popped from the socket and was laid upon his cheek. His unnatural appeal for revenge was such that I dropped the view on the floor.

"My God," I whispered.

"I have never seen such a collection," Miss Rathburn said, her hands folded tightly. "Usually, we see the spirits of beloved spouses or departed children. They are sad but never frightful. To borrow your friend's vocabulary, Doctor, we can deduce that these ghosts are her victims."

Reluctantly, I took up the viewer and looked again. This time, I counted. There were three men and three women. All appeared elderly, wrinkled and worn. I noticed clasped hands, the closeness of their ethereal bodies.

"Husbands and wives," I heard myself whisper. "Who is this woman?"

In that instant I focused my vision not on the milling shades, but on the figure in the chair. Though I had never really seen her face, her large, muscular hands became clear, as did the fashionable folds of her walking dress. My heart pounded so loudly I could barely hear Miss Rathburn's answer to my inquiry.

"She said her name was Lizbeth Maplecroft."

CHAPTER TWENTY-SIX

At last, we had found Miss Telfair's accomplice. Now we knew who collected the blood for the unholy rites. My pride in being the one who had uncovered the villain's identity was mitigated by my horror at what I had discovered.

As I hurried back to the hotel I could not banish the image from my mind. The eyes of Mrs. Maplecroft had been so blank, so fixed and soulless. Was she a willing participant in this dark work? Or was she also a victim, a pitiful pawn manipulated by Miss Telfair's black magic? Holmes's words returned to me, of how easy it would be for him to control mere mortals. He refused to do this; he understood the immorality of such actions. But if a witch like Alice Telfair was void of such concerns, and determined to gain even more power from the Fountain of Youth, what horrors awaited the world if she succeeded?

Miss Rathburn had given me the lady's address. Her photograph was to be delivered to a suite in the Hotel Alcazar. This magnificent hostelry faced our own hotel and was a sister to it. Graced with twin towers and lovely gardens, it was known for the conveniences it offered, including shops and restaurants within its arcade. It appalled me to know that we had wasted several days searching when our prey was just across the street.

One thing confused me still: Mrs. Maplecroft had been travelling with a child, a little girl who was so concerned for her mother's well being when I met them in New York. But where was Alice Telfair? The child and Miss Telfair could not be one in the same. Even the talented Irene Adler, who had bamboozled Holmes by pretending to be a slim youth in an ulster, could not pull off such a remarkable feat of deception. And Holmes, so much the master of assuming other personas, could not strike decades from his age with paint and props alone. The thing was impossible.

Could that sweet child belong to Miss Telfair, be the fruit of some unacknowledged romantic union? If so, then we must work even harder to save her. I had feared for one young woman's soul; now I was even more distressed over the fate of a child's.

Holmes had not returned to our suite. I considered setting out for the Alligator Farm, to find him, but as I opened drawers in search of the carriage tickets Miller had gifted us with, I heard a small thump. I lifted a folded shirt and saw a familiar artefact on the rich wood.

It was a simple silver ring, much like a man's wedding band. I lifted it, recalling its usefulness in our previous investigation. Just to be certain, I considered my reflection in the mirror as I slid the object onto a finger.

I vanished. I saw the image of the bed and the nightstand. I tugged the ring from my finger and immediately returned to my rightful place, my solid British frame blocking the reflection of the articles of furniture.

An insane idea possessed me. It was a busy hour, a time when most of the ladies of the Flagler hotels visited in their parlours or hosted little adventures, riding out together for the beaches, the Alligator Farm, or the Castillo. Most likely, Mrs. Maplecroft and her ward would be out of their rooms. What other evidence might I find there? Maybe I could even locate the map. It was doubtful that another opportunity would arrive so easily. Perhaps I owed it to Holmes to take the initiative. I even had the lady's room number in hand.

I recalled an old proverb: *fortune favours the brave.*

With new resolve, I crossed the courtyard between the hotels. The sun was bright and flowers were explosive with blooms. Dozens of ladies milled about, exclaiming over the beauty of the gardens. On the roadway parallel to the hotel, a gang of young men puttered on bicycles, saluting the ladies and performing tricks. No one took the least notice of me as I passed through the great casino and entered the hotel proper, making my way along the grand staircase.

I found a dark corner, slipping into it and waiting until an attractive young couple passed by, holding hands and giggling together, clearly a pair on their honeymoon. I could hear the orchestra tuning up in the dining hall and more distant splashing from the impressive swimming pool. With a deep breath I slid the ring onto my finger. I tested it by stepping in front of a waiter, who nearly ploughed me down for my troubles. Convinced of the magic's effectiveness, I made my way to Mrs. Maplecroft's suite.

I felt a thrill as I leaned against the door. I knocked and received no answer. Proving that my years with Holmes had not been wasted, I pulled my penknife from my pocket and began to work on the lock, which was more ornate than practical and surrendered easily to my assault. I pushed the door in gently, whisking myself inside.

The room was impressive, if not as ornate nor as remarkably furnished as its counterpart at the Ponce de Leon. There were beautiful chairs, a gilded mirror over a marble-lined fireplace, and delicate works of art on the wall. I stepped through the sitting room to the bedchamber. I saw two large steamer trunks at the foot of the bed. Ladies' attire was scattered over the linens, shoes and gloves hurled about as if the occupants had dressed in a great hurry, tossing aside rejected accessories. I noted a girl's delicate dress hung on one chair and tiny patent leather shoes placed beneath a window. There was a large armoire in the corner. It seemed to me the most likely place to hide valuables. I had my hand poised to open it when I heard the sound of the outer door squeaking on its hinges.

I whirled around, forgetting for a moment that I was still invisible and thus safe from detection by the room's occupant. Mrs. Maplecroft entered the suite, removing her hat with its voluminous veil as she closed the portal behind her. Thanks to her unguarded state and my friend's magic, I was able to tiptoe closer, entering the sitting room and making a detailed examination of Mrs. Maplecroft's features.

She was a very plain woman, possessed of a broad face and an ample double chin. Her cheeks were heavy and flushed red, perhaps from the unseasonable warmth the hotel's many fans did little to alleviate. Her frame was, like her face, broad and unremarkable, stuffed into a dull grey frock of material far too heavy for tropical climes. Once again I noticed her hands were oddly muscular, more like those of a farm worker than a true lady. As she passed by me, her perfume could not cover the odour of some exertion, and I noted a large patch of perspiration staining the fabric of her gown between her shoulder blades and under her arms.

She passed through the small sitting room into the bedchamber. I followed at a discreet distance, watching as she opened the armoire. I had promised myself I would not remain in the suite, should she begin to disrobe, as I did not wish to extend my investigations into the realm of prurient voyeurism. Mrs. Maplecroft fumbled about her skirts, and I had begun to turn around, pondering how I could achieve an exit without alerting her to the mysterious opening of the door, when I heard her whisper, "The job is done."

I whirled about. Mrs. Maplecroft was holding a hatchet, its handle still dripping with blood. I watched in horror as she removed a glass jar from the cabinet and, with the delicacy of an artist, coaxed the gore from the blade to the container. I saw snatches of hair and bits of bone fall into the jar, along with great clots of congealed blood.

My revulsion produced an unconscious sound. Mrs. Maplecroft twisted, looking directly at me, or rather, into the space where the gasp had originated. She lifted the hatchet, holding it up as stoutly as any Viking warrior had ever clasped a weapon, and began to advance.

Vainly, I sought an escape. The woman's hearing was obviously exceptional and she would detect my footsteps if I tried to flee around her. I could bolt for the door, but I feared the hatchet would go flying into my back, impaling me the moment my hand turned the knob. There was only one window. The room was some four stories above the ground; it was doubtful I would survive the leap. But I was steeling myself to go through the glass when a knock just behind me halted Mrs. Maplecroft's advance. Her eyes narrowed. She hesitated only for a moment before rushing back to the open armoire. I took advantage of this moment to slink to the side of the wall. Seconds later, Mrs. Maplecroft returned, fluffing her hair and making a quick daub at her sweaty cheek with her handkerchief.

She opened the door. A Negro maid stood there, holding the hand of a small girl in a stripped swimsuit. I recognized the little girl who had spoken to me in the hotel in New York.

"Here she is, Madame. You had a very nice swim in the ladies' pool, didn't you, dear?"

The girl beamed up at the woman, tugging gently at her starched apron. "I did! Thank you ever so much. I wish my mother was not afraid of the water."

Mrs. Maplecroft muttered her thanks and sent the maid off with a quick tip. I knew I had but one chance at freedom, and so I dodged behind the maid, bumping into her as I slipped through the gap. She closed the door, looking all around for the source of her encounter.

"Lord have mercy," she whispered, "I knew this place was full of ghosts!" She glanced down at the silver in her hand. "But you'll have to do more than that, Mr. Spirit, if you want Mary Alexander to leave! This job is too good to quit cause of some fool haint! You go on now and scare the white folks!"

She marched away with queenly dignity. I trailed her cautiously, waiting until I had turned a corner and found a private place to remove the ring from my finger. What a fool I had been, to embrace magic on my own!

I hurried back across the street to the Ponce de Leon. To my frustration, Holmes had not yet returned. I paced back and forth across the room, swearing with all an old soldier's fury. After an hour I could bear it no longer, and made my way once again to the centre of town. I had thought to hail a cab to take me to the Alligator Farm, in hopes of catching up with Holmes. But even as I reached the square, where the women sat with their baskets, I saw his lean figure strolling across the bridge. I hailed him and drew him to the seawall.

"Watson, you look rather perturbed. Do you still find the heat disagreeable?"

"Holmes, I know who the killer is! I know who has murdered all those people."

My sudden words took him aback. He insisted that before I speak further we sit down inside one of the establishments that passed for an American pub or saloon. Though it was still scandalously early, I welcomed a glass of good whiskey.

I told him of my morning's adventures, forcing myself to go slowly, to put everything in my story in precise order. My friend's eyebrows rose when I informed him of Miss Rathburn's remarkable camera and its ability to capture not only a sitter's personality, but also any spirits that hovered around him.

"I erred, Watson. I perceived our friend Tiger Tail as a man versed only in crude native conjuring. His abilities to work complicated enchantments are astonishing. The Shadows are in his bloodline."

"You spoke with him?" I asked.

"Only briefly," Holmes answered, with a dismissive air. "Continue your story."

I recounted the rest of it, from the discovery of Mrs. Maplecroft's bloody attendants in the photograph to my return to the hotel. At my description of my impatience and my donning of the magical ring, Holmes' face turned dark. Had he not been my dearest friend, I would have run from him at that moment, so fierce was his visage.

"That was a very foolish thing to do, Watson."

I fully confessed to my error, but refused to pause for any scolding. I told him what I had witnessed in the suite. Just as I was describing the blood-bathed hatchet, there was uproar in the streets. I looked through the open window and saw a crowd gathering some distance away. Several people were pointing to a small house, and a number of policemen were blowing their whistles. The cry of 'murder' reached our ears.

"What should we do?" I asked.

Holmes's reply shocked me. "Nothing. If this crime is a mirror of the others, there will be no clues. The pattern must hold: an elderly couple, a brutal death, and no robbery. No motive, no witnesses, no suspects."

"But we know who did this!"

"We have nothing more to go on but our accumulated experiences chasing this phantom monster," Holmes replied. "And the only evidence we could offer authorities would be a picture that resembles, as its author well acknowledges, a common if clever fraud. That, or the testimony of an invisible man! No, Watson, this is a difficulty we must resolve by improbable, but not impossible means." Holmes placed coins on the table and signalled for me to down the dregs of my glass. "Let us return to Miss Rathburn's establishment. I would like to see that photograph."

Together we walked through streets that were thickening with excited onlookers, as people passed the news that murder had been done only a few storefronts away. By the time we reached the corner of St. George Street, the area near the fortress was vacated, the tourist throngs having migrated toward the cries and confusion. Miss Rathburn was sipping tea in her small chamber, alone except for a motley coloured, flop-eared hound that lifted his head and gave us a surly sniff as we entered.

"Good afternoon, Mr. Holmes," she said, before either of us spoke. "Jack was just here and he said you might come by again. I take it Doctor Watson told you about my photograph?"

"He did," Holmes said. "I would like to see it."

She rose and guided us into the studio, the dog tagging at her heels. Holmes took the stereo viewer and examined the picture.

"I have never met this woman, and yet there is something vaguely familiar about her," Holmes said. "As if I have seen her face before, in some other context."

"She is surely a criminal," I said, "her name smacks of an alias!"

Miss Rathburn drew a hand along the back of the wicker chair. "I agree, Doctor. In fact, it sounds rather like the name of a house, not a person. I can just imagine some pretentious planter naming his estate 'Maplecroft.'"

Holmes lowered the stereo viewer.

"Lizbeth *of* Maplecroft," he whispered. He shoved the device into my hands, and without another word he raced from the room. Even though Miss Rathburn could not see his departure, she felt it in the quick rush of air and heard it in the hard slamming of the door.

"Oh dear. I suppose Mr. Holmes has had another brilliant idea?"

"I do not know. He seemed to have some inspiration," I agreed, "though I would be much more appreciative if he had chosen to share it with me!"

Miss Rathburn smiled. "I understand. Jack is also maddeningly close-lipped about his magic."

To calm myself and pass the time, I recalled a question that fitted with my friend's speculation as to the lady's paramour and his powers. "Is Jack a mortal who has studied magic, or was it born in him?"

Miss Rathburn's smile broadened, even as her face softened with affection. "He was born with his magic. Kinfolk on both sides of his family were conjurers, hoodoo men and wise women alike. He rarely speaks of his family, though. I know only that some of his relations were once slaves, and others were of the Muskogee nation, which settlers all lump together as Seminoles." She settled into the chair. The dog trotted over to her. "The people of St. Augustine think that he is an ignorant native showman, barely able to sign his names on the cards that I produce for him, but he has studied many great books of wizardry. Someday, we hope to travel, so that he can learn even more." She leaned down, and the affectionate dog put its head in her lap as she stroked its soft ears. "Of course, we must both make fortunes first, before we can afford to leave this town."

"He could use his magic," I said. "Anyone so gifted need not be poor."

"That would go against his standards!" she replied, with just a touch of heat, as if I had insulted her. "To use magic for personal gain would be beneath him. Surely your time with Mr. Holmes has taught you that!"

I felt blood rush to my face. I was poised to beg her pardon when the bell jangled. Hopeful that it was Holmes, I rushed into her reception room. Instead, a messenger in the hotel uniform of the Alcazar stood at attention. He gave me a sharp salute and handed me an envelope. I was fishing in my pocket for a tip, but he shook his head and took his leave as promptly as he had entered.

I felt Miss Rathburn step in behind me. "What is it?" she asked.

"A message from Holmes," I said. There was nothing scrawled on the outside of the envelope, but logic told me it could only have been dispatched by Holmes. I knew of no one else in the town that was aware of my location, or would need to deliver any orders. The words were typed, not handwritten. Later, I would ask myself how I could have been such a fool.

"It says 'Come at once to the Alcazar Hotel, to the archery arcade.'" I looked back to Miss Rathburn. "Perhaps he has arranged an interview with Mrs. Maplecroft."

"In that case, should you not stop first at your own hotel and retrieve your gun?"

I blinked. "Dear lady, how did you know that I travel with a firearm? Surely you are Holmes's equal in powers of deduction!"

She shook her head. "No, Doctor Watson, I am merely a fancier of your tales, which Jack reads to me. You forget that you have made yourself famous."

I exited with humiliated gratitude that the lady could not see a brighter flush of embarrassment than any that had previously stained my cheek. Recklessly, however, I ignored her suggestion. I was certain that if Holmes planned to waylay the murderess, he had his own much more capable weapons of magic primed.

I reached the passage that lead into the archery grounds, pausing long enough to bend over and catch my breath. My journey had taken me nearly a quarter of an hour, as the streets were still clogged with people gossiping and speculating about a double murder. I caught words as I hurried past, only slowing enough to weave between persons and not shove any bystander to the ground. 'Butchered' I heard, and 'hacked apart.' I took some comfort in knowing that whatever Holmes was planning, those innocent souls would soon be avenged.

The archery ground was empty except for a single boy in a sailor suit practicing at the butts. I looked all around, but caught no glimpse of Holmes. I checked my watch and wiped the sweat from my brow. Where was he? What had delayed him?

"Doctor Watson!"

That was not my friend's voice. The words were high-pitched and shrill, as if a child had called my name. I turned back to the archery range.

A beautiful girl with her golden hair tucked up stood only a few yards away. Though she was dressed as a boy, I instantly recognized the youngster from New York. She was the same girl who had been brought up from the pool by the maid. I tried to speak, but my words were hushed by my astonishment.

The girl was pointing a child-sized bow at me. The arrow poised to take flight was no natural weapon, but a shaft that glowed, radiating blue fire.

The girl released the arrow. It went straight into my heart.

CHAPTER TWENTY-SEVEN

I woke from one nightmare to another. I clutched at my chest, gasping for air. I could breathe and move. The darkness began to recede, but I had to struggle against it. Something heavy was thrown over me. Unable to see, I writhed and punched until at last I shed the obstruction.

I blinked. A heavy woollen blanket was crumpled on the floor. I was lying on a narrow bunk, atop a thin mattress. As I pushed myself up, my back met a wall. Still gasping, I was uncertain of anything except that I was mercifully alive.

Slowly, I calmed down and began to study my surroundings. I was in a tiny chamber, lit only by a flickering candle. It appeared to be some type of nautical cabin, but the windows were blackened to prevent me from gazing out of my prison. I felt a slight shuddering, and by concentrating intensely I could hear a low rumble, like the workings of a steam engine. I rose and tried the door, only to find it locked. There were a few items on a low desk that was clamped to the wall. I inspected them, startled to find that they were the merely contents of my own pockets, minus my penknife. Nothing in the small pile seemed capable of helping me make an escape.

I resumed my seat and recalled all that had happened. I placed my hand back to my chest, still uncomprehending of my survival. I had been shot. The pain had been piercing, unbearable. I had a vague image, like the last fleeting scenes of a dream, of my young assailant standing over me, the bow in her chubby hand and an expression of accomplishment on her face.

This was black magic, and I was its prisoner.

At last, I could bear the silence no longer. I curled my hand into a fist and banged on the door. I shouted and raged. I made threats, warning my captors of what Holmes would do to avenge me. No one answered my cries.

Desperate, I did the only other thing I could think of; I took the candle and turned it over onto the mattress. It caught the cheap fabric easily, and smoke roiled up from the bunk. Coughing, I once again pounded on the door, yelling 'fire!' as I continued to beat my fist on the panel.

Abruptly, the door flew open. I nearly toppled into the arms of a dark figure. He pulled me out of the cabin and shoved me against the outer wall before seizing a bucket and flinging water into the room. His action set off a great hissing and another pillow of smoke pushed against us. My rescuer caught my elbow, tugging me away from the cabin.

"You fool," he hissed. "Be quiet! Don't make this worse."

I looked around. The darkness was broken only by small pools of yellow light cast by delicate lanterns hung along the ship's railing. Beyond the boat, I could just make out a narrow river and the vague shadows of a dense, tangled swamp. Rich, alluvial odours assailed me, and I heard the soft lapping of a wheel against water. My mysterious companion caught my coat, dragging me forward to the bow of the vessel. He flung me down upon a pile of ropes.

A bright light flared and heat erupted from a fire that was suddenly lit in an iron brazier. I had read of such bonfires being used to guide ships along the rivers, but instead, the new light gave me my first clear look at my guard.

It was Jack Madison, the man also known as Tiger Tail.

I stared up at him. His betrayal of our cause reeked, and I ground my teeth in anger. "How could you?" I demanded. "Holmes told you the danger."

He turned and walked away without answering me. The shadows shifted. Mrs. Maplecroft replaced him. She did not speak, but hovered over me, her hatchet in hand, wielded as easily as a teacher might hold a ruler.

"Who are you?" I demanded. "Tell me your name, your real name. Why do you do these horrible things?" I continued, frustrated by her stubborn silence. "Are you free? Do you have your own will? Who are you?"

"Oh, do stop jabbering," another voice drawled. I twisted and found the little girl standing opposite, sneering at me. She was dressed in a simple, long robe like the worshippers had worn, and I noted a wand, much as Doctor Dee had used, in her hand. "Do not make me regret bringing you along. I'd just as soon throw you to the alligators as listen to you prattle."

"Who are you?" I asked

"I wasn't even after you when I sent the message," the child continued, ignoring my inquiry. She spoke with a pretentious air completely at odds with her tiny frame. "I wanted that blind bitch Rathburn, for a bit of insurance, to make sure my pet wizard behaves himself. Too bad you were the one who got the note instead. I think I'll turn that stupid messenger boy into a toad when I get back to town."

I stared at the girl. Softly, I repeated my question. "Who are you?"

"I am Alice Telfair," she said. "Surely you knew? No? What, silly man, did you think I was Lizzie's child?" Her laugh was ugly. "She likes to think I am like a child to her. But she is just a doll to me, a big doll that I can order to do whatever I please."

"How can you be so *young*?" I whispered. Her transformation was incomprehensible. The girl leaned down, placing a small bare foot on the ropes that formed my seat. "Was it the water?" I babbled. "Has drinking the water done this to you?"

She laughed sharply. "You idiot, you're as stupid as Lizzie, who let me enchant her without even a struggle. I thought you were rather thick in New York, when I tested the effectiveness of my glamour on you in the hotel."

I shook my head. "You are not skilled enough to do this." I recalled my friend's words, of how the casting of a glamour was difficult and required years of practice and excessive energy to maintain. Only the greatest Shadowborn wizards could wear one. "Holmes said it was beyond you."

Miss Telfair giggled. "Did he now? He never guessed this glamour was the gift my good friend Mephistopheles gave me?" I felt my stomach drop at this revelation. The child before me grinned and bounced, as if describing a favourite toy. "The Devil would not take my soul, but he was impressed by my spirit, my American gumption in calling him up from the depths of Hell! And so he gave me the power to cast glamours, to deceive anyone who might attempt to stop me. I am a child at this moment, but I do not have to remain a child. I can shed this skin whenever I please."

"I don't believe you," I hissed, still unwilling to accept the evidence of my own eyes.

"No? Then let me give you a demonstration. Lizzie killed for me just this morning, so I'm filled with power. Watch!"

She stepped backward, twisting her wand. Her skin broke apart and dropped down like the great shedding of a snake. In the place of a young girl now stood a beautiful woman, clad only in the thin gown that barely touched her thighs. She giggled at my astonishment and waved the wand again. Now she was a young man, with flaxen hair and a short beard. Another wave, another shedding, and Mrs. Maplecroft stood before me, her pasty rolls of unhealthy, repulsive skin not covered by the tiny dress. I looked away in horror and revulsion.

"I can be anyone, Doctor Watson," the false Lizzie said. "Old, young, female, male. I could even be an animal, if I chose to be. The Devil promised, as long as I offer the blood, I can change my form, so no one can ever catch me." She leaned down, her muscular hand tugging my chin, forcing me to look up into her flat, grotesque face. "I take it you do not like older women, Doctor. Perhaps you would prefer me like this."

She peeled away the flesh of her helper. I screamed at what emerged. To this day, I do not know how she did it, whether she grabbed it from my mind, or whether she had seen an illustration, or even in some past time observed us together.

All I knew was that my sweet Mary stood nearly naked before me.

"NO! You filthy witch, stop it! Leave her alone!"

Alice Telfair laughed shrilly, clapping her hands together. The sound was unnatural. Her amusement was that of a child, rather than a woman. I had squeezed my eyes shut against the

223

cackling abomination, but now I opened them, and saw that she had shrunk back to her original form, was again a little girl.

Mephistopheles's evil gift had truly put us off the scent.

"Why are you doing this?" I asked, my spirits sinking lower as my plight became more obvious. Even when Holmes learned that I had vanished, he would have no idea of who had summoned me. He would not know how or where to pursue my captors. I tried not to show fear, and out of pride refused to plead for my life. I sought to project a confidence I did not feel. "What do you hope to achieve by finding the Fountain?" I demanded of the witch. "You had the water your father stored, why did you need to come here?"

The child smiled. "So you did consult with my father before his death, as well as investigate his murder! I had thought he might summon Sherlock Holmes when I vanished and left him to rot. I had hoped he would shrivel and die like my poor mother did, but from what I was told his fate was far more gruesome." She settled onto a crate, motioning for Maplecroft to leave us. The boat was still moving, but I heard a slowing of the engines. "He told you everything, I take it? How like him, the snivelling coward. He was eager to study, but never to apply anything he learned, happy only when he could be the fat and prosperous patriarch, keeping us under his heel by rationing out the water. After he killed my mother, I knew I had to be free of him. I learned as much as I could before I stole the map, and had Mephistopheles been more cooperative, I would not have required further assistance to find the Fountain."

"I still do not understand---what more do you want? Why must you go to the Fountain?"

She frowned. "You are such a dullard I wonder how Holmes abides your company. Think, Doctor! It is so simple, and has been there all along, if you would just reason it out." At my continued confusion, she giggled. "Go on, shall we make it a contest? Guess! Guess!"

The boat's engine came to a halt. For a time we drifted. I spoke no more, despite the smug set of Miss Telfair's face. I had finished playing her horrible little game.

"No more to say, Doctor? It is just as well. Now come along like a good little puppy."

She rose and walked to the side of the vessel. Our ship had bumped clumsily against the bank of the river, and Tiger Tail was securing it with a rope tied around a cypress tree. When she sensed she was unaccompanied, Miss Telfair turned and gave me a quizzical look.

"I said, follow me."

"No."

Her eyes widened. I was reminded of the way a spoiled child's face shifts, from puzzlement to outrage, when a stern nurse denies him a bag of candy. Clearly, Miss Telfair was not accustomed to being countermanded in any way.

"What did you say, Doctor?"

"I said no. I will not follow you to the Fountain. I will not be a witness or a hostage."

"Then you will die!" she snapped. "Do you think I would hesitate to kill you?"

I did not answer. Miss Telfair lifted her wand and aimed it at me. I braced myself for whatever horrific execution she would deliver.

Her arm suddenly dropped. She pouted and rubbed the muscle near her shoulder, as if she had developed an intense cramp. The scowl on her face was easy to read; she was confused and annoyed, perhaps even a bit embarrassed. Defiant after a moment of reflection, she lifted her chin and tried again to take aim with her magical weapon. This time, when her arm fell, it drew a sharp cry of pain.

"I need not waste more of my magic on you," Miss Telfair said, blinking back tears. She turned to her minion on the shore. "Tiger Tail---finish him."

The man had placed a wide wooden plank from the bow to the sandy bank. Alice Telfair walked across it, closely followed by Mrs. Maplecroft, who carried her hatchet in one hand and a large carpetbag in the other. They disappeared into the darkness of the forest, but a moment later the witch's childish laughter floated back on the sullen evening breeze, a perversion of the excitement an innocent girl might express on first beholding a golden shoreline.

Tiger Tail approached me. I knew he was a wizard as well, a hoodoo man of great Shadowborn strength. My ending could hardly be more merciful in his hands.

He reached down and drew a blue-bladed hunting knife from his belt. The reflection of the moon raced across the steel, the last vision I would ever see.

Resigned to my fate, I closed my eyes.

CHAPTER TWENTY-EIGHT

"Get up."

The command was gruff, but not brutal. I blinked. Tiger Tail was bending down, cutting a length of rope. When I failed to respond, he seized my collar and hoisted me to my feet. Before I could speak, he was once again tugging me along the side of the ship. He opened the door to the cabin where I had previously been confined, shoving me inside.

"You will stay here," he hissed. "It is safer this way."

The door slammed behind him. The room was completely dark, as black and airless as a tomb. The candle was out, and though the chamber still reeked of smoke, there were no remaining embers for even the poorest illumination. Stumbling forward, I tried to force the door open. It would not rattle. I wondered whether it was locked with a key, held with a bar, tied with the rope he had cut, or bound by some magical spell. Any method was adequate, as there was no possible manner of escape for me.

I tottered backward, groping around until I located the bunk with the scorched mattress. I sank down on it, trying to clear my mind and calm my nerves. Tiger Tail had disobeyed his orders. Did my continued survival mean that a wizard's game was being played? What was his motive, what did he hope to gain from this strange form of cooperation with Miss Telfair? Was he perhaps Holmes's ally after all, or was he, like the witch, greedy for the Fountain's waters?

Something hissed. It was a sound like the rush of air from a steam kettle. I froze, listening intently, trying to catch the sound repeating. It was difficult to hear over the hammering of my own heart.

I had heard such a sound before. In the darkness I was once again in Helen Stoner's bedroom at Stoke Moran. In memory's eye I could see Holmes strike a match and lash forward with his cane. His voice came back to me, filled with revulsion.

"It is a swamp adder!...the deadliest snake in India!"

The hissing became louder. Instinctively, I hunched my arms and legs together, wedging my back against the corner of the room. I listened, but now the sound was gone. Another sound replaced it, a crinkle of fabric, followed by what I can only describe as a kind of oozing.

Was the snake on the bed? Or was it in the blanket on the floor? I vaguely recalled a shelf above my head; was the viper about to drop down my shoulders?

I willed myself to utter immobility. The noise stopped. Had I imagined it?

Without meaning to, I emitted a low breath. The hissing revived and was accompanied by an ominous rattle. I recalled the serpents in Tiger Tail's performance, especially the one the barker had referred to as a 'canebrake rattler,' whose bite would kill even the heartiest man almost instantly.

How long I sat there, sweating profusely, my heart hammering a thunderous cadence in my ears, I do not know. It was probably only a few minutes, yet it felt like hours. The rattling came and went, the hissing moved away, drew closer, moved away again. I could imagine the snake slowly canvassing its small home, aware of an intruder and determined to methodically seek him out.

Then, blessedly, the door was flung open and bright light poured inside the small chamber. I was momentarily blinded, but I heard a loud curse followed by the sharp retort of a small pistol.

"God in heaven, that was close! Doctor Watson, are you all right?"

I blinked, staring up at my savoir. Much to my astonishment, the figure in the doorway was not Holmes, but Miller. He shoved the derringer back into his pocket, kicking the snake---which had been on the floor beside me, poised crawl onto the bunk---to one side. He was clearly a superb marksman, as the bullet had shattered the reptile's head.

"I am," I whispered, moving slowly. Spikes of pain ran up my cramped legs, yet I was able to wobble from the room. The clouds had parted and a full moon now illuminated the scene beyond the boat. Holmes stood on the bank, accompanied by Miss Rathburn, who wore an unseasonably heavy shawl over her simple calico dress. I laughed, nearly hysterical from the sudden release of such unbearable tension, at the sight of the scrawny dog beside her. "How did you get here?" I asked my rescuer.

"You can thank your friend Holmes for that," Miller said, seizing a lantern and leading me toward the plank. "He's brilliant, in case you didn't know it! He figured it all out and came for me."

Holmes was considering the tangle of trees some distance from the bank, inspecting them with the intensity of an artist about to paint a masterpiece. "Watson, I owe you a thousand apologies," he said, turning toward me as Miller and I approached. "I was too eager to confirm my suspicion concerning Mrs. Maplecroft's true identity. Once that was confirmed, I was certain that the child and Miss Telfair were one and the same, united by the Devil's gift. When

I returned and Miss Rathburn told me of the message, I knew our enemy was at last ready to move. I am sorry that you were caught up in her snare."

I could not so blithely forgive him this time; I had been through too much. I said nothing, and only nodded when he also asked if I was unharmed. Miller, whose high colour spoke to his enjoyment of this adventure, quickly filled in the gaps.

"Mr. Holmes knew this witch would be headed for the Fountain of Youth and he needed a fast boat to catch her!" Miller made an expansive gesture, and I turned to see a vessel much like a police launch tethered just behind the riverboat. Like his carriage, it was painted in gaudy colours. Its bow was complete with a ludicrous wooden figurehead, a mermaid with massive bare breasts, bright red hair and an insipid expression on her face. "I call this my jungle cruise ship," Miller continued, still the showman. "I take tourists up the river, reveal to them the wonders of nature, let them blast an alligator or two."

Miss Rathburn placed her hand on Miller's arm. The gentle touch silenced him at last. "I think we should move on," the lady said.

Holmes reached into his coat and removed a Colt revolver, passing it to me. "It is not your preferred weapon, I realize, but it should be adequate."

"What use are guns against magic?" I muttered, even as I quickly checked the chambers and snapped them back into place. I jerked my head at Miller. "You've told him everything?"

Miller answered before Holmes could even draw breath to speak. "Oh yes. Quite remarkable! And I would never have believed such a ridiculous tale had Mr. Holmes not shown me that spectacular bee. What a clever little fellow. People would pay handsomely to see him perform his tricks. You know, you could charge more than two bits to...where are you going?"

"I suggest you keep up!" Holmes snapped, pausing only long enough to snatch the lantern from Miller's grip. The dog was whimpering and drawing Miss Rathburn behind him. She clutched her shawl more closely and allowed the cur to lead her. I took my place beside Holmes, with Miller bringing up the rear. For half a mile or more we followed the twists and turns of a tiny creek, a flow that was barely more than a trickle. It disappeared abruptly, leaving only a damp spot in the earth. The dog stopped, whining in frustration.

"This is the last known marker," Holmes said. "From here we must once again consult the map."

"But Telfair and her associates have it," I objected. "And you said it could not be copied."

"On paper," Holmes replied. "Our friend Jack Madison was more imaginative, and deduced how to produce an accurate replica. Miss Rathburn, if you will?"

The woman turned, holding the dog's leash for Miller to take. She lowered her shawl to her waist. I was shocked to see that the rear of her gown was split, the cotton fabric torn and trailing threads, as if crudely ripped by insensitive hands. The exposed white flesh of her back glowed pure and ethereal in the moonlight as Holmes moved his lantern closed.

Drawn on her flawless skin was a map. Indigo lines traced a path through the swamp, and strange, arcane symbols gave information as to paces and landmarks.

"The witch found Jack. She came to his show, yesterday," Miss Rathburn said. "She was a woman, not a child, and she came alone. Jack convinced her to show him the map, and he agreed to meet with her today, to take her to the Fountain. He memorized the map, but last evening he also drew it on my skin, to test the nature of the enchantment." Despite her blindness, she turned her head as if to study our reactions. "You no doubt consider me a hoyden, or worse."

Holmes plucked up the shawl, gently returning it to her shoulders. "On the contrary, Madame, I find you resourceful and brave."

"I should have told you his plans this morning, Doctor Watson. Jack went with Alice Telfair for his own reasons, which have nothing to do with wanting to drink that cursed water." Miss Rathburn shook her head. "He made me promise not to tell until it was over, but Mr. Holmes convinced me that anyone who can cast a glamour strong enough to make herself a child is a witch with superior powers! Jack needs our help, whether he wishes to admit it or not."

"I believe I know why Tiger Tail has gone with Miss Telfair," Holmes said. "You do not have to tell us and betray a confidence, Miss Rathburn, for I can deduce it. Your gentleman is after Miss Telfair for the same reason Miss Telfair broke every bottle of water in her father's cellar---to avenge the death of a beloved parent."

I saw it suddenly, and wondered why I had not seen it before, not read it in the man's reaction to Holmes's first statement. "The slave conjurer...Old Gator was Tiger Tail's father!"

"Who?" Miller asked, but Holmes ignored him. I saw Miss Rathburn make the smallest of nods.

"Jack told me that a man named Telfair purchased his father, when Jack was just a baby. His father was never seen again," the lady said.

"But revenge for that injustice has already been taken," Holmes said. "Mr. Telfair paid for his crime some time ago. Let us hope we can reach Alice Telfair and her minion before Tiger Tail does anything that might imperil his soul."

We resumed our progress, Holmes guiding us past landmarks that, to another explorer, would mean nothing: a petrified tree, a sudden sinkhole, an Indian's mark upon a rock. The dog began to show signs of picking up a scent and tugged more strenuously at the leash.

The tangled woods gave way to a clearing. And there, poised to halt us, was the fiendish green mist.

CHAPTER TWENTY-NINE

"What a marvel!" Miller declared. "I've never seen anything like it! And mind you, I've spent time in San Francisco!"

"And I in London," Holmes said with a touch of grim humour. "Watson will verify that in our city the fog descends and hangs in yellow, sickly miasmas. This, however, is a mist that earth is quite incapable of producing."

I understood his meaning. Only the Shadows, a world so corrupt and vile, could have belched forth such a putrid mass. It was like a sewer had spilled out the noxious waste of all the world's cities. The smell was such I was forced to put my handkerchief to my nose, fighting down the urge to retch.

"Without the ability to navigate by magic," Holmes said, "one might be absorbed into that fog for decades. Or be lost forever."

"Perhaps I should wait here," Miller bravely offered.

Holmes smiled at our companion's eagerness to remain behind. "An excellent idea. If you will stand guard beside that tree? Our business at the Fountain should not detain us for long."

Miller nodded, taking the lantern and assuming a sentry's stance at the base of a century's old oak. Holmes knelt, clawing his fingers into the dirt, removing handfuls of black soil and forest debris.

"It is not so difficult a spell for a true wizard, if impossible for a mortal to master," he said softly. "But it does require us to pass briefly through the Shadows. The mist is merely an extension of that horrible void." He looked to me with concern softening his features. "Miss Rathburn, as you already reside in darkness, it will have no terrors for you. But Watson, are you sure you can bear it?"

Memories of that passage fluttered back, but I banished them with a stern command. "Of course I can. I have no fear of Shadows."

"There is none stouter of heart than you, old friend," Holmes said. He turned his attention to his work, murmuring words in that strange, spider-like language and grinding the earth and its parts until I saw bright red droplets pearl on his fingers. I sensed the air around me change, felt pinpricks all along my skin. With the grace of a skilled cricket player, Holmes hurled the small bundle of dirt, twigs, and his own blood into the fog.

The putrid mist shivered and parted. A tunnel opened. The dog nearly pulled Miss Rathburn to the ground in its eagerness to plunge ahead. I peered around and noted that Mr. Miller had finally been awed into complete muteness. He stared wide-eyed and open-mouthed at the remarkable aperture before us.

Holmes took Miss Rathburn's free elbow and we moved forward.

Our passage was, mercifully, a brief one. I walked without impediment, as if the gnarled and twisted ground of the forest, which previously had been choked with obstacles such as roots, vines, and stones, was now as smooth as a city street. The green hue of the mist had departed, but we were still enveloped in a complete darkness. Once again, I was guided more by the sense of my companions than by any visual clues. Holmes kept up a low conversation, and I clung to his words. My breathing became shorter, each gasp a little spear in my lungs.

Daylight appeared. The darkness was banished in an instant, and we were standing amid tall trees with bright sunshine pouring over us. The change was instantaneous, miraculous. My relief matched the illumination.

I heard a voice chanting unfamiliar words. Holmes passed Miss Rathburn's hand to my arm with a silently-mouthed command to protect her. The dog whimpered, but a mere look from Holmes silenced it. Cautiously, I followed Holmes's lead, and together we peered around the trunk of the last massive oak tree on the edge of a clearing.

Before us was an oval pool approximately fifty yards in diameter, with a small outcropping of rock jutting some twenty feet above it. Mrs. Maplecroft sat on a fallen log, watching as Tiger Tail circled the fountain, dragging a long stick along its edges. In much the same way that Doctor Dee had surrounded the Faust Circle with libations and salt, the native conjurer paused from time to time and placed a twig or bit of cloth on the ground, whispering an incantation as he worked. Alice Telfair stood on the rock above the water, but she had shed her glamour. She was no longer an innocent child, but a young woman of great beauty. Her golden hair tumbled freely about her shoulders, and the gown that she had worn was barely long enough to cover her hips. She stood unconcerned for any modesty, watching Tiger Tail labour and hissing at him to hurry along.

"What is he doing?" I whispered.

Holmes did not answer, but the expression on his face was a rare one. He appeared confused, even baffled. I had rarely seen him scowl so deeply.

"I do not know. I am not familiar with his words or this rite."

I glanced sideways. Miss Rathburn was gripping my arm more tightly. She leaned against me, placing her words in my ear.

"There is no ceremony. He is speaking in his native language, mocking her as a fool."

I edged close to Holmes, whispering to him. "Tiger Tail is bluffing."

The dog was straining at its leash. There was a snap, as the cord broke. With a sharp bark, the animal bolted from our hiding place and dashed across the open ground. Mrs. Maplecroft sat frozen as a statue, as if unaware of the intruder. The hound ran to Tiger Tail, nuzzling against him. It came to me in a rush that the dog was the native's familiar.

"What is this?" Alice Telfair demanded. "How did that cur come through the mists?" She swung around, whipping the wand from the sleeve of her gown. "Who is there?"

Red light spat from the tip of the rod. It flew across the space and hit the tree like a bolt of lightning, instantly igniting the branches. Fire raced down the trunk, nearly searing our faces. We had no choice but to move forward, away from the conflagration. Holmes held up his hands in the style of a surrendering prisoner.

"Alice Telfair, you must not do this."

She signalled to Mrs. Maplecroft, who rose stiffly from her perch, her hatchet at the ready. "So this is the mighty Sherlock Holmes, the conjuring detective," Miss Telfair shouted back to Holmes. "I was warned about you, that you would follow me. You are most persistent."

"I thank you for the compliment," he said. "Allow me to offer you one in return. You are a very apt pupil of the magical sciences."

"But still only a mortal," she replied. Some secret, invisible command must have passed between them, because her female servant was steadily advancing on our party. "Do you know what it is that I want the most? The thing I seek?"

"To be of the Shadows," Holmes replied, so calmly he might have been discussing a case in the comforts of Baker Street. "You want to be a Shadowborn, as I am, because you know that such a heritage would give you more power and a form of immortality that draughts from the Fountain of Youth could never offer."

"You understand me, then," she said, with a strange quiver in her tone.

"I do," Holmes said. "When I watched the worshippers at the river and saw them being baptized, I grasped the connection you had made. You believe that when a mortal is immersed in these waters, which flow from the Shadows, he becomes a creature of the Shadows."

Miss Telfair gave a little cry of joy, pressing her hands together to her lips. She looked suddenly as sweet and naive as a debutante accepting a spray of posies. "Oh, this is wonderful! Mr. Holmes, no one else has ever understood. This is what I want to be! From the moment I read the dark books and cast my first spells I knew I should have been born in the Shadows. I was meant to have the blood of wizards in my veins!"

"You are not the first mortal to wish for such a thing," Holmes continued. He seemed unaware that Mrs. Maplecroft was only a few yards from our position. I kept my face to the vicious murderess, doing my best to shield Miss Rathburn between us.

"Many have desired exactly the change that you seek. But none has found it."

Miss Telfair held out her arms. "So you say. But I believe I can change. My heart says I can be a Shadowborn!" She stomped a bare foot and shook a clenched fist. "I am so tired of hearing NO! This is what I want and I will have it, no matter who stands in my way!"

"Then the Fountain has already cursed you," Holmes answered. "You are almost a century old, and have the ability to work mortal magic, but you have the weak mind and the sullen will of a spoiled child."

For a moment she seemed not to understand. She swayed on her perch as her rosebud mouth formed a silent circle of surprise.

"Let me be plain, Miss Telfair," Holmes continued. "You can not have what you seek because it is an impossible thing. Bathing in the Fountain of Youth will not transform you, and wishing that it would will not make it so. If you leap into the spring, all you will become is wet." Holmes scowled. "In short, you have behaved as a naughty little girl, a mewing brat, but instead of merely crying for the moon, you have done murder for it. Miss Telfair, it is time to grow up."

Her face turned scarlet with rage. She shrieked and the wand again ignited. This time my friend was ready, and he threw out one hand with a word of protective magic. A barrier went up, and the red heat from Miss Telfair's weapon swirled around us, like rain pouring from an umbrella. The witch gave another cry. Icy daggers erupted from the tip of her wand, peppering down and driving through the ground as sharp as stakes. Had any of them struck us, we would surely have been killed instantly.

"You can not win this battle," Holmes called to her, as she continued to fling bolts of power. Holmes deflected her magic with ease, so smoothly that her tantrums seemed to amuse him. "I am Shadowborn, you are of the mortal plane. Your abilities will never be as strong. Even your unholy blood magic will soon be exhausted and fail."

"Not if I harvest more!" she cried, swinging her hand at Mrs. Maplecroft. The woman came to life, the dullness of her gaze replaced with a sudden glow, a hideous radiance. She flanked us with unnatural speed, pitching her hatchet with the deftness of a circus performer. I pushed Miss Rathburn sideways as the hatchet somehow pierced the barrier Holmes had created. Mercifully, the weapon missed its mark. It drove into the ground, its blade tearing through the fabric at the train of Miss Rathburn's dress.

I never thought twice. I lifted my arm and fired at our assailant. Blood sprayed from Mrs. Maplecroft's shoulder. She fell without a sound, but Miss Telfair shrieked as her creature toppled.

"What have you done? I placed a ward on her! She was protected! This is not possible!"

Tiger Tail had watched our battle impassively. Now he stepped to the edge of the water, shaking his head at Miss Telfair. "What a mortal witch can do, a Shadowborn wizard can easily undo. You are too young and unskilled to even notice my unravelling of your spells. I stopped you from killing Doctor Watson and I removed your protection from this woman."

Holmes regarded his native counterpart with admiration. "Good show!"

Tiger Tail gestured toward Miss Telfair. "Now cease this bickering. Come down and surrender."

Holmes nodded. The glowing barrier around us faded. "It is over, Madame. You will gain no more power and you will pay for your crimes."

Miss Telfair looked back and forth, her breathing hard, her eyes wide and suddenly frightened, like those of a cornered animal. My odd sympathy for her returned at that instant. She looked confused, so very young. What had the water, offered for the kindest of reasons by an indulgent father, done to her mind as well as her soul? Holmes was right, the map---which no doubt lay in the carpetbag near Mrs. Maplecroft's body---had to be destroyed before it led any more fools to this cursed place.

"You said the rite was necessary!" Miss Telfair screamed at Tiger Tail. "You said the Fountain would change me after your ceremony was performed."

The native wizard looked to Holmes, then back to the witch. "I lied about the ritual," Tiger Tail said flatly. "I delayed because I knew Mr. Holmes would come to stop you. No ritual is needed for the Fountain to do its work."

"Not needed?" Miss Telfair said. Her face contorted, then she gasped in sudden delight, finding something wonderful inside Tiger Tail's words. "Not...needed! But the water does work!"

Everything seemed to happen at once. Holmes shouted a warning. And at the same moment, a look of evil triumph came over Miss Telfair. She flicked aside the gown. For one instant she posed like a golden goddess atop the grey stone, her naked body perfect and sun-warmed, radiating a primeval power all its own. She sprang from the rock, diving toward the beautiful, clear waters.

It still freezes my soul to think of what happened next. A thing broke through the surface of the Fountain in the same second that Miss Telfair's feet fatally left the stone. To this day, I could not say what exactly the monster was, except that it was dark green in colour, reptilian in form and roughly the size of an omnibus. Its massive jaws gaped open and the world shook with its roar as Miss Telfair plunged down toward the creature's hideous maw. She fell too fast to even scream or flail in terror. With a great snapping sound, the aquatic beast consumed her in one vicious bite.

The monster crashed back into the spring's depths. Water sprayed from the fountain in a high arc. Instinctively, Holmes whirled and threw his arms around both Miss Rathburn and myself while at the same moment summoning the force that had protected us from the witch's darts. The shield sparked and blazed, in much the same effect as the disreputable burning spring. We were covered with hot, hissing steam, but no moisture. Over Holmes's shoulder I saw that Tiger Tail had likewise produced a magical covering for himself and his whimpering dog. Water from the Fountain soaked the prone form of Mrs. Maplecroft.

"My God," I whispered, as the steam dissipated. "Is it over?"

"It is," Holmes said, assisting Miss Rathburn to rise. "And I fear Alice Telfair has reached the world of the Shadows, but not in the way that she intended."

The native conjurer dismissed his own ward and stomped toward us. "Mr. Holmes lied to her," he said, with menace darkening his tone.

"I am quite adept at telling falsehoods," Holmes replied curtly, "when they suit my purposes." He considered his counterpart with some anger. "At least my lie was harmless. Had she believed me and stepped away from the brink, she would still be alive."

"Jack?" Miss Rathburn reached out with trembling hands. Her lover took her in his arms. "What was it---I could only hear that horrible roar---was it an alligator?"

He spoke to her, but his eyes were locked to Holmes's face. "It was my father," he said. "Mr. Holmes told me what I had long suspected, that after Telfair purchased my father, he murdered him. Or, I should say, he tried to. But Telfair's shot was not fatal, and when my father's body slipped into the Fountain's water he became something different, something hideous, a reborn thing of the Shadows."

"Thus my falsehood, which was an attempt to save the lady," Holmes said. "Miss Telfair was correct in believing she would change. But as we have observed, a complete immersion in the water of the Shadows creates monsters, not miracles." He arched an eyebrow at his counterpart. "You told her no ceremony was required. You let her believe the Fountain would transform her."

"And I did not lie about that, did I?" Tiger Tail countered. "I merely neglected to tell her exactly what she would become, or what dwelled in its waters. It was her free choice to take that dive."

"You wanted her to die," Holmes said, with tart disapproval.

"Didn't you?" Tiger Tail countered.

A low moan diverted us. The injured woman on the ground was trying to move. Now regretting that I had so rapidly and unthinkingly fired at her, I hurried to make amends.

"You might have told me that ordinary weapons would pierce that shield," I snapped at Holmes. "I deduce that it only protects against magical assaults."

Holmes fought against a smile. "Do forgive me, Watson. It slipped my mind at the moment. Perhaps you should file that data away for some future investigation."

Ignoring my friend's smirk, I took Tiger Tail's knife and cut the bloody gown free from Mrs. Maplecroft's shoulder. My bullet had pierced her clavicle, but to my astonishment, I found the wound already mending. The water that sprayed from the spring had healed her.

A loud voice shattered our quiet wonder at the Fountain's amazing effects.

"I can't believe it! That was astounding! Tiger Tail, can you order that hideous creature to perform on cue?"

We all turned around. To our mutual astonishment, Miller was standing only a short distance away, beneath the trees. He began to babble, his words making it clear he had witnessed the finale if not the prelude of our 'entertainment.'

"That was stupendous! I've never seen anything like it. Imagine, we could build an amphitheatre around the pool, and feed the beast chicken carcasses to make him jump from the water. Think how much we could charge for admission!"

As Tiger Tail gathered up the carpetbag, and Holmes and I lifted the swooning Mrs. Maplecroft between us, I wondered if I alone noted that Miller's bald dome was glistening as if touched by morning dew.

CHAPTER THIRTY

"Lizzie Borden?"

Holmes nodded. The figure on the sofa stirred slightly in her sleep. The evidence of the bullet had vanished, and her grizzled hair was once again the golden-brown Holmes told me it had been in the days before she was accused of killing her father and stepmother in the narrow little house in Fall River.

"I sought out our friend Mr. Hanscom, because of the words Miss Rathburn uttered. Do you remember them, Madame?"

The lady photographer sat in the wicker chair in her studio. It was nearly dawn, and we were all exhausted from our evening's adventure, but Holmes felt it was important for everyone to be clear as to the facts of the matter. Only Miller had left us, pleading that he had to get home to his wife or face bunking down in his doghouse for untold nights to come.

It had taken us some time to return on the river from the site of the Fountain, following yet another fearful passage through the dark tunnel of the Shadows. Holmes had savagely berated Miller for attempting the journey on his own, but the man was so amazed by all he had seen that Holmes's sharp words went unheeded. He spent most of the trip mumbling to himself, occasionally bursting into a shriek of hysterical laughter. I feared his venture through the Shadows had driven him at least partially mad.

I was still amazed by what we found when we returned to the river. Miller's vessel bobbed at the water's edge, but the steamship I had been imprisoned on was nothing but a derelict craft, a crumbling skeleton of a boat, entwined with grass and vines, alive with the calls of birds and small animals. Tiger Tail's explanation confirmed Holmes's statement as to the magnitude of his powers.

"It was a wreck I found along the river. I recast it as a seaworthy vessel long enough to bear my cargo to the Fountain." He shrugged as if asked to explain an everyday action, such as drinking tea or reading a newspaper. "Enchantments on large, already decayed goods do not hold for long. That is why the snake squirmed into the cabin, Doctor Watson, because the magic was beginning to decay. I promise you I did not put the viper in your room."

I had accepted his words, but I was still giving him a wide berth and not turning my back to him. He now stood beside his lady, keeping one of her hands clasped to his.

"My words?" Miss Rathburn asked Holmes. "I do not recall saying anything important."

"You were the one who gave me the key to unlock the mystery of her identity," Holmes replied, standing over the sleeping figure. "You speculated that Maplecroft sounded more like a house than a family name. At that comment, I recalled that the infamous Lizzie Borden had made herself even more notorious by using her blood-soaked inheritance to purchase a hillside mansion. She further annoyed the Puritan townsmen by giving her estate a pretentious name. I needed only to consult my friend Hanscom, a former Pinkerton agent familiar with every aspect of the case, to receive confirmation that the lady who reposes before us now styles herself as 'Lizbeth of Maplecroft.'"

"Holmes," I said, recalling the vacant look in the woman's eyes as she had guarded me on the boat, and the stiff, mechanic quality of her movements, "is she an accomplice, or another victim?"

"That, Doctor, is the essential question. I believe that Miss Telfair made Miss Borden's acquaintance while in Boston, where Miss Borden travelled to indulge herself in theatrical excursions and shopping expeditions. Our 'Lizbeth' is a lonely woman, shunned by her neighbours and a pariah to her own kinsmen. But Alice Telfair had no such prejudices, because she found in Lizzie someone desperate for love and friendship. Even novice, mortal witches can cast spells of enthrallment, turning weak-minded fellow humans into their slaves. Alice Telfair knew she needed a minion to kill and collect blood; in Lizzie Borden she found an easily-entranced woman who could not only wield the axe, but would serve as a proper companion to an unmarried lady. Her value was enhanced when Alice Telfair donned her child-shaped glamour to elude us, an action that required an adult as a chaperone."

"So you do not hold her responsible for the murders, in Prague and London and here in town?" I asked. It infuriated me to think that these souls would never be avenged.

Holmes once again demonstrated his ability to read my mind. "The best revenge is served cold, Doctor. Alice Telfair has paid for her crimes in a most spectacular fashion. I predict that Miss Borden will awaken with no memory of her sanguinary part in this gruesome saga. She will be frightened and appalled to find herself among strangers. Therefore we will send her back to Fall River, where every day the good people of that town will punish her for her original crime with cold glances and swiftly turned shoulders."

"It also seems that Mycroft was in error," I pointed out. "He thought Miss Telfair's plans were more ambitious and would destroy the world. In the end, she was only interested in her herself."

"True," Holmes mused, "my brother may have missed the mark, just as I failed to imagine the possibilities of the Devil's gift to Miss Telfair." My friend's expression softened with rare humility. "But you have taught me an important lesson, Watson: every human soul matters."

"It is all so sad," Miss Rathburn sighed. "Those poor people murdered, merely because Alice Telfair wanted to be like you are Jack...and like you, Mr. Holmes."

"She was wrong to wish for such a thing," Tiger Tail muttered. "Mortals should not meddle with the Shadows."

"Perhaps Doctor Dee is correct," Holmes offered. "Our time is passing. The world should dwell in Sun, and our kind should be banished."

"What about the map?" Miss Rathburn asked. "The one my Michelangelo sketched on my back will be gone as soon as I can take a proper scrubbing. What will you do with the real one?"

Holmes looked to battered old carpetbag that Miller had carried from the boat, leaving it on the floor for us before departing for his home. The bag was such a perfectly dreary thing, so ordinary and unexceptional that one might stare at it for a hundred years and never see it. Yet inside was a creation of the Shadows, an artefact that had been the root cause of madness and murder. I regarded the bag as if a million swamp adders writhed inside. I would not have touched it for the world.

"The map to the Fountain of Youth is, I confess, still a mystery to me. I do not know who created it, or how it came into the possession of Father Olivarez, all those years ago," Holmes said. "But it must be destroyed. Once it is gone, the mist will serve as a protective boundary and the Fountain will never again be found.

Or," he added, with a small chuckle of whimsy, "if it is, some future detective and wizard can be summoned to deal with the consequences. I do not plan to return to this charming city."

He gestured for Tiger Tail to do the honours. The native knelt, opening the bag. For a moment his face was inscrutable. Then he held up the bag, shaking it, finally flipping it over and disgorging the contents. There was nothing inside expect a lady's hairbrush and a single red shoe.

Our sightless companion interpreted our stunned silence and immediately named the culprit.

"Miller!

CHAPTER THIRTY-ONE

That afternoon, Mr. Hanscom took charge of a befuddled Lizzie Borden or, as she insisted on being addressed, Lizbeth of Maplecroft. She warmed to the detective's sombre face, recalling him from the brief period before her arrest, when he had been employed by her family's attorney to find the truth in the matter. The stoic gentleman buried any distain he had for the murderous lady, gently escorting her to the train and assuring us that he would see her safely back to Fall River. I commented to Holmes that Hanscom seemed to have donned a glamour himself, to be able to restrain the urge to push Miss Borden from the speeding locomotive.

"To a detective, there is nothing more fascinating than an evildoer," Holmes corrected. "I have spent many productive hours in jail cells, listening to men who have committed unspeakable acts wax eloquent about their atrocities. The insight into the human mind and soul is well worth the unpleasant nature of their company." He raised a hand in salute as the train departed. "Perhaps in the long hours to come our friend will finally coax Miss Lizzie Borden into confessing how and why she killed her parents, thus bringing him some peace in knowing that he was correct in his deductions."

"Could she face the gallows again?"

"Never. The American system does not permit even the most vicious of murderers to be tried twice for the same crime."

Holmes led me through the crowds that were awaiting transportation to the Flagler hotels. We walked at a brisk pace as Holmes informed me of his next plan.

"We must persuade Miller to surrender the map. I realized afterward how easily he did the thing. There was another carpetbag on the floor of his ridiculous jungle cruise vessel, perhaps left behind by a lady tourist. He swapped them while we were travelling back to the city." Holmes's cane beat a sharp rhythm on the sidewalk, and there was such a purposeful set to his face that the people of leisure quickly stepped aside and regarded him as a curiosity, rather like a lion taking a stroll down the Strand. "I doubt that idiot has any true grasp of what he has obtained and how dangerous it is. To him, it is probably nothing more than an unique souvenir of our visit."

"Can you simply overpower him and wipe away his memories?" I asked, thinking that would be the most efficient way to retrieve the stolen goods and insure that Miller did not reveal Holmes's most closely guarded secret to the world. My friend shook his head.

"I could do it, but I will not. Do you recall the words I said to you in London? Such an act would be a violation of my promise to never harm humanity. We must find another way." Holmes gestured for us to make a turn, leading the way to Miller's office on Aviles Street. "Perhaps he will listen to reason. And, if not, maybe he is not above being bribed."

To our amazement, the office was abuzz with activity. Secretaries were clattering on type writing machines, and telegraph boys were running in and out with messages in hand. Men in heavy suits were seated against the wall, staring in an unfriendly manner at each other. Before Holmes could make an appeal to the lady who seemed to be bringing order to this chaos by forcing guests to sign a register, a door to an inner chamber opened and Miller pushed a tall gentleman with black and silver hair from his presence.

"I should have known you're too much of a Scotsman to see the potential! Five hundred shares, bah, you'll need to be willing to pony up for a thousand before we can do business, Peter Mackintosh!"

The rejected man smacked his silk hat to his head and shoved past us with the look of a highly offended robber baron. The lady rose to call another name, but Miller, catching sight of us, shouted her down.

"No, Claudia, hold the pack off for a while. These are just the fellows I want to see!"

He drew us inside, past the vicious stares of the other potential investors. The door slammed hard behind us. I barely kept from gaping in wonder at the sudden change in the man. In a matter of hours he had shed at least thirty pounds, and his head was now proudly sporting chestnut waves of hair.

"Mr. Holmes, Doctor Watson, how good to see you. Please sit down! I had meant to drop a note of thanks to you at your hotel but, as you can see, I am rather busy. What a day it has been!"

Signs of industry were everywhere. Crude, hand-drawn posters were tacked to his wall, as well as maps with bright arrows attached, pointing to a spot along the San Sebastian River. Telegrams and letters were scattered about his desk, and with great pride Miller thrust a printed program into my hand. It was so fresh some of the ink had smeared. It bore an engraving of an Indian resembling Tiger Tail, as well as a mermaid and the looming visage of a conquistador in full armour. Across these figures were the words:

FABULOUS FOUNTAIN OF YOUTH!

MIRACLE WATERS DISCOVERED BY SPANISH AND GUARDED BY SEMINOLES!

YOUTH GUARANTEED WITH ONE SIP!

EXPEDITIONS DEPART TWICE DAILY

My friend gave an audible groan as he read over my shoulder. "Mr. Miller, you can not do this."

"Well, it's my map now!" the prompter replied saucily. "The rightful owner is dead and I have found it. I deserve it, for my part in the adventure, I think." He picked up a small model of his river vessel and waved it at us. "If not for my boat, you'd never have found that place. The map is the least you owe me."

"You do not understand---" Holmes began, but Miller cut him off, waving a hand sparkling with a garish gold and diamond ring.

"I understand perfectly! The Fountain is magical. Look at me, I was merely sprinkled with water and now I have hair again! It's wondrous!"

"It is deadly," Holmes stated. "It brings on corruption of the soul."

"Bah! Now, examine this," Miller continued, heedless of Holmes's multiple attempts to interrupt his enthusiastic presentation. "I'll buy a fleet of jungle boats for the day trips, and invest in a larger riverboat for the overnight cruises. Once that is done, I'll build a hotel on the site, a huge hotel with restaurants and shops and casinos, with ragtime music playing in the swamps and pony rides just for the kiddies. I'll put that ass Flagler out of

253

business, I will! My Fountain of Youth will become the greatest attraction ever dreamed of in Florida or in the world for that matter!" Throughout his speech, he directed our attention to his sketches, drawings that showed, in the crudest manner, plans for a hostelry and a boardwalk of amusements. In his art, the Fountain itself had shrunk to a mere pinprick, surrounded by all types of gaudy entertainments.

"And what do you think I can charge for a cocktail of pure water? A dollar? Ten dollars? A hundred dollars? The world will beat a path to my door when our newly-elected President McKinley returns to Washington looking like a sprightly lad of fourteen. Yes, indeed, I will become the richest man in America, and all the elderly will rise from their rolling chairs and call me blessed!"

He dropped back in his seat, gripping his lapels, already basking in imagined glory. Holmes drew a deep breath.

"What have you done with the map?"

"It's in a place you will never find it! Not even the great Sherlock Holmes could get access to it, it's so well hidden. I have no plans to show it to anyone except a Mr. Menendez," he said, glancing at a message scrawled on a piece of paper. "He sent his man around this morning with this note, promising to provide capital to fund my venture to eighty percent if I will meet him tonight and show him proof that I have found the Fountain."

"That is stupidity itself!" I blurted, at the end of my patience with the promoter. "Surely you realize he plans to rob you."

"That he might," Miller chuckled, opening a drawer in his desk and removing a sizeable handgun, "but I will be prepared. I trust you recall what a good shot I am, Doctor?"

Holmes rose from the chair. His face looked suddenly old, the sadness adding decades to the lines across his brow.

"Mr. Miller, I will state this one last time. You have seen the magic the Fountain can work, but you have also seen the pain and suffering it inevitably causes. You can not reach the Fountain of Youth without the assistance of a wizard, and none in this city will aid you."

Miller shrugged. "I can find other magicians. You two are not the only ones on the earth."

"You have no manner of locating a true Shadowborn wizard, Mr. Miller. You will find only charlatans and frauds," Holmes predicted, "and you will waste your money and your life in the process. I warn you, the map itself is cursed. Whoever owns it is followed by a dark shadow, an unknown and unseen figure. I swear to you, this dark thing is capable of committing murder in a manner so ghastly even the torturers of the Inquisition would be appalled." Holmes extended his hand. "Please, Mr. Miller, for the safety of your life and your soul, give me the map. Build whatever 'attraction' you may dream of, tell all the lies your fevered brain can imagine. You might well become a man of wealth and fame in the process, and I will not begrudge you your success. But return the map to me so that I can fling it back into the Shadows where it belongs."

Miller glared at my friend. "Get out," he hissed.

Holmes made a short bow. I followed him through the doorway. As we were stepping onto the street, Miller bellowed for his next investor to be admitted.

"Watson," Holmes said, "did you notice anything peculiar about the message which Mr. Miller consulted?"

We had begun to walk down the street, retracing our steps toward the square. "Only that it was written in Spanish. I would not have given that fool credit for knowing the language."

"Neither would I," Holmes said, halting before a whitewashed wall. "This is the public library," he said, "and home to the St. Augustine Historical Society. I suddenly feel the need to do some research."

Selfishly, I hoped he would not request my assistance, and to my great relief he suggested that I return to the hotel or enjoy a final afternoon of sightseeing in the town. I left him at the door of the institution. He was humming a soft Iberian tune.

**

"Try these now," Holmes said, gently returning the tinted spectacles to their owner. For the past hour, we had been guests at Miss Rathburn's tidy bungalow, dining on Southern fare of fried chicken and okra, with lemonade and ice cream. Tiger Tail had joined us, and for some time he and Holmes had been mulling over a way to place a delicate enchantment on the lady's glasses, so that the spectacles would replicate the effect of her cameras and allow her to see the world at all times. The native's dog (who I had learned was actually not his familiar, but merely a beloved pet) whined for treats, while the lady's white cat eyed the flop-eared interloper with feline contempt. It was a sweet domestic scene, a pleasant counterpoint to our dark and violent adventures in the Oldest City.

"Did the magic work?" Tiger Tail asked as Miss Rathburn patted the dark glasses into place. "Do they let you see?"

She turned her head in my friend's direction. "They do! Oh, Mr. Holmes...why did you not tell me that you are such a handsome man?"

Tiger Tail growled like his namesake. "Temperance, give those spectacles back to me and let me break them!"

"I think my work here is done," Holmes said, waving aside the lady's profuse gratitude while consulting his pocket watch. "But Doctor Watson and I have one more appointment to keep before we depart on the morning train."

This was news to me, but I did not object. As we walked along the twilight streets of the town, a thought crept into my brain. I struggled to phrase it properly.

"Holmes, you say that a Shadowborn wizard can cast and maintain a glamour. If that is true, why does Tiger Tail---or rather, Jack Madison---not cast a disguise for himself, and make his appearance that of a white man, rather than one of mixed ancestry? If he did so, he could wed his beloved."

Holmes considered my inquiry sombrely. "There are two objections to that, Watson. The first is the amount of magical energy required. Even the oldest and strongest of the Shadowborn cannot maintain a glamour for an extended period. Alice Telfair could only don hers because of its satanic origin." Holmes swung his cane to his shoulder. "But the second objection is, I believe, closer to the truth. Tiger Tail knows Miss Rathburn loves him for who he is, not for who he could pretend to be. The laws of the country matter little to such a tender emotion." Holmes took his stick and clattered it against a fence like a small boy. "But what would I know of love?"

I found I had no answer for that question.

Holmes pointed across the seawall to a small sailboat. "Our transportation awaits."

"Where are we going?" I asked.

"To observe Mr. Miller's rendezvous with his client," Holmes said, urging me to take care along the slippery steps. "And to bring this case to its conclusion."

"But he did not tell us where he was meeting the man."

"And since when has such an omission stopped me? Watson, can you handle the sails?"

I confess that I am not much of a nautical mate, but with a bit of instruction from Holmes I was able to perform my duties correctly so that the little boat could be launched into the river. The wind was brisk that evening, and we were soon making swift progress down the channel toward the sea. Holmes took the tiller, pointing out various landmarks to me as we glided along. In a short time the city was left behind us, and there was nothing on either bank except river grass, tangled trees and scrubby bushes, some of which sprouted leaves that looked like barbed sabres. The air became heavier, tinged with salty spray, and I knew we were very near the ocean.

A strange sight appeared at the final bend in the river. It was a single stone tower, a relic that might have been transported from an ancient castle in Wales or Scotland, with a rounded sentry box jutting from one side. It had clearly been abandoned for some time, and the wilderness was working to reclaim it. A small wooden dock was the only sign that it held some interest for tourists, perhaps those who came out to sketch its picturesque deterioration.

Miller's gaudy jungle cruise vessel was tied there. I looked back to Holmes.

"How on earth did you know?"

"He foolishly gave me the name of his mysterious associate, the one who sent his man with the message. Once I knew the name, it was only a matter of an hour's researching to find the ground he would choose, because it was the scene of a former crime and an excellent spot for potential bloodletting."

I was silent in confusion. Holmes shook his head. "Was the potential investor not familiar to you, Watson?"

"It was...Menendez? Yes, I seem to have read of someone with that name, but it was in a history book. Wasn't he the captain who---"

Holmes silenced me with a quick gesture of his hand. I followed the motion and saw a figure walking at the top of the tower. He was only a silhouette, but a tiny red point marked the tip of the cigar he was smoking.

"Let us make one final effort to save this fool's life," Holmes said, tossing me the rope. I secured the boat and together we walked up the rickety steps to the tower's battlements. Miller had seen the boat, but not our faces, and he gave a cry of dismay when we appeared in the moonlight.

"Now see here, this is persecution!" he snapped. "Don't think you'll take it from me, Mr. Holmes. I'll shoot you both, and never do a day's time for it!" He plucked the gun from his coat pocket and waved it fiercely in our direction. "Protecting oneself from assault qualifies as justifiable homicide!"

"Mr. Miller, I have no intention of trying to take your possession from you by force," Holmes said, far too calmly. I suppose he was accustomed to such, but I would never grow blasé when a gun was pointed at my head. "I am merely giving you one final chance to save your life and soul."

"Your melodrama does not impress me, sir. What, do you think you can conjure that monster from the Fountain of Youth to gobble me up?"

"I could do many things," Holmes replied. "I could kill you in ways mankind has not yet imagined. But I will not. The choice of life and death is yours."

Miller never wavered. I wondered if that slight sprinkling of water from the Fountain had so quickly corrupted him, or if it had merely stoked the already blazing fire of greed in his soul. "I will give you to the count of five," he snarled.

"I need no lessons in mathematics," Holmes answered. "Come, Watson, it is time to depart."

Without another word we descended the steps. I presumed we would board our vessel and make our way back to the city.

Holmes halted.

Waiting on the dock was the dwarf.

"My God," I whispered. The little man was clad in the attire of a monk, his frayed brown robe dragging across the wooden boards. Beside him was an ancient chest painted with grinning skulls and Latin inscriptions. The ornate brass cross on the lid produced a strange luminescence, casting a low light on the dwarf's repulsive features.

This time, the evil figure did not smirk or vanish into thin air. Instead, he watched us approach and spread his hands in a gesture of welcome.

"At last we meet," Holmes said. "Let me be clear that I do not appreciate your games, the way you have taunted my friend in hopes of making him question his sanity. Nor do I approve of the deaths you have caused, in the Paris hotel, or the station in Prague, or by your summoning of the Kraken, which stole away the lives of two heroic British sailors. You will have much to answer for when you stand before the seat of Judgement."

The man made a grimace. He opened his mouth, revealing a grotesque, mutilated tongue.

"Your lord is cruel, I understand. But even eternal silence and undying servitude is no justification for murder." Holmes folded his hands on his cane. "I wish to speak with your master."

The dwarf crouched to lift the lid of the box.

CHAPTER THIRTY-TWO

A hideous figure rose from the chest, propelled without any sense of exertion, like a body lifted upright on a board.

It was a skeleton clad in a conquistador's armour. A tarnished silver breastplate dangled from its ribcage, and greaves still protected the bones of its arms and legs. An open-faced helmet of fantastic workmanship was fixed on its head and stiff leather boots covered its feet. A sword of Toledo steel was belted over the pelvis. The rest of the corpse's costume, a blouse and doublet, were tattered and rotted, as if they had laid with the body for hundreds of years.

Only the face had some vestiges of skin, across the eyes and brow. The eyelids opened, the bare jawbone clacked and clattered. What came from the repulsive thing was a rapid jabbering of Spanish. I did not understand how it could even speak, as it clearly lacked lips or a throat, its vocal chords long since having crumbled into dust.

"Would you like me to translate?" Holmes inquired pleasantly. I tore my horrified gaze from the spectral creature.

"You will have to."

"This gentleman is Don Pedro Menendez de Aviles, the founder of the city of St. Augustine. He read the secret memoirs of Ponce de Leon, and from the famous conquistador he learned there was a Fountain of Youth in the land of La Florida, but a green mist guarded it and only a great conjurer could find his way to the source. Indians had passed on this tale to Ponce de Leon, who held it as little more than a fable, but Menendez took it as truth and vowed that nothing would stop him from finding that magical place. In his quest he became a man of legendary cruelty, willing to do anything in order to drink this water.

"In 1565, his master the King of Spain ordered him to build a settlement in the land of flowers, a bastion against pirates and invaders. But while his men felled trees and constructed a fort, Menendez captured and tortured native shamans until he found one willing to take him to the Fountain. He travelled only with his captive and a dwarf named Rodrigo. It was Menendez who drew the map, which the passage through the Shadows enchanted, so that it could never again be copied on parchment. Menendez filled dozens of bottles of water before he returned to the half-constructed fort. There, he took a blade and, without hesitation, cut out the illiterate dwarf's tongue so the little man could tell no tales of their adventure. But the native magician---who, like me, was a Shadowborn Halfling---was so horrified that he slipped his chains and turned himself into an eagle. Quick-witted, Menendez blasted the eagle with a harquebus. The great bird fell beyond the walls of the fort, and Menendez paid him no more heed. You will recall what I told you before, Watson, about the mortality of my kind?"

"A Halfling wizard is mortal when he dwells in the human world of Sun," I said, my mind filled with the awful memories of the time when Marie Laveau was about to attack an unconscious Holmes, and only my quick actions had spared his life. "So the wound to the bird was also fatal to the man."

Holmes nodded. "And to Menendez's great misfortune, Father Olivarez, a priest with the expedition, witnessed his shot and the eagle's fall. The padre had a kind heart, one that could not bear to watch even a dumb animal suffer. He went in search of the bird and found the shaman turned back into human form, dying on the rocks beside the bay. The great Indian conjurer told him of the miraculous Fountain of Youth, of the map, and of Menendez's perfidy. With his dying breath the native wizard cursed both Menendez and his dwarf." Holmes's grey eyes narrowed, glittering with his gift. "A wizard's curse is a terrible thing."

"It was a curse of immortality?" I asked.

"After a fashion," Holmes said. "Rodrigo would linger as a spirit, able to dissolve and reform his body at will. But the dwarf's vile master was condemned to lingering shame for his evil deed, ordered to retain his soul and his bones, but not his flesh, until the map was destroyed."

Menendez's jawbone clacked. I stepped away and averted my gaze, unable to watch the gruesome machinations. Holmes listened and afterward resumed his narration with the air of a tour guide in the Castillo.

"Menendez had thought to profit from his cruelty. He planned to take the map and the bottles of water to Spain, where they would be treasures more priceless than the gold of Cortez or Pizarro. But Olivarez, who had buried the poor shaman and tended to the dwarf's mutilations, vowed that such meanness would never be rewarded. A short time later, while Menendez was busy at this very place, slaughtering unfortunate Frenchmen who were victims of a shipwreck, the padre took the map and the bottles of water and departed for the interior of La Florida. He disappeared for decades, while Menendez---who had been cursed with immortality of mission but not of flesh---followed him."

The undead conquistador's right hand reached out, finger bones snapping in fury. The dwarf produced a pike and placed it in his master's grip. With strange yet stately dignity, the animated skeleton began to walk up the pathway to the tower, his servant skipping merrily behind him. I understood now how Olivarez and Telfair had been murdered, and I knew what would surely occur next.

"Holmes!" I cried, "We must stop them!"

"The wizard's dying curse is the only one that can never be broken, not even by a wizard of equal power," Holmes said. "And Miller has made his choice."

I turned back to the path. The skeletal warrior and his escort had vanished. I grabbed my friend's sleeve.

"Holmes, surely you can't---"

He signalled for silence. For a long moment, all was still, I heard nothing but the chirping of crickets, the splash of a fish leaping in the river, and the persistent whine of a mosquito.

Then there was a shot, followed in rapid succession by five more. A scream came from the top of the tower. Long and lingering, it swirled, rose and fell, then slipped away, chronicling a death too ghastly to contemplate.

Silence reclaimed the world. Minutes passed. Finally, the dark figures reappeared, striding down from the tower.

Menendez had been reborn to his flesh. He was now once again a proud man, with a thick black beard and swarthy skin. He clutched a tightly rolled parchment in his left hand. I noted that the paper was soggy with blood. His right hand was on his gore-coated sword, and I gripped my cane more tightly, though it would have been a poor weapon against such a foe.

To my surprise, he offered a bow to my friend, and his servant did likewise.

"Muchas gracias, Don Sherlock Holmes."

He passed by us, boarding the sailboat. The mute dwarf jumped over the rail and began to work the ropes. In moments, they were nothing but a dot along the river, gliding back toward the city.

"What will he do?" I asked.

"He will go to the mist that surrounds the Fountain of Youth and fling the map into its depths. And with that action, the cursed spot will once again be hidden forever."

"And what will become of them when that action is completed?"

"They will take the rest so long denied, their bodies crumbling into dust. May God have mercy upon their souls."

I looked back toward the tower. "And Miller?"

"Will be accused of having absconded with several hundred dollars in investments. He will be remembered as a scoundrel, the first of a long line of Florida tourism promoters to bear such a epitaph, if I perceive the future correctly."

Holmes bent down and picked up a shell some previous visitor had left on the dock. He tossed it into the river, and I watched as the ripples spread in an ever-widening circle.

"Well, Watson, we have a very early train to catch in the morning. It would be best if we borrowed our friend's steam launch and returned to our hotel."

"Is it right to take his boat?" I asked.

Holmes jabbed his cane back to the tower. "I see no reason not to. Miller will not be needing it."

CHAPTER THIRTY-THREE

"With luck, we should be in New York in less than two days," Holmes said, consulting the timetable as we waited at the station. "And from there we can board one of the finest liners to London. Unless, of course, you would prefer to take our return passage on the *Friesland*."

I shook my head. "I think we have earned a more pleasant journey than your brother's toy can provide. I also think that I will refer to it in a story someday," I added, much to Holmes's wry amusement, "but of course I will designate it as the 'Dutch steamer' which 'nearly cost us both our lives.'"

"Your readers will find you maddening, Watson."

"If only I could tell them the truth. Holmes, your adventures deserve to be recorded!"

He shook his head. I understood that this was an old argument he would prefer not to have. I yielded with a modicum of grace, thinking to myself that I would pass the long hours of our travels by drafting a manuscript despite his prohibitions. Even if it could never be removed from the Library of the Arcane, at least it would exist, and one reader would have the pleasure of following our quest. I was just about to light a final cigarette before boarding when a familiar voice hailed us.

Miss Rathburn was dressed in the height of fashion, as was her escort. Despite a few glares and sour looks from other denizens of the station lounge, who no doubt found their behaviour inappropriate, Tiger Tail proudly held his lady's hand in the crook of his arm.

"I could not allow you to leave without this," Miss Rathburn said, as the sharp whistle from the conductor made us aware there was little time for pleasantries. She withdrew an envelope from her reticule. "It is the photograph I made of you, Doctor. You should only view it with a stereoscope, for its maximum effect."

"You should not have troubled yourself," I chuckled. "This was taken after I fell into the grave in the plague cemetery," I reminded Holmes, "and I was hardly a handsome subject!"

"Doctor," the lady said, with gentle urgency. "You need to see it."

Holmes took her hand and kissed it. "Thank you, Miss Rathburn. You are a most exceptional woman." He glanced to her companion. "I hope all is settled now."

Tiger Tail nodded solemnly. "All is well."

I added my thanks and my best wishes for the couple's happiness. The conductor was shouting all aboard, and we took our leave. Just as we reached our car's steps, however, Holmes halted and gestured through the cloud of steam building about the wheels.

The strange, pale boy in the dark clothing stood there, his eyes solidly fixed on Holmes. I felt the unnatural chill return. Holmes crossed to the child, and to my surprise he knelt down and gently laid a hand upon the lad's frail shoulder.

"Write what you see," he told the boy. "Turn your visions into stories. Your weird tales will make your burden bearable."

With that advice, Holmes rose and together we barely gained our seats before the train began to move. Holmes lowered the window of the stifling compartment, directing my attention back to where the boy still stood, his cold gaze fixed on our position.

"One hoodoo man knows another," Holmes quoted softly, offering a final wave. As the train's wheels started to turn, a woman raced up and claimed the child, scolding him loudly. I heard her words as we pulled away from the station.

"Howard Phillips Lovecraft, don't scare me so! You awful boy, where have you been?"

CHAPTER THIRTY-FOUR

And so my Lady Hypatia, you now hold the story that can never be told. I pray that you have found it entertaining, that it has thrilled you in some way, or at least amused you in an idle hour. Holmes once again proved his mettle, as both an investigator and a wizard, and while I can claim no laurels for myself, I take some measure of pride in having insisted that he take this case. Even if my faith in Alice Telfair was betrayed, I find that in making the acquaintance of Tiger Tail and his lady, I have had my love for humanity renewed.

But there is an epilogue to this story. It will explain why this manuscript, rather than myself, in person, is before you. It concerns the picture that Miss Rathburn presented to me as I embarked on my journey home.

At first, I dismissed it from my mind. I spent my time making notes, and later drafting this document. Indeed, it was not until we were aboard the *Majestic*, on the final night of our cruise back to Southampton, that I again thought of the photograph. A number of gay young people were gathered in a salon, amusing each other with a stereoscopic viewer. When they exited for the evening's dancing, I retrieved their abandoned device and took it down to our cabin. Holmes, in his usual misanthropic humour, had rejected an invitation to dine with Captain Smith and was busily sawing away at a borrowed violin, subjecting the instrument to all the tortures of the damned. I ignored him and retrieved the envelope from my carpetbag. I pulled out the card and slid it into the metal holders, then adjusted the distance for my own less than youthful eyes.

At some point---I cannot say how long, for I truly lost all sense of time---I was aware that Holmes had stopped playing. I lowered the viewer. Numbly, I handed it to him. He examined the image. After a moment, he placed the device on the bed beside me and walked out without a word.

I realized I was staring at my hands. More time had been lost to me, as I wandered once again in distant lands of memory, with pain and loss has my twin companions. My neck was stiff and sore, my entire body ached when I moved. But finally, I understood what I must do.

With my tie loosened, my collar undone, I climbed up to the stern of the ship. The photographic card dangled between my fingers. For how long I stood there, studying the stars above the churning ocean, I do no know. I was only aware of unmanly tears rolling down my cheek and how fiercely my eyes burned.

I looked one last time at the image, letting every detail of it sear into my brain. Then I released the card, watching it spiral down and disappear in the blackness of the waves.

Holmes was beside me again. I had not heard him approach. Before I could even acknowledge his presence, he placed a heavy coat around my shoulders. "It is cold, Watson," he said, before vanishing into the ship's shadows.

There was nothing more he needed to say. We understood each other perfectly.

You are so brilliant, my dear lady. I am certain you have known what was on that card. Perhaps you even sensed it many pages ago, when I told you of the photograph being snapped in that small studio, by an enchanted camera that captures the dead.

It was Mary; my late, beloved spouse, Mary Morstan Watson, was standing just behind me. Her soft hands were on my shoulders, her face was a perfect oval of love and beauty.

She is with me still.

Author's Note

One of the joys of being a historian is becoming acquainted with people and places that have great stories. And one of the most enjoyable aspects of being a writer of fiction is the freedom to take these stories and give them different twists, seeking not complete historical accuracy but rather a historical spirit to infuse a work with memorable settings and characters. *Shadowblood* has begged, borrowed, and shamelessly stolen a number of its denizens and settings from the past, and in the spirit of fairness I am willing to point them out.

The myth of the Fountain of Youth is essentially a Victorian invention. There is no credible evidence that Ponce de Leon was actually searching for such a place when he stumbled upon Florida's pristine beaches. But the conquistador's futile quest made for a wonderful legend, one repeated in hundreds of variations in untold numbers of children's books. A modern tourist attraction called the Fountain of Youth exists in St. Augustine, but the gullible should be warned that it is nothing more than an artesian well.

In 2010, French researchers positively identified a mummified head that had for decades resided in a tax collector's attic as the remains of King Henri IV. Though unable to use DNA testing on the grisly relic, the scientists were able to identify lesions, scars, and an ear piercing that were well-known attributes of the king who was assassinated in 1610 and desecrated in 1793. A quick web image search will uncover Holmes's freakish witness to Mr. Telfair's murder!

Doctor John Dee was a sixteenth-century scholar with vast expertise. His work in mathematics, alchemy, and astrology, as well as his claims to have regular consultations with angels, made him a wonder of the age. He served Queen Elizabeth I as a kind of court wizard, and also spent time at the court of Rudolph II, the Holy Roman Emperor who was far more interested in the occult and magic than in ruling his large and unwieldy domain. Gotz (who I fictionally domesticated to be Doctor Dee's servant) was also a marvel of the times, with a metal prosthesis that allowed him to continue brawling across Europe, shouting his catchphrase (which roughly translates to 'kiss my ass!') for decades.

Prague is one of Europe's most beautiful capitals, a city filled with architectural masterworks from many centuries. The clock tower, bridge, cathedral, and tombs that Watson described are aspects of the town that I fell in love with during my own journey to Prague in 2010. There is a Faust house, and the legend of Faust needs no further explanation, as Marlowe, Goethe, and many others have so cunningly told the tale of man's hubris and the devil's deals. The Golden Lane sits just below the castle; it was once the street where goldsmiths and other servants of the sovereign lived. Though sadly decayed by the late 1800s, today it is a pleasant tourist walk, and across Prague there are many places that sell exceptional dumplings and goulash.

St. Augustine was Florida's original tourist city. Before the Civil War it was known primarily as a haven for people suffering from tuberculosis (then called consumption) and other pulmonary complaints. In the 1880s, Henry Flagler, the business tycoon and co-founder of Standard Oil, honeymooned in the city and fell in love with it. He decided to build a spectacular resort, the Hotel Ponce de Leon, just a block off the old square. He went on to build the Alcazar and complete a third hotel originally called the Casa Monica and renamed the Cordova, creating a community of glamorous venues for his elite guests. Today, the Ponce de Leon houses Flagler College, but visitors can still tour the marvellous rotunda, dining hall, and ladies' parlour, which have been restored to their Gilded Age elegance. The Alcazar is now the Lightner Museum of Victorian art and furnishings, as well as home to offices and expensive shops, while the Casa Monica has been reborn as a hotel. All the sites mentioned in my novel (with the exception of Rathburn's Photography Studio and Miller's Tourism Office) are real places where a modern visitor can spend many happy hours, though the St. Augustine Alligator Farm is much changed from its 1890s appearance. Alligator wrestling---which Tiger Tail gave a display of---is still practiced in Florida, as thrilling as it was when Seminole promoters discovered its lucrative nature in the early years of the twentieth century. And Holmes's prediction of air conditioning did come true, much to our relief. In the 1840s, Dr. John Gorrie of Apalachicola made the initial experiments in refrigeration, which led to the ice machine and later to the principle behind air conditioning.

Lizzie Borden is an American icon of mystery. Historians and armchair sleuths still debate whether she killed her father and stepmother in their strange Fall River home. Whether guilty or innocent (and for the record, I hold that she was guilty as sin!), her lawyers successfully manipulated the gender conventions of her day and played to the belief that no real lady could have committed such a heinous crime in such a horrible manner. Had Lizzie merely poisoned her parents (and there is a suggestion that she tried this method earlier, but failed) one has little doubt that she would have swung from the gallows. It was the method that the jurymen could not accept as valid; nice spinster ladies simply did not use hatchets! After her acquittal, Lizzie Borden sought to reinvent herself, purchasing a mansion that she called Maplecroft and signing herself as Lizbeth. She also travelled occasionally and was rumoured to have had a lesbian affair with an actress. She died in 1927, an embarrassment to her community, though today she is something of a minor tourist industry in Fall River, where bold travellers can book a night at the bed and breakfast that now exists at 92 Second Street.

The Pinkerton agent O.M. Hanscom, a superintendant from Boston, was hired by the Borden family attorney to clear Lizzie's name and find the real killer. He spent only two days in Fall River before abandoning the case and, in the words of the affair's original chronicler he "departed as mysteriously as he came."

Stereoscopic pictures were a passion of the Victorian age, and their viewers were prized possessions. An early form of 3-D imaging, the most popular cards showed exotic landmarks and landscapes, as well as humorous posed scenes. Spirit photography emerged following the Civil War, with perhaps the most famous example being William H. Mumler's photograph of a spectral Abraham Lincoln embracing his widow. Fans of antiques can find examples of both these art forms in stores and flea markets.

Father Olivarez is a figment of my imagination, but Don Pedro Menendez de Aviles is not. While hopefully not cursed to wander as a skeleton, the founder of St. Augustine was not exactly a nice guy. He murdered Frenchmen at Fort Caroline (in present-day Jacksonville) and finished off over a hundred French survivors of a shipwreck close to the current spot of the Fort Matanzas National Monument, where Mr. Miller met his (fictional) demise. Modern readers might shudder at such casual cruelty, but in the minds of sixteenth-century Spaniards, there was no shame in dispatching the 'heretics,' as French Protestants were considered.

While I have played a bit fast and loose with the transportation in this story, especially the wondrous 'bigger on the inside' *Friesland* and the nonexistent *Andromeda*, the *Majestic* was a vessel of the White Star Line. Did Holmes reject an invitation to dine with its captain because he had a premonition about the man's future? After all, Captain Edward John Smith gained immortality as the captain who went down with the *Titanic*.

And finally, there's that strange little boy. I had just discovered the wonders of H. P. Lovecraft's fiction when I began work on *Shadowblood*. Astute readers will perhaps notice a few names and phrases shamelessly lifted from the Lovecraft canon, but, in my defence, I offer that Lovecraft was unselfish in terms of his creations. He built a dark world that many lesser talents have plundered for almost a century. While there is no evidence that Lovecraft ventured to St. Augustine as a child (he was born in 1890), he did arrive in 1931 and explored streets and buildings even older than those in his beloved New England. For the sake of fiction, I offer that his grandfather---who was instrumental in raising the young H. P.--- was comfortably wealthy, so perhaps the boy and his mother did travel southward. If there was ever a hoodoo man haunted by shadows and blood, it was this great American master of horror.

Also from MX Publishing

Close To Holmes

A Look at the Connections Between Historical London, Sherlock Holmes and Sir Arthur Conan Doyle.

Eliminate The Impossible

An Examination of the World of

Sherlock Holmes on Page and Screen.

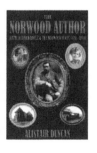

The Norwood Author

Arthur Conan Doyle and the Norwood Years (1891 - 1894) – Winner of the 2011 Howlett Literary Award (Sherlock Holmes book of the year)

www.mxpublishing.com

Also From MX Publishing

In Search of Dr Watson

Wonderful biography of Dr.Watson from expert Molly Carr – 2nd edition fully updated.

Arthur Conan Doyle, Sherlock Holmes and Devon

A Complete Tour Guide and Companion.

The Lost Stories of Sherlock Holmes

Eight more stories from the pen of John H Watson – compiled by Tony Reynolds.

www.mxpublishing.com

Also From MX Publishing

Watsons Afghan Adventure

Fascinating biography of Watson's time in Afghanistan from US Army veteran Kieran McMullen.

Shadowfall

Sherlock Holmes, ancient relics and demons and mystic characters. A supernatural Holmes pastiche.

Official Papers of The Hound of The Baskervilles

Very unusual collection of the original police papers from The Hound case.

www.mxpublishing.com

Also From MX Publishing

The Sign of Fear

The first adventure of the 'female Sherlock Holmes'. A delightful fun adventure with your favourite supporting Holmes characters.

A Study in Crimson

The second adventure of the 'female Sherlock Holmes' with a host of sub- plots and new characters joining Watson and Fanshaw

The Chronology of Arthur Conan Doyle

The definitive chronology used by historians and libraries worldwide.

www.mxpublishing.com

Also From MX Publishing

Aside Arthur Conan Doyle

A collection of twenty stories from ACD's close friend Bertram Fletcher Robinson.

Bertram Fletcher Robinson

The comprehensive biography of the assistant plot producer of The Hound of The Baskervilles

Wheels of Anarchy

Reprint and introduction to Max Pemberton's thriller from 100 years ago. One of the first spy thrillers of its kind.

www.mxpublishing.com

Also From MX Publishing

Bobbles and Plum

Four playlets from PG Wodehouse 'lost' for over 100 years – found and reprinted with an excellent commentary

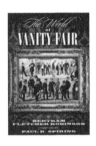

The World of Vanity Fair

A specialist full-colour reproduction of key articles from Bertram Fletcher Robinson containing of colour caricatures from the early 1900s.

Tras Las He huellas de Arthur Conan Doyle (in Spanish)

Un viaje ilustrado por Devon.

Also From MX Publishing

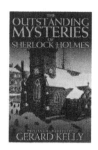

The Outstanding Mysteries of
Sherlock Holmes

With thirteen Homes stories and
illustrations Kelly re-creates the
gas-lit, fog-enshrouded world of
Victorian London

Rendezvous at The Populaire

Sherlock Holmes has retired,
injured from an encounter with
Moriarty. He's tempted out of
retirement for an epic battle with
the Phantom of the opera.

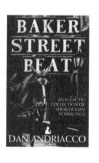

Baker Street Beat

An eclectic collection of articles,
essays, radio plays and 'general
scribblings' about Sherlock
Holmes from Dr.Dan Andriacco.

www.mxpublishing.com

Also From MX Publishing

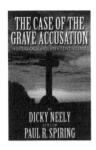

The Case of The Grave Accusation

The creator of Sherlock Holmes has been accused of murder. Only Holmes and Watson can stop the destruction of the Holmes legacy.

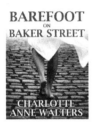

Barefoot on Baker Street

Epic novel of the life of a Victorian workhouse orphan featuring Sherlock Holmes and Moriarty.

Case of Witchcraft

A tale of witchcraft in the Northern Isles, in which some long-concealed secrets are revealed including about the Great Detective himself.

www.mxpublishing.com

Also From MX Publishing

The Affair In Transylvania

Holmes and Watson tackle Dracula in deepest Transylvania in this stunning adaptation by film director Gerry O'Hara

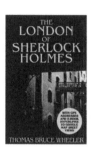

The London of Sherlock Holmes

400 locations including GPS co-ordinates that enable Google Street view of the locations around London in all the Homes stories

I Will Find The Answer

Sequel to Rendezvous At The Populaire, Holmes and Watson tackle Dr.Jekyll.

www.mxpublishing.com

287

Also From MX Publishing

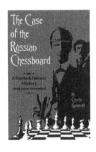

The Case of The Russian Chessboard

Short novel covering the dark world of Russian espionage sees Holmes and Watson on the world stage facing dark and complex enemies.

An Entirely New Country

Covers Arthur Conan Doyle's years at Undershaw where he wrote Hound of The Baskervilles. Foreword by Mark Gatiss (BBC's Sherlock).

www.mxpublishing.com

Lightning Source UK Ltd.
Milton Keynes UK
UKOW06f1016230516

274818UK00001B/149/P

9 781780 920474